Praise for The Ant & Bea Mysteries

'Bea and Ant are a delightful crime-solving duo and I'll very happily join them again for another clean-up in a Costsave aisle.'   *Crime Review*

'Ant and Bea are fabulous creations and I really felt part of the Costsave community by the end. I can't wait to see what they get up to next!'   SOPHIA BENNETT

'This odd, appealing pair prove a formidable match for the surprising killer. Readers will look forward to their next outing.'   *Publishers Weekly*

'I love spending time with Bea and Ant! A simply delightful crime-cracking duo.'   CHRISTI DAUGHERTY

'Rachel Ward provides warm characterisations, convincing dialogue, deliciously awkward romantic liaisons, a wicked wit to make you giggle and a plot to keep you guessing all the way to the check-out. It's a treat!'
Bradford on Avon Mini Book Festival

'I absolutely loved *The Cost of Living*. Crime just where you least expect it, and one of my favourite ensemble casts.'
K.J. WHITTAKER

'Starring the most unlikely but endearing detective pairing since Morse and Lewis, *Dead Stock* is a charming, heart-warming page-turner. Agatha Christie meets Car Share and Coronat̶   A NADIN

Rachel Ward is a best-selling writer for young adults. An avid reader of detective fiction, *The Ant & Bea Mysteries* is her first crime series for adults. Rachel is married with two grown-up children, and lives in Bath.

Also by Rachel Ward

The Cost of Living
Dead Stock

EXPIRY DATE
AN ANT & BEA MYSTERY

RACHEL WARD

SANDSTONE PRESS

First published in Great Britain by
Sandstone Press Ltd
Willow House
Stoneyfield Business Park
Inverness
IV2 7PA
Scotland

www.sandstonepress.com

ISBN: 978-1-912240-98-2
ISBNe: 978-1-912240-99-9

Cover design by David Wardle at Bold and Noble
Typeset by Iolaire, Newtonmore
Printed and bound by Hussar Books, Poland

There's a lot in this book about dads, so this is dedicated to Ozzy, who has been the best dad ever to Ali and Pete. It's also for my mum, Shirley, who continues to support, encourage and inspire.

Prologue

She'd planned for this. Knew just what she needed to take, where to go, so that she'd be ready when the time came.

It wasn't what she wanted. She never thought things would turn out like this, but not everything can be fixed. Sometimes you just have to get out to keep yourself safe. Walk away and don't look back.

There was a noise outside, a car door slamming. She froze. Surely he wasn't back yet? Her mouth was dry, her heart hammering away in her chest as she listened. There were footsteps on the gravel drive. Someone was walking up to the front door. No, she thought, please God, no.

Not now.

1

'It's meant to be summer, isn't it?' said Ant, glumly, looking at the pattern of muddy footprints leading from the front entrance to the 'Lunchtime Meal Deal' cabinet where a cluster of men in high-visibility jackets and heavy work boots were making their selections. 'I mean, can't they wipe their bloody feet?'

'Don't think we're getting summer this year,' said Bea. 'Or rather, we've had it. Those few nice days in May. Reckon that was it. No suntan for me.' She sighed, remembering the most recent photo Jay had sent her – a selfie on a beach in Thailand, with the sun setting behind him, its golden rays glinting on the glass bottle of beer he was raising to his lips. Wish you were here, his message had said. Yeah, she thought, watching the rain splatter against the floor-to-ceiling window of Costsave's shopfront, I wish I was, too.

'You'd better fetch your mop before you get it in the neck from Neville,' said Dot. 'Oh, talk of the devil—'

Neville was stalking over towards them, clutching his clipboard. 'Anthony—' he said, but Ant was there before him.

'I know, I know. The floor. I'm going.'

They all watched him slouch away towards the back of the store where the cleaning trolley was kept.

'He's doing his best, Neville,' said Bea. 'You got to admit, it's not easy with building works here, there and everywhere and blokes trailing mud into the shop.'

'I'm not saying conditions here aren't challenging, while the drains are replaced, but it's important to keep on top of things, Beatrice. Keep the mess to a minimum for our customers. They're the ones that matter, after all.'

'It's not just here, though, is it? They're digging up the High Street for some reason, and there's the second phase of the factory flats under way. Kingsleigh's just one big building site at the moment.'

'You can't make an omelette without breaking eggs,' said Neville, somewhat gnomically.

'Huh?'

'Costsave needs its new drains. The town needs improving. A bit of disruption will be worth it in the end.' He set off back to the customer service desk.

'I suppose he's right,' said Dot. 'It's nice to see things happening in the town. It's needed a facelift for a while. And more housing.'

'We haven't got a housing problem, according to this week's *Bugle*,' said Bea. 'Did you read what our town council leader said? "We're lucky that we don't see homelessness in Kingsleigh."'

'Huh,' said Ant, who was trundling the cleaning trolley slowly past the checkouts, 'what he means is he doesn't have to step over anyone on his way home from the pub. No one's kipping in shop doorways. He doesn't see it, because it's hidden.'

'How are you getting on at Nat's house?' said Dot. Ant had moved in with his brother Stevo's girlfriend's family when his mum had swapped her council house in Kingsleigh for one in Cardiff a few months before.

Ant pulled a face. 'I'm not there anymore,' he said. 'Got a bit crowded. Shame, 'cos her mum's a bloody brilliant cook.'

'Where are you now, then?'

'Saggy's.'

'Oh blimey,' said Bea.

'It's all right,' said Ant, although the flatness of his monotone suggested otherwise. There were thunderclouds gathering above the customer service desk. 'I'd better get on, before Nev blows a gasket.'

Bea and Dot both had customers approaching. They swivelled back into position, ready for action. Dot had a gaggle of builders clutching their meal deals. Bea groaned silently inside when she saw who hers was. A good-looking man in a shiny suit would normally be a bonus, but not this one. This was Dave, the abusive husband of one of her favourite customers, Julie. He was a surveyor for the contractor digging out Costsave's drains, so he'd been in and out of the store more often than usual over the past few weeks, and he always seemed to make a beeline for checkout number six.

'Hello, Bea,' he said, sliding a packet of beef and horse-radish sandwiches towards her.

'Hello,' she said, beeping his shopping through as quickly as she could, avoiding eye contact.

'What about this weather, eh? Still, seeing you brightens up my day.'

Bea cringed. 'That's three, ninety-nine, please.'

He held his debit card near the contactless reader and Bea was reminded how Julie didn't seem to have a card of her own. She always paid in cash, spending the housekeeping that she was allowed that week, Bea supposed.

'Do you need a receipt?'

Her eyes met his briefly. He seemed to be amused at her stonewalling. There was a flicker of a smile at the edge of his mouth. 'No, no need, darlin'. See you soon.'

Bea shuddered as he walked away. That was one big

disadvantage to working on the checkouts. You were a sitting duck. People knew where to find you.

'Once a creep, always a creep,' said Dot, who'd been listening with one ear as she served her builders.

'Tell me about it. He doesn't get the hint, does he? And he's always bloody here these days,' said Bea. 'Tell you who I haven't seen for ages, though. Julie and the kids.'

'That's odd. They're normally in most days, aren't they?'

'Yeah, and she usually comes and sees me. Now I think about it, it must be a couple of weeks or more since I saw them.' Dave had left the store now. Bea could see him walking across the car park in the rain. 'It's like they've disappeared off the face of the earth.'

2

'Ooh, don't mind if I do.' Bea's mum, Queenie, took an amuse bouche from a passing tray. It was a curl of smoked salmon sitting on a mini-pancake, with a wisp of dill on top. Bea watched as she picked off the dill and ate the rest.

'What are you going to do with that?' she asked, nodding at the greenery.

Queenie looked around for somewhere to put it.

'Give it here.' Bea put it in her mouth and gave an experimental chew, then swallowed it down.

'Nice?' said Queenie.

'Not particularly. Perhaps it needed the salmon to go with it. Anyway, I preferred those teeny burgers. They were yum. Can you see any more?'

'No,' said Dot, who was standing with them, 'but I think Bob's got hold of something. He's over there, look.'

Bea scanned the room. It was huge, with a bar at one end and big windows along one side overlooking acres of sports fields and the river beyond. Just in view were the hoardings marking the edge of the next phase of building at the former factory site. From here on the first floor, she could see over the top, where building work was carrying on, even at six o'clock in the evening, with two diggers scooping out the footings for the next tranche of housing. Costsave's drains might be important to the people who worked there, but the factory redevelopment was at the heart of the supposed revival of the town.

The room was packed with people in smarter than usual clothes, standing in groups, making small, but very noisy, talk. Bea spotted Eileen and Dean in one corner. Although peace had broken out between her and Dean, Eileen was still very prickly, and, Bea found, best avoided. Dave was there, too, in a cluster of people including a man in a lounge suit with a shiny gold mayoral-style chain round his neck. Ugh, thought Bea, so many people to avoid. Safer to stay in this corner. She saw Bob, making his way through the crowd. He had a tray in one hand and was lifting it over the top of people's heads as he manoeuvred his substantial bulk through.

'Great to see you here, Maggie,' he said when he reached them. Bea still winced to hear him use her mum's real name. 'And you, Dot, of course.'

'Thanks,' said Queenie. She was getting out and about more these days, and even worked two days a week in the launderette, but this was the first time she'd been in a crowded room like this. Bea gave her arm an encouraging squeeze. 'I couldn't turn down the chance to come and have a look at the new club.'

'Yeah, it's a bit nice, isn't it? A step up from the old social club,' said Bob. He lowered the tray, revealing ranks of mini-sausages, lined up like soldiers ready for inspection. He held the platter out towards Queenie and Dot. 'Sausage, ladies?'

'No thanks,' they said in unison, then caught each other's eye. Dot winked, and Queenie nodded and smiled back. Ever since they had worked out that Bob was trying to romance them at the same time, they had both kept him at arm's length.

'Like that, is it?' he said, colouring up just a little. He

popped a sausage into his mouth and looked morosely out of the window.

Ant wriggled into a space next to Bea, then reached across her to grab a handful of sausages from Bob's tray.

'Oi!' Bob protested. 'Get off me sausages. What are you doing here, anyway? Your family never worked here, did they?'

'So what?' said Ant. 'Free country, innit? Anyway, I'm Bea's plus one tonight, aren't I?'

'Um, yes. Yes, he is,' said Bea, improvising. 'I asked Ant because I thought he might like to see the new gym and stuff here.'

'Hmph.' Bob went back to looking out of the window.

'What's up with him?' said Ant.

'Mum and Dot just owned him.'

Ant grinned. Waiters were moving through the crowd now with trays of thin glasses each containing an inch or so of something fizzy. Ant wolfed his sausages down and picked up two glasses from a passing tray.

'Here,' he said, handing one each to Queenie and Dot, then he grabbed two more and gave one to Bea. He sniffed his glass and took a swig, downing the whole contents of his glass in one gulp.

'Steady, mate,' said Bea. 'You're meant to keep this for the toast. Look, they're getting ready to do speeches and stuff.'

'Damn. I'll grab a couple more.' Ant dived into the crowd, in the waiter's wake. He returned with one glass for him and one for Bob. Bob was staring out of the window, and Dot had to tap him on the shoulder to get his attention and pass him his fizz.

'There's something going on out there,' he said. 'They've stopped work on the site.'

'Well, it is getting late,' said Bea. 'I expect it's just knocking-off time.'

'No, I think it's more than that. I—'

Someone had set up a microphone stand on some staging blocks at the far end of the room and now a tall man, with a dome of balding head glistening with sweat, tapped it, sending an unpleasant knocking sound booming out of the speaker near to Bea's ear.

'Okay, okay. Evening, ladies and gentlemen. Evening. Settle down, please.' The room started to hush and everyone turned to face the speaker. 'Welcome, everyone, to the new Factory Quarter Sports and Social Club. Some of you know me – I'm Pete Banner, the manager here. We were all sad to say goodbye to the old club, but I think you'll agree that we've got a fantastic new facility for the whole community. I'm delighted to welcome our *very* special guest, Malcolm Sillitoe, the chair of the town council, who will officially declare us open. Malcolm?'

He stood aside from the microphone and moved backwards, slightly bowing as he went and sweeping his arm round to invite Sillitoe to step forward. Ant leaned sideways towards Bea and muttered, 'If he stoops a bit lower, he'll actually be able to get his tongue up our Malcolm's arse.'

Bea batted Ant's arm – 'Shush, Ant. Stop it' – but she couldn't help smiling. Sillitoe took a moment to look around the room, smiling and nodding at people he knew. As he launched into his speech, Bea's heart sank. He had all the smug hallmarks of someone who enjoyed the sound of their own voice very much indeed. She turned her gaze towards the window as his voice drifted over her.

' . . .rich heritage . . .moving forward . . .quality housing . . .'

Bea shuffled closer to the window. Bob was right. There was something going on out there. All workers in their bright jackets and hard hats were clustered round one of the diggers.

' . . .dynamic town with a bright future ahead . . .'

Ant pulled at Bea's sleeve. 'Look, Bea.'

'What?' She faced the front again and could see a guy in a high-vis jacket was talking to Dave in a very animated way. Dave, in turn, beckoned to Pete, who stepped to the front of the stage and leaned down so Dave could whisper into his ear. He frowned and seemed to be asking Dave to repeat himself, then turned a very odd shade of off-white. He straightened up and moved towards the microphone. He hovered for a moment or two, obviously hoping that Sillitoe would notice him and give way. The councillor, however, was in full flow and kept going.

By now, there was a little ripple of excitement buzzing through the room. There was an audible 'Ooh' from the crowd as Pete wrestled the microphone out of its stand and stepped away from Sillitoe, who stood, open-mouthed, at being interrupted so abruptly.

'I'm sorry, ladies and gentlemen, due to circumstances beyond our control, we're going to have to bring this evening to an end.'

Out of the corner of her eye, Bea noticed a flashing blue light. She glanced round. Two police cars were drawing up by the building site hoarding.

Someone booed and another voice called out, 'What circumstances? What's going on, Pete?'

'I'm afraid I can't...the thing is...' He floundered for a minute, at a loss, then emitted a little groan. 'You're going to find out soon enough. There's a problem with site B, the new footings. They've found something. They've found a body.'

3

For a moment, everyone was quiet, digesting the news.

Bea's first thought was of the Kingsleigh Stalker and the terrible events of the previous winter. He was safely behind bars now, convicted of one actual and two attempted murders, but had there been other victims? Someone unreported, unmissed?

People were starting to file out of the room. The waiters were going round collecting up glasses.

'That's a shocker, innit?' said Ant. He was looking out of the window. Another couple of police cars had arrived. Inside the hoarding, people in white head-to-toe bodysuits were by the digger now and the group of builders in their high-vis jackets had been moved back behind a barrier of yellow tape.

'Yes,' said Bea. 'I wonder who it is. Do you think it's another one, you know, like Ginny?'

Ant puffed his cheeks out. 'Who knows, Bea? Doubt it. Our man didn't cover his tracks, did he? He just attacked people and left them in the street.'

'I keep thinking, even now, it could've been me. I mean, why did Ginny die and I survived?'

Ant put a comforting arm round her shoulder.

'No point thinking like that. It is what it is. It's terrible about Ginny, but we're all glad you're still here.'

'And now this.' Below them people were starting to leave the building and straggle towards the car park, or along the pavement, back towards town.

'But this could be anything, mate,' said Ant. 'Wasn't the factory built on a Roman villa or something? Could be ancient bones, hundreds of years old. We don't know, do we?'

'No, we don't. You're right. Better go home, I suppose.'

Ant and Bea turned away from the window. Queenie, Bob and Dot were in a little huddle at the side of the room, deep in conversation. Dot nudged Bob when she saw them walking over and they all stopped talking and put their game faces on.

'I'll give you all a lift home, shall I?' said Bob. 'Or shall we go to the Legion or somewhere? We're all dressed up, after all.'

Queenie shook her head, grim-faced. 'I just want to go home, Bob. If you don't mind.'

'Are you all right, Mum?' said Bea.

'Yes, love.' Queenie clutched her handbag a little closer to her and started walking towards the door. Bob went with her.

'What's up with her?' Bea said to Dot.

'Nothing. It's just a shock, isn't it? Another body turning up in Kingsleigh. We've had more than our fair share over the past year. It's not nice, is it?' There was something about the way she wouldn't quite look Bea in the eye that set alarm bells off.

'Dot?' said Bea. 'What aren't you telling me?'

Dot pressed her lips into a tight little line. 'Not now, Bea. Not here.' She trotted a few steps across the plush carpet to catch up with Queenie and Bob.

'Bloody hell, Ant. Did you get all that? What's going on?'

But she was talking to thin air. Ant was going round the room stuffing hors d'oeuvres into his mouth. She hurried over to him. 'Ant! Stop it!' He looked at her, baffled.

'What? They'll just chuck it out, Bea. Here, help me with this.' He spread out a paper napkin on a side table and started piling little sausages into the middle.

'If you want a lift back, then you'd better come with me now. Bob's got his car.'

'No, it's all right, Bea. I'll finish up here and then walk. I'm not in a hurry to get back to Saggy's.'

'Is it all right there? Have you got your own room?'

'Nah. Well, they've got a sort of lean-to at the back. I'm on a sun lounger in there, but it's where their washing machine is, and the dryer, and the dogs. It's a bit crowded.'

'You could come to ours, you know, but it would only be the sofa.'

Ant smiled. 'Thanks, mate. I'm all right. I'm tough, me, aren't I? Saggy's is just temporary until I get a flat from the council or something else turns up. It's all good. Hey, don't miss your lift.'

'Okay. I'll see you tomorrow, yeah?'

'Yup. Night, Bea.'

Bea headed towards the exit. Dave was aiming for the door at the same time. He was frowning, and there was tension in his jaw, but he switched on a smile when he saw Bea, stopped and indicated that she should go first.

'Shame the party's over,' he said. 'I noticed you earlier. Didn't have a chance to say hello.'

Bea couldn't think of anything to say. She hurried out of the door and down the stairs, keenly aware of him following her. Once into the fresh air, she spotted Tom standing by a break in the hoarding. He wasn't in uniform now that he had a new job in the CID, and was wearing a rather tight T-shirt under a black jacket, and jeans. She jogged across the road.

He was talking on his radio. She waited until he finished to ask, 'Tom, what's going on?'

He looked pleased to see her. Ever since he'd found out that Jay was away for the summer, he had been texting Bea, and ever-so-casually calling round to checkout number six on a regular basis.

'Bea, you look nice,' he said. 'Were you at that do, too?'

'Yes, but never mind that.' Although she wasn't actively encouraging him, due to previous shady behaviour when he tried to date her while still living with the mother of his little boy, part of her was glad that he'd noticed the effort she'd made. She'd managed a pretty good attempt at a messy Meghan-style bun and her boat-neck top was really rather sexy. 'What's happening?' she said.

'How much do you know?'

'Pete, the manager, just said that they found a body.'

'Yeah, well that's all we've got for now,' he said. 'The digger driver's being treated for shock, though. Saw a hand sticking out of the edge of the area he was turning over.'

'A hand on its own?'

'No, looks like there's a whole body in there. The scene of crime guys are going to uncover it, gently though, bagging up the soil for evidence as they go.'

There was something at the back of Bea's mind, a nagging, awful thought that crystallised as she stood talking to Tom. She didn't know whether to tell him or not.

'The hand,' she said, 'did it look male or female?'

Tom's radio crackled into life. 'Sorry, Bea, I've got to get on. Look, I'm going to be busy, but give me a ring, yeah? Let's grab a drink sometime soon.'

He was gone before she got the chance to say that if the body turned out to be female, she had a horrible idea that she might know who it was. A thought that had taken a while to form wouldn't go away now. It was screaming inside her head like the worst migraine. A thought, or rather a name: Julie.

4

They drove home in silence. Bea stared out of the window at the drizzly streets. In her mind's eye she was replaying Dave's reaction to the find at the factory. Had he shown any sign of anxiety or remorse? He'd been frowning, hadn't he, but then he launched into the normal low-level flirtation at the doorway. If it was Julie's body that they'd found and he was behind it, then the man had nerves of steel. He must be some sort of psychopath, she thought. She shivered and turned her attention to the others in the car. They all seemed lost in their own thoughts – there was no banter or chat.

The car pulled up outside Bea and Queenie's house.

'Here we are, then,' said Bob.

Bea reached for the door handle, but Queenie didn't move. The air inside the car was heavy with unspoken words. Bea remembered again how they'd all gone quiet back at the club when she'd joined their group. She took a deep breath.

'Okay, before we get out, I want to know what's going on.'

'I don't know what you mean,' said Queenie.

'It's like someone slapped you all in the face with a wet fish or something.'

'It's nothing, love,' said Queenie.

'Don't give me that, Mum. I'm not stupid. There's something up and you're all in on it.'

Silence again. Bea caught Dot looking at Queenie. Bob cleared his throat and shifted in his seat.

'Will one of you tell me what's wrong?' Her voice was too loud for the small space, but she didn't care.

'Okay, okay,' said Queenie. 'But let's not do this here. Come on inside, everyone. I'll put the kettle on.'

They climbed out of the car and trooped round the side of the house. Bea unlocked the kitchen door. It still felt strange coming home to an empty room. She and Queenie had looked after a large golden retriever for three months, until her owner, Charles, who had been in hospital, was able to take her back home. Since then, she'd been wondering on and off if they should get their own dog.

Bea filled the kettle and put four tea bags in the pot.

'Have you got anything stronger, Maggie?' said Bob.

'You're driving, aren't you?' Queenie said.

'Just one.'

'Actually, I could do with a drink,' said Dot. 'I could nip down to the corner shop, if you like.'

'No, no,' said Queenie. 'I've got sherry, or whisky. Might be some gin there, too.'

'Should be brandy for the shock, shouldn't it?' said Dot. 'Whisky will do me, though.'

'Yeah, that'd be great,' said Bob.

'I'll join you, then.' Queenie reached for three glasses out of the cupboard. 'Bea? Do you want one?'

Bea had an ominous feeling that she was going to need one, that the next few minutes were going to bring things that she didn't want to hear.

'Yes. Okay,' she said. 'I'll have some Coke with mine, though.'

They took their drinks through to the lounge. Bea sat on the sofa next to her mum, and Bob and Dot each settled in an armchair. There was silence again. Bea put her drink down on a coaster on the coffee table. The others took nervous sips and nursed their glasses. No one seemed keen to start the conversation.

'So?' said Bea. 'What is it? What's going on?'

Bob, Dot and Queenie looked at each other again. Then Queenie turned slightly in her seat, angling her knees towards Bea.

'The thing is, you probably don't remember anything about it, but there was a girl, a young woman really, who worked at the factory. She went missing fourteen years ago. She was never found.'

'A girl?'

'Her name was Tina.'

'Tina? The Tina that used to babysit?'

Queenie's pupils went wide with alarm. 'So you do remember. Yes. That Tina.'

'I knew she was missing because there were posters all over town.'

Queenie sighed. 'We tried as hard as we could to shield you from it all. You were only seven. I didn't want you growing up scared.'

Bea couldn't help noticing the irony. Her mum had spent six years confined to their house by agoraphobia. It was only in the last few months that she'd been getting out and about again.

'So what happened? Tell me.'

'It was a terrible time, Bea. The thought that a girl could just disappear. She went to an evening do at the old social club and she never came home. Didn't turn up for work the next day. She'd just gone. Her parents were tortured by it. We all were. It was the not knowing.'

'Perhaps we do know now,' said Dot. 'God, what an awful thing. She's been there all that time.'

'Now listen, you two,' said Bob. 'You're both jumping to

conclusions. We don't know anything and it won't help to speculate.'

'Strange, though, isn't it? We were back at the rebuilt club, after all those years, and now this.'

'When was it, exactly, Mum?' said Bea. 'When did she disappear?'

'2005, love. Summer of 2005.'

'It felt like everything changed that summer,' said Dot. 'We won the Olympic bid and then the next day there were all those bombs in London. And everything changed in Kingsleigh, too. Tina disappearing felt like the end of an era. The end of happy, innocent sort of times.'

'They *were* happy days before that, weren't they?' said Queenie. 'The kids were all still little. Me and Harry. You and Darren, Dot. And you and your Babs, Bob.'

'Hmph, Darren!' huffed Dot, rolling her eyes. 'It certainly all changed for me that year. I wised up to him.'

'But you were happy before that. For a while.'

'Yes, I was, I suppose.'

'And your lovely Babs. She was a diamond, Bob, wasn't she?'

Bob looked down into his glass, which was nearly empty. He seemed to be struggling with something.

'Yeah. She was,' he said, quietly. 'She was everything to me. That was the summer we found out, though. 2005. Bloody hell.'

'Found out what?' said Bea.

'She had breast cancer, love,' said Queenie, quietly.

'Oh, I'm sorry. Sorry, Bob.'

'It's all right, Bea. It still hurts. I still miss her, but it was a long time ago now.'

'It was all a long time ago,' said Queenie. 'But it's going to come back now, if it is her down at the factory. If it's Tina.'

'Well, better wait and see,' said Bob. 'We'll know soon

enough.' He drained his glass and stood up. 'I'll get off home now. Do you want a lift, Dot?'

Dot swirled the remaining amber liquid round in her glass and then set it down on the table. 'Yes, please. I feel like an early night. Think I've had enough of today.' She stood up, too, and Queenie showed them out. Bea could hear them starting to say their goodbyes at the kitchen door, and then their voices went quieter and the door clicked. Queenie had gone outside with them. Bea could still hear the low murmur of conversation, but not what they were saying.

She picked up her drink and padded into the kitchen. She stood close to the door and listened.

'It's all coming back again. What a nightmare.' This was her mum's voice. Bea held her breath, straining to hear more. Now Bob and Dot were chiming in, talking over each other.

'We don't even know . . .'

'We're all here for you . . .'

'Yes, I know. I'm sorry. It's all about that poor girl, not me. I'm sorry to make a fuss.'

'Don't be silly. Try and get some sleep.'

'Yes. Thank you. Goodnight.'

Bea sprang away from the door and went over to the fridge. She had the door open and was reaching for the bottle of Coke as Queenie came back in. 'Bit strong for me,' Bea said. 'Just having a little top up. Do you want another one?'

She looked round. Queenie's eyes were red and her face flushed and blotchy. 'Mum! What's the matter?'

Queenie strode quickly through the kitchen. 'Nothing, darling. I'm all right. It's just that girl. That poor girl. I'm going to go to bed. I'll see you tomorrow.'

And she was gone, leaving Bea with the awful feeling that she'd only been told half a story, and that the other half might be something that she really didn't want to know.

5

The staff room was abuzz with gossip about the body at the factory, although as far as Bea could tell, no one actually knew anything more about it than they had done the evening before. By the time she got to Costsave, there had been no official announcement from the police, either, although Twitter told her that Avon and Somerset Police had called a press conference for ten o'clock that morning. She'd texted Tom first thing to try and get the inside track, but he hadn't got back to her.

George, the manager, took her place at the front of the room, flanked as usual by Neville, her deputy, and Anna, her office manager.

'All right, everyone, settle down. In a moment I'll ask Neville to go through the stats for May, which were, I've got to admit, a little disappointing. I know morale is suffering at the moment with the disruption caused by work to improve our facilities, so I've got an important announcement.'

Everyone's ears pricked up. George was starting to get a reputation for doing things differently. Could this be the start of employee bonuses? Maybe a partner-style deal like some other chains?

'Some of you may be aware that the local council has been funding an arts worker to develop cultural activity in the town. I've met with them and they have put me in contact with a wonderfully talented woman called Candy Argos. We'll be meeting her at our huddle tomorrow, but until then I'd like you all to think about getting involved in this exciting initiative...' She paused and looked round the room at a sea of expectant faces, then announced, triumphantly, 'The Costsave Choir.'

Her words were met with a variety of noises, none of them musical – groans, a volley of laughter, and someone calling out, 'Say, whaaat?'

George held her hands up. 'I know, I know. Bit of a surprise to spring on you, but, trust me, this is going to be great. It's not just for budding Whitneys or Marias, it's for everyone.'

'Do you mean, like, compulsory?' Ant asked.

'No, no, of course not. It's in your own time for the most part, although I will allocate some team-building hours to this. We'll also look at having rehearsals at different times of the day so various shifts can take part. Listen, guys, I've got to nail down the details with Candy and see how we can make this work, but I'm putting a sign-up sheet on the noticeboard today—' she waved a piece of paper in the air in front of her '—and I'm signing up! I'd love you to, too!'

She looked around, expecting more of a reaction. Feeling sorry for her, Bea started clapping. For an agonising moment or two, in which she wanted to be swallowed up by the coffee-stained carpet underneath her feet, she was the only one but then others started joining in and eventually there was a short round of applause.

'Okay, everybody, thank you. Now, over to Neville for our stats report...'

'Are you going to be signing up, Dot? You've got a lovely voice,' Bea asked as they made their way to the checkouts.

'Yes, I think so. Why not? I hardly go out anywhere anymore. Since I did my hip in, I've become a bit of a hermit.

Be nice to do something different. You'll do it, won't you?'

'Um, not sure. Maybe. Not sure it's my sort of thing.'

'Come on, Bea. Sing first, pub after?'

'Well, if you put it like that . . .'

Bea's first customer was, of course, Smelly Reg. Never a voluble person, he didn't even grunt today. He just put his *Racing Post* and a sliced loaf on the conveyor belt, handed over his money without a word and left, trailing the characteristic odour of tobacco and unwashed crevices behind him.

'What's up with him?' said Dot.

'Dunno. I suppose even Kingsleigh's brightest and best have an off day.' Dot gave an amused snort and turned back to her first customer. There were fewer builders than usual, buying their snacks on the way into work, and Bob reported that all work at the factory site had been suspended for the day.

'The whole thing's ground to a halt.'

Bea felt a pang of anxiety. When would they announce who had been found there? She kept a keen eye on the flow of customers through the checkouts, hoping to spot Julie after all.

Later, she was pleased to see Keisha pushing a trolley round the aisles. Keisha was the previous occupant of checkout six. She'd stopped working at Costsave when she had had her baby, Kayleigh, who was being treated for leukaemia. Kayleigh's Wish was the store's official charity, and they'd managed to raise enough money for a special pushchair and for the family to have a holiday in Florida. Bea waved at Keisha as she walked past and was pleased when she headed for her checkout with her full trolley.

'Hiya, doll,' said Bea. 'No Kayleigh today?'

'No, she's been doing really well for the last few weeks. She's at nursery today. We're trying a couple of half days a week to see how she gets on.'

'Wow, that's brilliant. She's come a long way in the past year.'

'You can say that again.'

Keisha carried on loading her shopping onto the belt while Bea beeped it through and packed it into bags.

'Is that the same nursery Julie's Mason goes to?'

'Yes. Mason's a sweetheart. He's always been really good with Kayleigh. Hasn't been there for a while, though.'

'Oh?' Bea tried to keep it casual, but she was itching to know more.

'I've not seen him, or Julie, for three weeks now. It was a bit weird. He just stopped coming to nursery, just like that. I do wonder if . . .' She walked closer to Bea and lowered her voice. ' . . .I wonder if she's done a bunk.'

'I've been thinking that. I've not seen her in here, either. Do you think that's what's happened? She's left him.'

'Maybe. I wouldn't blame her if she had.' Keisha looked meaningfully at Bea, and Bea nodded. They'd both seen the bruises under Julie's makeup.

'No, me neither. Would she have told you, though, if she was going? Were you close to her?'

'No, not that close. The kids had a few playdates, but only a few. Kayleigh's been tired from nursery so we've not been doing much the other days.' She went back to her shopping. It was all loaded up so she pushed her trolley along to the packing area.

'I'll let you know if I hear anything.'

'Thanks, Keisha.'

When it was time for Bea's break, she didn't head straight into the staff room, but instead collected her phone from her locker and went outside. The back of the store was out of bounds due to the drainage works, so she found a quieter spot in the corner of the car park, perched on a low wall, and rang Tom.

'Bea! This is a nice surprise.'

'Hey Tom, are you down at the factory?'

'Yeah. There's a lot of standing around at the moment. It's fascinating, though, Bea, watching how they record the scene, take it apart. This is it, girl. This is what I was born to do. My first big case as a detective.' She could hear the excitement in his voice.

'What's happened so far, then? Is the body out?'

'It's all under wraps now. There's a big tent up, but I do know they've uncovered her. They're going to move her to the mortuary as soon as possible, probably in a couple of hours' time.'

'Her?' A pulse of alarm flushed through her, making her stomach tighten and her scalp prickle.

'Dammit. I shouldn't have said anything. Bea don't breathe a word to anyone, okay? You've got to promise. If I get done for leaking information that's me finished before I've even started.'

'I won't say anything, I promise. But it's definitely a woman, yeah? Is it . . . I mean, can you tell how long she's been there?'

'I can't say any more, Bea. There'll be an announcement as soon as possible but I reckon it might take a few days. There's the whole issue of identification and telling relatives. It's all got to be done properly.'

'Yeah, I can see that. I swear I won't talk about it.'

'To anyone. Not even your mum.'

Bea saw Ant walking round the side of the store. He scanned the car park and spotted her, his face brightening. He started walking towards her.

'No, I promise. Tom, can I tell you something? It's not official or anything. Just something I'm worried about.'

'Of course. Fire away.'

'There's a woman, a local woman, who's usually in

Costsave every day, but I haven't seen her for two or three weeks. No one has.'

'A woman?'

'In her late twenties, early thirties, two little kids.'

'Perhaps she's just shopping somewhere else, Bea.'

'Maybe, but the kids haven't been to nursery. I'm worried in case – no, it sounds silly when I say it out loud – in case, she's the one at the factory.'

'That's a big leap to make, Bea. Besides, it's only one body. No kids.'

'Am I being silly?'

'No, not at all. Any information can be useful. Text me her name, just in case. Look, I've got to get on, but we'll catch up soon, yeah?'

'Okay.'

'And mum's the word about the victim.'

'Of course. Bye, Tom.'

'Bye.'

She killed the call, as Ant reached her.

'Here's where you're hiding,' he said. 'I wondered where you were.'

'I'm allowed a bit of peace and quiet, aren't I? Just now and again.'

His eyebrows shot up. 'Blimey, keep your wig on. I'll leave you to it, then.' He started walking away.

'No, you don't need to. I'm sorry!' Bea called after him. He stopped and turned around. 'Come back.'

He joined her on the wall, brought out his packet of cigarettes and lit one up.

'So what's up with you, then? You missed showtime in the staff room. Everyone's going silly about this choir thing. Kirsty and Eileen started singing "Mamma Mia". Then Bob joined in. I didn't know whether to laugh or cry, or film it for YouTube.' He was smiling, looking for her reaction. 'Bea? Bea, something really is wrong, isn't it?'

'It's this body, Ant. The body at the factory.'

'Oh yeah. Nasty business, but nothing for you to worry about, surely? This is a proper police investigation – definitely not one for me and you.'

'I don't really know why, but somehow it feels personal. It all got really weird last night. My mum and Dot and Bob were talking about a girl that used to work there, who disappeared fourteen years ago.'

'Tina Robbins? Yeah, they were all talking about her at Saggy's this morning. But what's that got to do with you?'

'She used to babysit me.'

'Really? Whoa.'

'Yeah and they were all really secretive, and my mum was upset.'

'I reckon the whole town's going to be upset, though. Like I said, nasty business.'

'But there's something else, too. If the body isn't Tina, then I think it might be Julie.'

'Julie? Who's that?'

'You know. The customer with two kids and the creepy husband who beats her up.'

'Julie and Dave. Gotcha. Why on earth would the body be her?'

'She's disappeared, Ant. I haven't seen her for ages, and Keisha said that her little boy hasn't been to nursery for three weeks.'

'Maybe they've all had a bug, or she's taken the kids to visit their grandma or something. You really are jumping to conclusions there, Bea.'

'But what if I'm not?'

'You are.'

'But what if I'm not?'

He stubbed out his cigarette and jumped off the wall,

holding out a hand to help Bea up. She held it, and as she stood up, he pulled her towards him, like a dancer, then twirled her round. Finally, he drew her close and gave her a hug.

'Ant! What are you doing? Stop it!' Bea wriggled free.

'You worry too much. You're a worry pot. Come on!' He grabbed her hand again and started running towards the store.

6

'Where are we going?'

'Up to the staff room, Bea. We're both going to sign up for the choir. Reckon you need it.'

Bea was intending to sign up for choir anyway, but she sensed an opportunity. 'I really don't want to,' she said, as they climbed the stairs to the staff room.

'Come on, Bea. It'll be a laugh.'

She stopped abruptly, forcing Ant to stop too. She looked behind them, checking that they were alone.

'Okay,' she said, 'I'll do it, on one condition.'

'What is it?'

'I'll try the choir with you, if you try the literacy club at the library.'

Ant groaned and leaned against the wall.

'I won't be any good at it, Bea. I had eleven years of school, on and off, and I couldn't get it then.'

'This is different. It's relaxed, one-to-one help. I had a word with the woman who runs it.'

'Huh! Interfering much, Bea!'

'Not interfering, Ant. *Helping*. Anyway, turns out it's Maureen, Neville's wife, who's in charge.'

'What!? That's it, then, total humiliation. No thanks, Bea.'

He tried to push past her, but she blocked his way solidly and put her hands up to his shoulders.

'Ant, she's really nice. She's not Neville-ish at all. She's kind and sort of twinkly. This is it, Ant. It's your chance to start sorting things out for yourself. Once you can read, the world will be your oyster.'

'Never had an oyster. I'm not fussed about squidgy things in shells.'

She gave his shoulders a little shake. 'Forget seafood, Ant. Just promise me you'll try the class.'

Ant sighed. 'Will you come with me? Moral support and all that?'

'Yes, Ant, I will. Thursday evenings at six o'clock. Shall we start this week?'

'Yeah, all right then.'

They bustled upstairs and into the staff room. There were already eight or nine signed up on the choir list. Perhaps George was onto something, thought Bea. She added her and Ant's names.

Her first customer after breaktime was Dave. For God's sake, she thought, and pasted on a fake smile.

'Hi Bea,' he said. 'You're looking lovely today.'

The smile stayed, fixed, as she countered, 'I haven't seen Julie for a while. She okay?'

He did a double take. She wondered for a moment if he was going to turn nasty: she'd seen flashes of his temper before. Instead, he looked her evenly in the eye and said, casually, 'She's away, Bea. Taken the kids on holiday.'

'Oh? Somewhere nice?'

'Swanage. Caravan park,' he said, without missing a beat. 'I couldn't get away because of work.' He put his food into a plastic bag.

'You must be missing them. That's three pounds, ninety-seven, any time you're ready.'

'First time we've been apart like this. We got together when I moved here, twelve, no thirteen years ago, and that was it. Wedded bliss. Ball and chain.' He was deliberately making eye contact now. 'I'm quite liking the freedom. Time off for good behaviour. I can do what I like. See who I like.'

He was brazenly staring at her now. She really wanted him to go away now, but there were harsh disciplinary procedures for workers who told customers to piss off.

'That's three pounds, ninety-seven,' she repeated. 'You do contactless, don't you?' She looked meaningfully towards the card reader.

'Oh, right, yeah.' He paid and gathered up his things. 'See you later, Bea.'

'Feel like I need a shower,' said Bea to Dot.

'Hmm. Doesn't get the hint, does he?'

'Did you hear him say Julie's on holiday?'

'Yeah. That's good, isn't it? I should think the time away will do her the world of good. And those kids.'

'If it's true. If she is away.'

The rest of the day passed slowly. Some of Bea's regulars were in and she enjoyed talking with them, but it felt like a cloud was hanging over Kingsleigh. There was none of the usual banter, just discussions about the body at the factory. 'Have you heard?' 'Yes, terrible, isn't it?'

When five o'clock came round, Bea felt a little pang of sadness. Normally this was the time that Jay logged in to Dot's checkout. He was a student by day and worked at Costsave in the evenings. She remembered first seeing him walking towards her, with Neville at his side. There'd been something there from the start – chemistry. And they'd had five months of fun and warmth and rolling on and off the mattress on the floor in his student digs. God, she missed him.

She and Dot logged out of their terminals and went

upstairs to get changed. In the locker room, they stood next to each other at the mirrors, repairing their makeup.

'Dot, my mum was really upset last night. Can you tell me what's going on?'

Dot's eyes flicked to hers and away again. She pretended to be concentrating on reapplying her lipstick, although it looked fine to Bea.

'It's just resurfacing memories, Bea. A lot of stuff happened that summer. Grown-up stuff.'

'I am twenty-one, you know.'

'I know, darlin', but you weren't then, and there's some things it's better not to know about your parents. If your mum wants to tell you, then she will. Don't push it, though.'

'I don't like secrets.'

'Ha! Everyone's got secrets, Bea. Did you tell Queenie everything you and Jay got up to?'

'No!'

'Well, then. Some secrets are meant to be kept.'

7

Bea and Queenie stuck to their usual routine that evening. Pizza for tea, because it was Tuesday, then watching the early evening news, the soaps and whatever drama was on at nine. Everything was normal on the surface, but everything felt strange. There was an invisible wall between them. Bea heeded Dot's advice and didn't ask her mum anything out of the ordinary and Queenie didn't offer any openings, keeping conversation to the usual, safe topics. Bea went into the kitchen to make their bedtime cuppas just before the end of the ten o'clock news. The kettle was mid-crescendo when her phone rang. She flicked the switch to quieten the kettle and answered.

'Hiya, Bea. I've just got home. Been a long day, but I wanted to let you know, you don't need to worry about your friend. The body's been there several years, but not hundreds. It's not Roman or anything.'

'Does that mean it's Tina Robbins?'

'It's looking that way. It hasn't been formally IDed yet, Bea, so please don't tell anyone. I just wanted to stop you worrying about this Julie.'

'Her husband says she's on holiday anyway.'

'Really? Well, that's great. So you can sleep well tonight, then.'

'Yeah. I suppose.'

'Bea, you've got nothing to worry about. Your friend's fine. The body here isn't your problem. Perhaps you need a holiday. Perhaps *we* could have one, when this is all over. You and me.'

Bea sighed out loud.

'Tom, we're not even . . .I mean, I've got a boyfriend.'

'Yeah, but he's not here, Bea, is he? And I am. Time to give me another chance, I reckon. You know you want to.'

'Tom—'

'I'm knackered now. Gotta go to bed. I'm going to leave you with that thought, though. Don't write me off, Bea. I'm on the up and up now. You and me, we'd be good together.'

'Goodnight, Tom.'

'Night, Bea. Love you.'

The call ended. Bea shook her head. He was a trier, you had to say that for him. Love you, though. That was new. But he'd said it so casually, it didn't really mean anything, did it?

'Who was on the phone?' Queenie said when Bea took her tea through.

'Just Tom.'

Her mum sat bolt upright. 'Was it news? Is he at the factory?'

Bea set her mug down on the coffee table. 'Mum, you know I can't tell you.'

'So, it was. Have they identified Tina?'

'Mu-um. No. Not yet anyway, but it's looking more likely. Don't tell anyone I told you, okay?'

'No, of course not. Was that it?'

'Well, he sort of asked me to go on holiday with him. I don't think he was serious, but I don't think he'd say no if I said yes, if you see what I mean.'

'He's still got the hots for you.'

'Yeah, but I'm with Jay, aren't I?'

'Are you? Is he still messaging and everything?'

'Yeah.'

Bea had been a bit taken aback when Jay announced he was off for the summer, and even more nonplussed when he'd asked her to go with him. Apparently, it hadn't occurred to him that she couldn't afford the flights. She'd briefly wondered about taking out some sort of loan but had received a very sharp lecture from Queenie about the evils of living 'on tick', so had told him 'no'. Now she was wondering if she'd been too hasty. People took out loans all the time, didn't they? Couldn't she just get a credit card like everyone else?

'You should go out there, Bea. Go to Thailand.'

'I haven't won the lottery, Mum.'

'No, but I've got fifty quid saved from my job now. You could have that, and then maybe take out a little loan.'

'You've changed your tune! What about the demon debt? I thought you were dead against borrowing money.'

'I was. I am, but you deserve a holiday. You'd be able to pay it back eventually, wouldn't you? You've got a steady job.'

The more she thought about it, the more she liked the idea. Bea picked up her phone and started searching for flights. She was pleasantly surprised to find they weren't as much as she'd thought. 'Do you know,' she said, 'I think I might. I'm going to ring Jay.'

She went upstairs, her head full of palm-fringed beaches, crystal clear water...and Jay. Bloody hell, what on earth had she been thinking when she laughed off his invitation. Of course she should join him. You're only young once, aren't you? She got comfortable on the top of her bed and, without thinking what time it might be in Thailand, typed in a message.

'Wanna chat?'

Jay replied straight away with a Skype request, and then there he was on her screen.

'Hey, babe. What's up?' The image was quite dark, like he was inside a room with the blinds down. He looked woozy and rumpled, like he'd just woken up. His voice was so quiet, she could only just hear him. She tweaked up the volume on her phone, but it didn't help much.

'Do you still wish I was there, Jay?'

'Yeah, course.'

'Well, I'm going to book flights!' Her voice was squeaky with excitement. She watched for his reaction to mirror hers. Instead, there seemed to be a time delay as he processed the news. He looked away from the camera and then back again.

'Great,' he said. 'That's so cool.' The words were okay, but it was the tone that bothered Bea. His voice was still low, still measured.

'Do you mean it?' she said.

'Of course. When are you coming?'

Behind him, a shadow moved. Then Bea heard another voice, a girl. 'Who is it, baby?'

Bea felt like her bedroom was spinning. 'Who's that, Jay?' she asked.

'Nothing. No one,' Jay said, quickly, but Bea wasn't sure if he was saying it to her or to the girl. She felt hot tears welling up. She killed the call and put the phone down on the duvet next to her. The tears trickled down her face and she wiped them away with her hand. That was that, then, she thought. Out of sight, out of mind. She'd been living from call to call, message to message, and he'd been . . .

Damn, damn, damn.

It was going to be summer in Kingsleigh, after all. Another staycation in the south west's premier small market town no one has ever heard of. Bloody hell.

She heard Queenie coming upstairs. She listened as she used the bathroom and then shut her bedroom door. The wind had picked up outside and the rain was battering against the window. You've got nothing to worry about, Tom had said. Now she'd got nothing to look forward to, either.

She slipped out of bed and padded downstairs. She found a glass in the kitchen and fetched the whisky bottle from the cupboard. Oh Jay, how could you? I thought you were different. She didn't add Coke this time, and the whisky burned her throat as she sipped at it. She sat at the kitchen table, with the bottle in front of her, forcing the drink down. She poured another one. Her throat was starting to feel warm, rather than painful. In fact, she had a warm glow all over. After another glass – or was it two? – she stood up unsteadily and put the bottle away.

She'd left her phone on the bed. The screen was glowing with notifications when she picked it up again. Three texts, two call requests and a voicemail. She stabbed at the display and listened to the voicemail.

'Bea, it's not what it looks like. Come on, let's talk. I miss you, baby. I really miss you.'

The phone buzzed again. Another text. She snorted her contempt and turned off the phone, watching the lights flare for an instant and then die. She lay down under the duvet. The whisky had numbed her a little, but not enough to sleep. As she listened to the rain against the window, she tried to think of anything except Jay, but none of these other thoughts brought much comfort. She pictured the rain battering down onto the white tent at the factory. She wondered if the forensic team were still working there, in the middle of the night. She thought of Tina's family, waiting for the news they'd been dreading for fourteen years. And was it raining in Dorset, too? Was Julie tucked up in bed with Mason and Tiffany, listening to the sound of rain on a caravan roof in Swanage?

However hard she tried, though, her thoughts came back to a dark room on the other side of the world, with Jay and another woman, and she ended up crying herself to sleep.

8

'Oh no,' muttered Bea. 'Not today.'

George was standing at the front of the staff room with someone who could only be their new choir leader next to her.

Candy Argos was not what Bea had been expecting. She had pictured a clichéd choirmaster, along the lines of the vicar in *Dad's Army*, but Candy Argos was in her late thirties or forties, with cropped black hair, a round face and round glasses to match. She was wearing jeans and a bright pink T-shirt under a black blazer-type jacket. She was looking round the room, smiling at everyone.

'You all right?' said Ant, as Bea started to move towards the door.

'No. I can't do this, Ant. I'm going to hide in the bogs.'

She eased her way through the gathering and headed for the door.

'Bea, we're just about to start,' George called out. Bea went all clammy as everyone turned to look at her.

'I'm just . . .I just need a . . .I won't be long.'

'Okay, we'll wait.'

What? thought Bea. They'll wait? For God's sake. Now she had to go to the toilets, stay there a believable time and come back again. What a farce! She spent a minute or so checking

36

her makeup. Her eyes had been so puffy this morning, she'd had to apply layers of soothing balm, primer and concealer, and had reached for her largest megalashes to hide behind. She didn't look too bad, but she felt terrible.

She walked back to the staff room and when she appeared in the doorway, George nodded and made her first announcements. Bea weaved her way back to Ant.

'Dodgy tum?' Ant whispered.

Bea held her index finger up to her mouth and he took the hint and stood, eyes forward. George cantered through the announcements and was soon introducing Candy to the room. She took a step forward and boomed, 'Good morning, everyone! You probably look at me and expect me to lead you into a gospel chorus, and I *could* do that, and maybe we will, but I'm interested in any music which will set your hearts soaring, will make you smile, will set you free.'

Bea resisted the urge to shout, 'Amen!' To be honest, despite her gloom, she was starting to get interested. Candy's speaking voice was musical. She couldn't wait to hear her sing. She didn't have to wait long. 'Don't worry, I'm not going to make you sing today. Only kidding, of course I am! Here we go. Okay, everyone, stand square, relax your shoulders. We're going to start with some breathing. In, two, three, four. Hold it!' She stood on tiptoe and pointed to the ceiling, 'And out, two, three, four. One more time. Long breath in. Just let it happen, two, three, four and hold it, and out. Now, repeat after me. Hey-oh!'

And she was off. Call and response. It was only achingly embarrassing for the first few rounds and then, as people joined in, they started to relax and the volume grew and by the end Candy was firing off fancy trills and the Costsave crew were bravely trying to follow and everyone ended up laughing and there was a little ripple of applause.

'Okay, that was just a little taster. I see that many of you have signed up already. Please add your names today. Our first rehearsal will be right here on Friday. I'll be looking for a different place to rehearse. I don't mind if you haven't done this before. I don't mind if you don't have the best voice in the world. We can't all be Beyoncé. Some people tell me that they can't sing. But I *know* that everyone can sing. You are all welcome. Thank you, everybody. Thank you!' She started applauding, turning around to include everyone, and she got a full-on round of applause back. The whole room was buzzing.

Bea had enjoyed it, but as the meeting broke up, she felt the sunshine that Candy had generated dissipating and storm clouds gathering over her head again, and she was first out of the door. Ant pushed past the others to catch up with her.

'Bea, what's wrong?'

'I can't talk about it. Just leave it, okay?'

'Are you ill?'

'No, nothing like that.'

He pulled a sympathetic face and left her to head for the shop floor. Dot caught up with her as she was nearing the checkouts. She took one look at Bea, reached into her pocket and handed her a packet of extra strong mints.

'Cheers, Dot. Does my breath smell or something?'

'No, course not, but I can see you're struggling today. Those mints are so effing strong, you can't think about anything else when you've got one in your mouth. Thought it might help.'

'You're a doll.'

They settled into their checkouts and each ran through their own warming-up routine. They logged in to their terminals, adjusted the height of their chairs, and checked the change in their cash drawers. Then Bea applied some hand sanitiser, while Dot stretched and wiggled her fingers like a concert pianist about to perform.

The doors were opened, the public trickled in, led, as ever, by Reg. Bea died a little as she saw him heading her way. At least he wouldn't expect cheery banter, she thought. She took an extra strong mint from the packet and was pleasantly surprised that its vapour masked Reg's familiar aroma.

At lunchtime, she sat with Dot on the sofa in the staff room. They talked about the previous night's TV, and what was in Dot's magazine. Bea took her meat paste sandwiches out of the fridge, where she'd left them earlier, but couldn't even be bothered to unwrap them. Her appetite had deserted her.

'Wanna talk, love?' said Dot, looking at the untouched clingfilmed parcel.

'Think I'll go for a bit of fresh air,' said Bea. 'I'll see you later.'

She headed down the stairs and round the side of the building, and almost bumped into Ant. 'These are for you.' He handed her a little bag of Maltesers.

'Oh, what's this for?'

'You just looked like you needed them.'

'Ha, you and Dot both have very accurate antennae.'

'Huh?'

'Doesn't matter.' She opened the packet and offered it to Ant.

'Nah, they're for you.' She shook the packet, temptingly. 'Oh, all right then, just one. You have the rest, though.'

She popped a chocolate into her mouth and let it dissolve on her tongue.

'You don't have to tell me what's wrong,' said Ant. 'Life just sucks sometimes, doesn't it?'

'It certainly does. I couldn't talk about it this morning, but I feel a bit less fragile now. Jay's been cheating on me. I skyped him and he was in bed with someone else.'

Ant frowned. 'What an idiot! Cheating on you *and* answering your call when he was doing the deed.'

'He is an idiot, isn't he?'

'Hundred per cent. I'm sorry, Bea. I thought he was one of the good guys.'

'Hm. Me too. I guess he's just a guy.'

'We're not all bad.'

'"Not all men",' Bea used her index fingers to make speech marks. 'That's a thing, isn't it?'

'Dunno, is it?'

'Yeah. Whenever someone complains about shitty man stuff on Twitter or Facebook or something, a man always comments, "It's not all men, I'm perfect" sort of thing.'

'Oh, sorry. It's true, though. Not all men do "shitty man stuff". Some of us are nice.'

Bea was nearing the end of the little packet of chocolates and wishing it had been bigger.

'Have you ever cheated on someone, Ant?'

He scuffed the sole of his shoe on the tarmac. 'No, not really. I've seen two girls at the same time, not the *same* same time, which would have been *awesome*, but, you know, at different times.'

'Did they know about each other?'

'No, but it was all casual. It wasn't like boyfriend–girlfriend stuff. No commitments. So I don't think it counts. I would never cheat on you, if we ever...you know...'

'Course not,' Bea said, choosing to ignore the assumption that them getting together was a possibility, 'because I'd cut off your Brussels sprouts and put them in the deep fryer.'

Ant winced and covered his crotch with his hands. 'Yeah, you would,' he grinned.

'Yeah, I would. What about Ayesha? Would you cheat on her?'

The grin was wiped from Ant's face.

'Nah, I wouldn't and I didn't. I'd never have...'

'Have? What's happened?'

'It's over, Bea. Has been for a few weeks.'

'Really? Why?'

Ant hunched his shoulders. 'We couldn't meet at hers 'cos her family hated me, and we couldn't meet at mine because I haven't really got anywhere. If you've got nowhere to go, nowhere to be together, it's difficult. Then her parents decided to send her off to a sort of summer camp in America for six weeks and before she went she broke up with me, said it wouldn't be fair to keep me hanging on.'

'So her parents broke you guys up? That sucks.'

'Yeah.'

'I should buy *you* some Maltesers.'

'Chocolate can't solve everything.'

'No, but it can go a long way. Thanks for these.' She crumpled up the packet and squashed it into the palm of Ant's hand.

'Oi!' he said, trying to stuff it down the back of Bea's neck. She dodged away and started running back to the staff door. They were still playing this odd sort of tag when they found Dot standing in the corridor upstairs. She looked stunned.

'Where have you two been?' she said.

'Just outside.'

'Have you heard?'

'Heard what?' said Bea.

'It's online. The police have issued a statement. The body at the factory's been identified. It's Tina Robbins and they're treating her death as foul play. They're saying she was murdered.'

9

That evening, Bea and Queenie watched the evening news in silence. A reporter introduced the piece on the factory murder, standing by the old, wrought iron gates at the entrance to the site.

'Yes, sad news today as police confirmed that the body found in the foundations of the new site B development at the former chocolate factory in Kingsleigh has been identified as that of local girl, Tina Robbins, who disappeared in 2005. Earlier this afternoon they held a press conference.'

The programme cut to footage of a plain clothes officer addressing the camera. 'Today we had confirmation that the body found recently at the Factory Quarter in Kingsleigh was that of Tina Robbins. Tina disappeared on 25th June 2005, after attending an evening party at the Factory Social Club. Extensive enquiries at the time were inconclusive, but the case remained open, with officers following up any leads they could. This has now moved from a missing person's case to a murder enquiry. Tina's parents, Derrick and Nikki, are very bravely here today.' The camera panned sideways to a couple who sat behind the table next to him. The woman was hunched up, looking at her lap. Bea could see the muscles of her face moving as she fought back tears. The man was grey-faced. He didn't look at the camera but stared fixedly at the piece of paper held with both hands as he read out their statement:

'Today, the news that we were dreading has been confirmed. We, and our daughters Hannah and Serena, are heartbroken. We are grateful to Kingsleigh Police who have kept us informed about the search for Tina for the past fourteen years. At least now we will be able to say goodbye properly.

'We ask for the media to let us grieve in peace, and are now appealing again for anyone with any information at all to come forward. Please, don't let another family go through what we are going through now.'

He carried on holding the paper, staring at it, even though he had finished. Next to him, his wife was sobbing quietly into a handkerchief. The camera cut back to the detective. 'And I would add to that, we in the Somerset and Avon Police have promised Tina's family that we will not rest until her killer is brought to justice. Somebody knows what happened that night. Maybe somebody watching this right now, and if it is you, we ask you to put this family out of their agony and come forward. They deserve answers.'

The item returned to the reporter, who appeared to be blinking back tears. 'Obviously, it's a very emotional time here in Kingsleigh. Earlier, I talked to people in the street to see how the town was reacting to the news.'

'Turn it off, Bea. That's enough, now.'

Bea was shocked at the curtness in her mum's voice.

'No, Mum. We might see someone we know.'

Queenie shifted uncomfortably in her chair. 'What do they expect them to say, though?'

'Shh.'

They both watched as there were a series of mini-interviews with people they had obviously just stopped on the High Street, all expressing shock and sadness. Bea

43

recognised one of them as a Costsave customer, but hadn't seen the others before, until Neville appeared on the screen, looking even more like a startled chicken than usual. 'Well, obviously, this is terrible news for the town and for Tina's family. Our thoughts and prayers are with them.' The next interviewee was an older woman, who seemed to be wearing someone else's teeth, emitting an audible whistle with every sibilant 's', 'I never thought Kingsleigh was that sort of place until last year. Now I'm wondering if he was a serial killer. Terrible, it is. Terrible.'

The reporter signed off the piece by talking directly to the camera again.

'Local sources have told me that the police have ruled out a link to the Kingsleigh Stalker, who attacked young women in the town at the end of last year, but there's no doubt that today's news has stirred up painful memories here, and there's a feeling that local people won't rest easy until the killer who struck all those years ago is caught. Back to the studio.'

Bea didn't switch the TV off, but she turned the volume right down. She'd been fighting back tears herself as she watched Tina's parents. She'd expected Queenie to be in floods, as she often cried at the soaps and even reality shows, but she was dry-eyed, almost stony faced.

'That's just the start, isn't it?' said Queenie. 'The TV and the press will be all over this town like a rash. Just like they were before.'

'I don't remember much of that.' Bea recalled being told that Tina was missing, and there had been posters up on lampposts and in shop windows, but that was about all.

'No, because we tried to shield you from it. You were only seven. We didn't want you being frightened or having nightmares.' A little muscle was twitching at the side of her left eye. 'Come on, Bea, let's have another cuppa.'

By the time Bea had brewed up and brought two mugs of tea and a plate of chocolate digestives into the lounge, the soaps were starting and Queenie started to relax a bit more. They settled down for their daily dose of drama. In between programmes, Queenie reached forward and took another biscuit. 'Have you booked your flights?' She looked at Bea expectantly.

'No, Mum. I'm not going.' Bea tried to keep her voice casual. All the focus on Tina's murder had temporarily pushed Jay to the back of her mind.

'Come on, Bea. You deserve a holiday. I could maybe manage more than fifty, if it's the money ...'

'Mum, I'm not going because we've ...well, we've broken up.'

'What? When?' Queenie sat straight up in her chair.

'Last night. I don't want to talk about it, okay?'

'Bea—'

'All right! He was cheating on me. We're done. Silly to think it would keep going, really. So, no, I'm not going to Thailand.'

'Oh, I'm so sorry, Bea.' Queenie put her mug down on the coffee table and leaned forward to reach for Bea's hands, but Bea shook her off. She wasn't in the mood for comfort right now. 'Perhaps you should go away somewhere else, then.'

'Where? With who?'

'I don't know. One of the girls from school, or ...' she trailed off.

'Honestly, Mum,' said Bea, 'if I didn't know you better I'd think you were trying to get rid of me.'

Queenie laughed, but there was something forced about it. Bea looked at her. 'Mum, *are* you trying to get me out of the way?'

'No, of course not. You might want to ...I mean, with all this unpleasantness, it's not nice, is it?'

'You mean, it's not nice with a murderer roaming round Kingsleigh? We've already been there, haven't we, with the bastard that killed poor Ginny?'

'Exactly. I'm worried this will bring it all back for you. I don't want you upset.'

'There's someone else out there. Someone who killed my babysitter and buried the body. I'm bound to be a bit upset, but going away won't help.'

Queenie was ashen-faced now, and Bea felt a sharp stab of anxiety.

'Mum,' she said, 'what do you remember about that day? The day Tina went missing?'

Queenie picked up her mug again, even though there were only dregs left in it. 'Not much,' she said. 'There was a do at the social club that Friday night, like usual. Nothing out of the ordinary. There was a band, people played skittles in the back. Everyone was just unwinding, having a drink. Then we went home. No one knew she was missing until she didn't turn up for work the next day.'

'She was working on a Saturday?'

'The factory ran twenty-four-seven, Bea. She worked on the production line but also took her turn in the shop like the others. I think she was due in the shop that day.'

'What about that evening? Was there anything unusual?'

'No, it was just a standard Friday night out.'

'Tina didn't babysit me that evening?'

'No, we got Shareen from next door. Do you remember her? Tina was at the club for a while, early on. I didn't see her later.'

It was all so bland, so plausible, but Bea wasn't buying it.

'Mum, is there something you're not telling me?'

'No, love. There's nothing to tell.' Queenie turned the mug round in her hands. There was a mark on the surface of the china and Bea watched as Queenie picked away at it with her fingernail. 'I'm sorry about Jay. He was a bit, well, different, but he seemed like a nice lad.'

Bea sighed. She really didn't want to talk about it.

'Well, turns out nice lads will still cheat on you on holiday. And I was just sitting at home, waiting for him like an idiot.'

'You're not an idiot, love.'

Bea didn't linger downstairs for very long. She had a bath and tucked into bed with her laptop perched on her legs. Her mum may have said she wasn't an idiot, but she was certainly taking her for a fool because something didn't ring true about all this, and changing the subject to Jay like that had just piqued her curiosity even further.

She opened her browser and typed 'Tina Robbins Kingsleigh'. The first couple of screens were current articles, reporting on today's announcement, but Bea soon found sites relating to the older story, when Tina was a missing person. She scrolled through until she found a feature article from a national paper, 'The Girl Who Disappeared – Five Years On Her Family Are Still Looking For Answers.' 'Aha, here we go,' she said to herself. 'Let's get to the good stuff.' She was a quick reader and it didn't take her long to skim the first section, which was a description of the events of Friday 26th June 2005. It wasn't much different from Queenie's account. What was new was the next section – the investigation. The article described the leads that were followed in some detail and listed persons of interest to the inquiry, those who had been taken into custody for questioning more than once. Bea scanned the names and then stopped. She could feel bile rising up, pressing into the back of her throat. It couldn't be. She swallowed hard and looked again.

'Oh no. Oh no, no, no, no, no.'

Bea slammed the laptop shut. She kept her hands on top of the lid, pressing down, as if somehow she could stop the words she had read from escaping into the open, keep them hidden, locked in. But, of course, it was too late. What she'd seen couldn't be unseen. It was there now, in her head. It would never go away.

One name that kept coming up in the investigation, a man who had been interviewed three times, but never charged, someone who many people thought had got away with it – Harry Jordan. Her dad.

10

It couldn't be right, could it? There must be a mistake. Reluctantly Bea opened her laptop again. The article was still there. Her dad's name was still there.

She felt hot and cold at the same time. The feeling at the back of her throat became more urgent and she started retching. She had to throw back the covers and run to the bathroom. She knelt on the floor and hung her head over the toilet, trying to calm down, take some deep breaths, but every time she thought she was feeling better, the words came back to her, and her body went into spasms of revulsion. It went on for several minutes until she was exhausted.

Gingerly, she got to her feet and went over to the basin. She ran the cold tap and splashed her face. She caught sight of herself in the mirrored door of the cabinet above the sink and thought how weird this all was. She looked like herself, and the bathroom was the same as ever, but everything felt utterly unreal. She had no idea what to do now. She perched on the side of the bath and tried to think clearly.

Everything she thought she knew was wrong.

Her dad had been the best dad in the world. She'd idolised him, right up until he died, nearly seven years ago. He was steady and funny and loving, the centre of her world. It felt like her childhood, all those happy memories, weren't real. Nothing was what it had seemed.

Things were starting to slot into place; the whispered conversation between Queenie, Bob and Dot the night the body was found, the looks that people were giving her at work. It felt like everyone – *everyone* – except her had known about this. It felt like her whole life had been a lie.

There was a knock on the door.

'Bea? You in there? You all right?'

A new emotion was added to the mix boiling away inside Bea – righteous indignation. Queenie had hidden so much from her. She'd lied and lied. Bea stood up and was over to the door in two strides. She unbolted it and wrenched it open, coming face to face with her mum who had been pressing her face to the door, listening for a reply.

'Oh!' Queenie said, taking a step back. Then, reading the expression on Bea's face, she retreated further.

'Why didn't you tell me?' Bea bellowed at her.

'Tell you what?' said Queenie, standing at the head of the stairs now, cowed by Bea's fury.

'Don't pretend you don't know! Dad was a suspect! He was interviewed several times! Didn't you think I had a right to know?'

Her mum started scratching at her wrists, a habit that usually made Bea go soft inside, want to hug her, but not today.

'Like I said, Bea, I was trying to protect you.'

'Yeah, okay, when I was seven, but what about now? I asked you straight out this evening and you lied!'

'Yes, I know. I'm sorry.' The marks on her wrists were bright red. There were even some little pinpricks of blood beading onto the surface. 'Can we sit down and talk about it, Bea?'

Bea didn't want to sit. She had so much adrenaline

pumping through her system, she wanted to scream and shout, or smash something up.

'I can't, Mum,' she said. 'I just can't.'

She couldn't stand the thought of being shut away in her bedroom. She needed some fresh air, so she grabbed her phone, pushed past Queenie and clattered down the stairs.

'Where are you going?' she heard Queenie say. Bea didn't answer but picked up a long mac to cover up her pyjamas, slipped her feet into the crocs that Queenie kept by the kitchen door to go to the bins in, and went outside. She was putting her arms into the coat sleeves and wrapping it round her as she walked round the side of the house. She could still hear Queenie's voice. 'Bea! What are you doing?'

Bea had no idea where she was going. She just needed to get out. She crossed the road and walked towards the rec. It was ten o'clock but there was still a little light in the sky. She walked across to the children's play area, through the gateway in the little fence and sat down on a bench. She badly wanted to talk to someone.

Her first instinct was to ring Dot, but Dot must have known about her dad – that must have been what she and Bob and Queenie had been talking about. They were all part of a conspiracy of silence, keeping her in the dark, treating her like she was still a child. Not Dot, then. How about her schoolfriends? They were all students now. At least two of them were away, travelling like Jay and the third might as well have been away – she and Bea had only met up once this summer and it had been a bit awkward.

Bea sighed. She scrolled back up her list and dialled Ant's number.

He picked up straight away. There was the sound of a television blaring out in the background.

'All right, Bea? Hang on, I'll go outside.' The background

noise receded, and she could hear him properly. 'What's up, mate?'

'I just . . .things are just . . .'

'Bea?'

'I dunno. Everything's just shit, Ant.'

'Where are you? Your voice is weird.'

'I'm on the rec. In my pyjamas.'

'You're what now? Never mind. Hang on. I'll come over. Take me two minutes on my bike.'

'Okay. See you soon.'

There was a group of teenagers hanging round the youth shelter on the other side of the grass. Bea knew they'd clocked her, but she ignored them and hoped they wouldn't come over. Apart from that there was just a dog walker, walking slowly along the edge of the park, vaping as he went. Bea shrivelled inside when she realised it was Dean and his dog, Tyson, and shrivelled further as they changed direction and started walking towards her. She wrapped her mac more tightly around her, but there was no disguising the bottom of her Disney Princess pyjama legs sticking out from beneath the hem of her coat.

As they got closer, Tyson started whining and straining on his leash. Bea knew that this was friendliness, not aggression, and she gently ruffled the dog behind its ears when he put his paws up on her lap.

'You're not really meant to have dogs in this bit. There are signs.'

Dean shrugged. 'Bothered,' he said, in reply. 'Aren't any kids about, are there? Are those your pyjamas?' His grin was almost a leer.

'Yeah,' said Bea, deciding to brazen it out. 'Just wanted some fresh air. Couldn't be arscd to change.'

'Fair enough.' There was silence for a few seconds. Adversaries for a while, an uneasy truce had reigned between them since just after Christmas when Bea had decided not to grass on him to the police, but an awkwardness remained.

'Here,' said Dean, and Bea wondered what was coming next, 'are you all right?'

She looked at him, surprised. The weaselly face looking back at her seemed genuinely concerned. 'Oh,' she said. 'Yes. I mean, sort of.'

He stepped forward as if he was going to sit next to her, then thought better of it and instead crouched down and started fussing Tyson. Now he and Bea were almost eye to eye.

'If you're in some sort of trouble, I could, you know . . .help.'

'That's, um, that's kind, Dean.'

She thought about asking him if he'd heard rumours about her dad, but at that moment a figure on a bike appeared at the corner of the field and started pedalling rapidly towards them.

'Ah, here's Ant,' said Bea.

Dean looked round. 'Oh, are you two . . .? Ha! Always thought you would. I'll leave you to it, then.' Before Bea had a chance to deny anything, he stood up and started walking out of the play area. He went out of the little gateway as Ant was dumping his bike and jumping over the fence. 'All right, mate?' Dean held his fist out towards Ant, who, surprised, met it with his. Without looking back, Dean carried on walking.

Ant jogged up to Bea. 'Was he bothering you?'

'No. He was . . .well, nice.'

'Nice? Dean?'

'I know.'

'Anyway,' he said, plonking himself down on the bench. 'What's up?'

Bea looked across the park. The teenagers were kicking a can around now, larking about. 'I don't know where to start.'

'Is it Jay? Has something else happened?'

'No, it's Queenie.'

'Your mum? Have you fallen out with her?'

'Yeah. Sort of. We had a row.'

'That's not like you.'

Bea sighed. 'I know. The thing is, she and Dot and Bob and everyone really, have been lying to me, or at least, treating me like a baby.' She paused, not wanting to say the next words out loud. Ant said nothing, letting her get her thoughts together, giving her space. 'It's my dad. He was a suspect when Tina disappeared. He was interviewed several times.'

'Oh shit.'

'Yeah. I mean, it can't have been him, because he was just the nicest man ever. It can't have been him, Ant, but why wouldn't Mum even tell me about it?'

'I dunno, Bea. Have you asked her?'

'No, I just got really mad. Honestly, I could've slapped her. That's why I came out. Just took myself away from her. Away from that house.'

She was leaning forward now, with her hands clamped between her knees. Ant had been mirroring her, but sat back a little so he could fish in his jeans pocket for his cigarettes. He lit one up.

'I know you don't, but do you want a drag?'

Bea had tried smoking before, but hadn't got on with it. Now she took the cigarette, put it to her lips and drew the hot smoke into her lungs. It caught in her throat and she started coughing violently. For a moment, it felt like her airways had shut down. She couldn't catch her breath and her eyes watered until tears trickled down her face. Ant took the cigarette off her and rubbed her back, until finally she could breathe again.

'Jesus,' he said. 'You're not a natural smoker, are you?'

'No,' said Bea, wiping her eyes with a crumpled up old tissue she'd found in her coat pocket. 'Think I'll leave that to you. Ant, what am I going to do?'

'Bea, you're gonna have to talk to your mum.'

'I can't. I just can't.'

'You can, mate. Just sit down together, keep it calm. You two, you've got a brilliant relationship. This is just a wobble. You'll get through it.'

'I don't know, Ant.'

'Do you want me to come in with you? Act as a sort of referee?'

Part of her wanted that very much, but she knew that this was something between Queenie and her. They were a family of two, had been for a long time. They needed to sort it out themselves.

'No, it's okay. I'll do it. I might ring you afterwards, though. If it's not too late.'

'Don't worry about the time. I won't be asleep. Saggy's dogs snore so bloody loudly, it's criminal.'

Bea took a deep breath. The sky was dark now. The air had turned cold. The teenagers were trailing out of the park in ones and twos. It was time to go home. She stood up and started walking past the roundabout and the climbing frame. Ant followed her. He picked up his bike and wheeled it alongside.

'Ant,' she said, as they neared her road, 'had you heard about my dad?' He looked embarrassed. 'Ant, please.'

'I didn't know before, but I heard something at work. Just gossip. It didn't make any sense to me, and it still doesn't. You knew your dad. From what you've told me, he was solid. Look, I've been through all this with my dad. On the telly. In the papers. Don't worry about what people are saying. Go and talk to your mum, Bea.'

'She might have gone to bed by now.'

'Well, if she hasn't, ring me after. I'm not in work tomorrow, but I'll catch up with you, yeah?'

'Okay. Thanks, Ant.'

She watched him fling his leg over the crossbar and cycle down the road, then she pushed open the gate and walked towards the house.

11

Queenie was waiting in the kitchen. She was sitting at the table, with a glass of whisky in front of her.

'Sit down, love,' she said, as Bea closed the door.

'Drinking on your own. Not a good sign.'

'Do you want one? It might be good for, you know, the shock.'

'All right, I suppose.'

'Sit down. I'll do it.'

Bea's hands were shaking. She clasped them together to try and still them, and waited while her mum poured whisky into two glasses, topping up her own, which she then set on the table between them. Bea's anger was subsiding a little and a terrible, churning anxiety was starting to replace it.

'So, you'd better tell me everything,' said Bea, her voice trembling. Did she really want to know, after all?

'What do you want to know?'

'I want to know why anyone would even think Dad might have done it. Weren't you at the club together? What happened?'

Queenie sipped at her whisky, then nursed the glass on the table in front of her.

'We were at the club, Bea, and it was just an ordinary evening, but I left before he did. He was having a good time and I'd had enough. I was getting a bit of a headache. I didn't want to drink any more, so I left him to it. I went home on my own.'

'And when did he get back?'

'Much later. Around midnight.'

'When the club closed? Bit late for chucking out time.'

'The club closed at half ten. He said he went for a walk, to clear his head.'

'Walking for an hour and a half round Kingsleigh? Did you believe him?'

Queenie took another sip, then looked Bea straight in the eye.

'This is your dad we're talking about, Bea. Of course I believed him.'

'But the police didn't.'

'They were interviewing everyone. It's their job.'

'Who else was there that evening?'

'Loads of people – Dot and Darren, who was her partner at the time, don't suppose you remember him. Bob and his Babs, although they left early. Babs wasn't feeling very well. Eileen and her Alf, Dean's dad. There was a band, and a singer. And Tina, of course. She wanted to see the band, I think. That's why she said no to babysitting that night.'

'And there was nothing else unusual about that evening, apart from Dad coming home late?'

'No. Well...'

'Mum?'

'Dot and Darren had a row. It got a bit...heated.'

'Was that normal?'

'It was getting normal by then. They had a bit of a fiery relationship. It probably wasn't anything, but he did storm out of the club.'

'Did the police interview Darren?' Bea knew they had done – his name had been in the online feature, too.

'Yes, they did. Like I said, they talked to everyone.'

Bea's hands had stopped shaking. She trusted herself to reach for her glass and start sipping her drink.

'I wish Tina had babysat that night,' she said. 'I wish none of this had happened. I liked it when she did babysit. She was nice.'

'You would say that,' Queenie sniffed. 'She used to let you stay up, and put bloody nail polish on you. On a school night, sometimes!'

Bea frowned, surprised at the harshness of her mum's tone.

'Didn't you like her?'

'I didn't say that, did I? She was all right.'

'She was beautiful.'

'She had something about her,' Queenie conceded, 'but she knew it.'

There was an odd sort of silence. Bea was shocked at how unsentimental Queenie was about Tina.

'Who do you think did it, Mum?' said Bea.

'I don't know, love. I can't think of anyone I know who'd do something so awful. Maybe it was someone we didn't know, like one of the band, or something.'

Queenie had finished her drink and was turning the empty glass round in her hands. Bea took a deep breath. There was something she had to ask.

'Honestly, Mum,' said Bea, 'is there any part of you that thinks it was Dad?'

There was a pause and then Queenie looked at her, quite steadily.

'No, Bea. He wasn't perfect, but he'd never kill anyone, never hurt anyone.'

Soon afterwards, they both went to bed. Bea rang Ant.

'Everything okay?' It was surprising how reassuring she found his voice.

'Sort of. I'll tell you all about it tomorrow. Just wanted to ring to say I survived.'

'Glad about that, mate. You and Queenie all right now?'

'Not all right, but a bit better.'

'Good.' Bea heard an alarming snorting noise in the background. 'Bloody hell, Bea, did you hear that?'

'Was that a dog snoring?'

'Other end, Bea. Jeez, what's this dog been eating?'

'Sweet dreams, Ant.'

'Ha! As if. See you tomorrow.'

She shut down her phone and resisted the urge to open up her laptop and keep digging. She'd seen and heard enough for one day, but her brain wouldn't switch off. She kept replaying her conversation with Queenie. Where had her dad been for that crucial hour and a half? Why had Queenie been so cold and dismissive of Tina? And one other thing – *he wasn't perfect*. What did that mean? Her mum and dad had always been happy, hadn't they? They'd had the ideal marriage, cut cruelly short by Harry's cancer. Bea had nothing but good memories of him, still felt cheated that he wasn't there anymore.

He was perfect. He *was*, she thought to herself, and then realised how childish it sounded. Nobody's perfect. We are all an odd mix of good and bad. But there was bad, and there was wicked, and nothing anyone would ever say would convince Bea that her dad was a murderer. And if half of Kingsleigh thought that he was, well, she'd just have to prove them wrong.

12

The weather was picking up, starting to show signs that it had remembered what it was meant to do in June. A few fluffy white clouds scudded across a blue sky as Bea walked into work the next day. She hardly noticed, preoccupied as she was by the catastrophe threatening to swallow her up.

In the High Street, she heard heels clicking on the pavement behind her. 'Bea! Wait for me!'

Bea groaned inwardly and kept walking. Although there was a big age gap, she counted Dot as one of her best friends, or at least she had until she'd found out that Dot was part of the conspiracy of silence around Tina and her dad. The clicking of the heels got louder, and Bea could hear Dot puffing and panting, as she ran faster and drew level.

'Bea! It's me!' Bea half-turned her head. 'Didn't you hear me?'

'Oh, hi,' she said.

'This is better, isn't it? Bit of sunshine at last?'

'Mm.'

'Bea! Bea, stop walking for a minute.' Bea rolled her eyes but stopped walking. 'Can we talk?' Dot was badly out of breath. She was perspiring, too, and peeled off her cardigan as they stood facing each other.

'We're talking, aren't we?' Bea couldn't keep the truculence out of her voice.

'I mean, properly. About your dad.'

'Oh.'

'Your mum rang me last night. She was really upset.'

'*She* was upset? I was upset, and I had every right to be. What did she tell you anyway?'

'Nothing, really. She was worried about you. Said you'd had words and stormed out. We had a little chat and then she said she could hear you coming back.'

'I can't do anything, can I, without people talking about me!'

'Not people, Bea. Your mum and me, and we weren't talking about you – well, we were – but only because we were worried about you. Because we care.'

'So do you think my dad did it? Is that what you're all protecting me from?'

Dot's face crinkled with concern. 'No! No, I don't. Harry was a lovely man. I don't think for one minute that he killed Tina.'

'So why not just tell me he was a suspect?'

'Look, Bea, nobody's perfect. And no one wants to find out stuff about their own family. Not really. Some things are just better off buried.' She suddenly realised what she'd said and looked stricken. 'Oh God, I didn't mean—I just—'

But Bea wasn't worried about Dot's clumsy use of language. She was fixated on something else Dot had said. *Nobody's perfect.* The same words that Queenie had used. What was it about her dad that made them say that?

Dot was properly flustered now. She drew out a tissue from her bag and blew her nose, then found another one and started dabbing at her face.

'Dot, forget about it. It doesn't matter. It's just words,' said Bea. 'But tell me, what did you mean when you said my dad wasn't perfect?' Dot practically hid behind the tissue now. Bea reached out and put her hand on Dot's and gently, but firmly, drew it down so that she could look Dot squarely in the face. 'Dot, why wasn't my dad perfect?'

Dot blinked rapidly. She was so hot and bothered now that her eyeliner had smudged at the edges.

'It's not for me to tell you,' she said. 'You really should ask your mum.'

'She's hardly told me anything.'

'Well, try again, Bea. If you really want to know, that is. Sometimes it's better not to.'

'You're worrying me now. I hate that everyone knows stuff that I don't. It makes it all seem really bad. Can't you just tell me?'

'I can't, babe. I wish I could. Anyway, "Let him who is without sin", et cetera. Darren and me had enough problems of our own around then. I wouldn't expect your mum to tell you about them.'

Bea tried not to betray the fact that Queenie had told her about Darren storming off, but she could feel a tell-tale blush spreading into her cheeks.

'So will you tell me about Darren?'

Dot frowned. 'It's ancient history, Bea. I hardly think about him anymore, even though he's my Sal's dad. Neither of us has heard from him, except the odd Christmas card every now and again. Why would you want to know about him?'

'I want to understand what happened the night Tina disappeared. There were so many people I know at the social club that night. I want to put a picture together.'

Dot looked around and dropped her tissues into a nearby rubbish bin.

'So you can solve the crime? Really, Bea, I know you like investigating stuff, but this is too big, too personal. You've got to leave it to the police. It's their job.'

'But what if they're like everyone else? What if they listen to people who say it was my dad? He's not here to defend himself.'

Dot rested a hand on Bea's arm. 'Bea, they're not going to go on gossip. They work with evidence. For a start, they've got, you know, a body now. They'll be looking for DNA and stuff, won't they?'

'I can't just do nothing, Dot.'

'Well, for the time being, you've got to push the weekly offers and keep the money coming into your till.' She checked her phone. 'Oh my gawd, Bea, we're late! Come on!'

They both started running along the street, past the post office, the pound shop and the Indian takeaway. They clattered round the corner and up to the zebra crossing. A rather startled driver braked as he saw them approaching, then smiled and waved them across. Bea and Dot both smiled back as they recognised Bob.

'We're not that late, are we, if Bob's just getting here?' said Bea, but Dot was trotting across the car park, heading for the staff entrance at the back of the store. Bea stopped running and watched her, and wondered if she had just been conned in order to avoid a tricky subject. She also realised that Dot had run, or slow-jogged, at least a couple of hundred metres on her new hip and she felt a little surge of pleasure that her friend was back to full health. Whatever happened, she'd always be friends with Dot, wouldn't she?

Even with the latest news hanging over the town, the sun coming out had lightened the mood, and prompted people to buy more salad, ice lollies for the freezer and even disposable barbeques. George bustled through the shop floor, inspecting the shelves. She breezed past the checkouts with Neville in tow.

'We need to get sun cream and after sun onto the shelves and make sure we keep the seasonal aisle topped up. I think there were more picnic sets in the stores. We've got room for them now. Let's go and check.'

She seemed to exude a positive energy. If anyone could turn Kingsleigh Costsave into a top earner, she could, thought Bea. She realised that her next customer was waiting.

'Sorry, I was miles away,' she said, looking up and smiling.

'No problem.' He was youngish, maybe early thirties, clean-shaven with blond hair cut very short at the sides, but longer and floppy on the top. He was wearing slim-legged trousers, an open-necked shirt and light jacket. He looked positively wholesome. 'Hope it was somewhere nice.'

She raised her beautifully maintained eyebrows and he grinned apologetically.

'The place, miles away. Sorry, silly thing to say. Don't mind me.'

She grinned and started processing his shopping. 'No, I was still in Kingsleigh, I'm afraid.'

'There's a lot going on, isn't there? The news about that girl. Terrible.'

'Mm, yes.'

'Did you know her?'

Bea looked up sharply, caught off-balance by the oddly personal question. 'Um, yes,' she said. The guy pulled a sympathetic face, and Bea felt herself softening in response. 'She used to be my babysitter, actually.'

'Really? This must be very upsetting for you?'

'It's horrible,' said Bea.

'That kind of makes you involved. How do you feel?'

'I'm sorry?' she said, confused. Behind her, she was aware of Dot turning her chair round.

'Excuse me,' said Dot, with a voice that could cut glass. 'Are you paying for those things? Because if not, I think you should leave.'

The man took a step back and held his hands up. 'No

offence. I was just interested, that's all.' He fumbled in his pocket and drew out his wallet, found his debit card and paid. 'It's what everyone's talking about, isn't it?'

'Yes, but not everyone asks such personal questions,' said Dot. 'Most people have more respect.'

They both watched him gather up his sandwiches, banana and drink and leave the store. Bea had a sick, uneasy feeling inside.

'You all right, babe?' said Dot.

'Yeah. That was weird, though, wasn't it?'

'Journalist.'

Bea's uneasy feeling crystallised into something more alarming, something close to panic. 'Journalist? How do you know?'

'Look who he's with now.' Dot nodded her head towards the large glass window next to them, through which they could see the main customer car park. Bea followed where Dot was looking and saw her customer talking to another man, near one of the trolley parks. The other man had his back to the shop, but there was no mistaking his distinctive combover and parka-style raincoat, worn even on this sunny day. This was Kevin, the photographer for the local press. At that moment, they both turned and looked at Bea, and Bea felt herself growing hot underneath her polyester Costsave tabard.

'Shit, Dot, you're right,' she said. 'He wasn't just doing a random vox pop, like you see on the telly. He knew who I was. The fucking nerve of him!'

Behind them, somebody cleared their throat. Dot and Bea swivelled round to find Neville clutching his clipboard and glaring at them.

'Something interesting out there, ladies? Could I trouble you to turn your chairs this way and actually serve some customers?'

'Neville, that bloke out there's a journalist. He was just in here, asking me questions.'

Neville peered outside. 'Questions? What about?'

'About Tina, the girl they've found.'

'Ah.' He came closer to Bea's checkout. 'Beatrice, it's my duty to ensure that this workplace is a safe place for you and all the other staff. If someone is harassing you, I'll have no hesitation in evicting them from the store, or calling the police.'

'Um, thanks, Neville. I appreciate that.'

'Costsave looks after its own,' said Neville. He flashed Bea what she assumed was meant to be a reassuring smile, and stalked off back to the customer service desk.

'Good old Nev. He's not so bad, after all, is he? His heart's in the right place,' said Dot.

'He knows, though, doesn't he? About my dad. He never asked why that journo was asking me questions, because he knows. Oh God, Dot, everyone knows. Everyone thinks it was him.'

13

At lunchtime, Bea braved the staff room, but soon wished she hadn't. Was she just paranoid or did people go quiet when she walked through the door? Were they talking about her when they gathered in little clusters? There were definitely surreptitious glances thrown her way. There were also people studiously ignoring her. Bea tried not to let it get to her. She made a cup of tea for herself and Dot, and they sat on one of the sofas. She opened her plastic lunch box and looked at the sad cheese sandwich that lay within, but couldn't muster enough enthusiasm to pick it up.

Anna came into the room. She scanned around and made a beeline for the spare place on the sofa.

'Hiya, Bea,' she said, setting out her packed lunch on her lap, a healthy option as usual – salad with beetroot and feta, with fruit wedges for afters. 'You okay? Neville said you had the press sniffing round earlier.'

Bea didn't know whether to be offended that Neville had talked about her behind her back or pleased that Anna was being so open. She settled on the latter.

'Yeah, it was weird. He just pretended to be an ordinary customer, but then started asking quite personal stuff.'

'That's out of order. We'll keep an eye out for him now.

If there's any sniff of trouble, we'll get rid of him. After all, none of this is anything to do with you.'

'Well, yes, sort of. Except that it is. I knew Tina. People think my dad killed her. It feels like it's a whole lot to do with me.'

'Bea, you were a child then. What your dad did or didn't do is separate from you. None of us are responsible for decisions taken by our parents.'

'No, but you feel sort of obliged to make things better, put things right. Or defend them. After all, he's not here to defend himself.'

'Mm, I'll always be grateful to you, Bea, for finding out who killed my Joan' – Joan had been Anna's Burmese cat, a victim of the Kingsleigh Cat Killer – 'and I know you like getting stuck into things, but if I were you, I'd try and sit this one out. Let the police do their thing. Just look after yourself and your mum.'

Bea sighed. There was a lot of sense in Anna's words.

'That's what I've been saying,' said Dot. 'The police can do stuff none of us can. Leave them to it. Come on, Bea,' she gave Bea's arm a little squeeze, 'eat your . . .whatever that is.'

'Cheese,' said Bea. 'Probably the boringest sandwich in the world, but I'm not really hungry.'

'Here, have some of these.' Dot leaned over, lifted up the top layer of bread, carefully placed a row of Twiglets onto the cheese and then put the top layer down again.'

'Twiglets! Yum!' said Bea.

'So gross!' said Anna, in mock horror, spearing a baton of red pepper and dipping it into a puddle of hummus.

They ate in companionable silence. Bea, trying not to think about Tina, found her mind turning instead to Julie. She remembered how worried she'd been before the body at the factory had been identified and realised that the feeling was still there. Whatever Dave said, Bea would still be worried about Julie and her two children until she had evidence that they were okay.

'Anna,' she said, 'can you look at people's Costsave saver card use on your computer?'

'No. That's a regional office sort of thing. Why?'

'I'm worried about one of my customers. I haven't seen her for ages and I wondered if you could check whether she's used her card anywhere, not just in K-town.'

Anna started nibbling a slice of mango. Juice threatened to run down her chin and she dealt with it deftly with a tissue. 'Well, I can't check, but I know someone who can. Give me the name and I'll see what I can do.'

'That'd be brilliant, Anna. If she's used her card in the last two or three weeks, at least I'd know she was okay, or buying food, anyway. It'd be one less thing to worry about.'

'If I can do that for you, I'd be happy to.'

In the afternoon, Bea spotted two young men, Tank and Dean, coming into the store. Tank, built like a brick outhouse, was walking slowly round the shop, pushing one of the small, shallow trolleys, shuffling his feet. Dean slouched along next to him. Tank had suffered a brain injury just after Christmas, when Ant and Bea had got tangled up in another investigation. He had spent several months in hospital having rehab, but was at home now, continuing his physio and being gently encouraged to tackle everyday tasks by his mum and occasional occupational therapists. Eileen, Dean's mum, came bustling up to them, and had a brief chat before getting back to setting up the merchandise on one of the end-of-aisle displays.

When they were ready to pay, Tank and Dean came to Bea's checkout. Bea watched Tank put his shopping on her conveyor belt. Each movement was deliberate and slow, but he managed to transfer everything from his basket without dropping it.

'Hi there, how are you?' she said, brightly.

'Good . . .thank you.' His speech, too, was slow and the words rather indistinct, but he could make himself understood. 'Is Ant here?' Ant had used his first aid skills to help Tank when he was in dire straits and ever since, he and Tank had a bit of a mutual appreciation thing going on.

'Not today, I'm afraid. It's his day off. Not sure where he is.'

'Tell him I said . . .hi.'

'Will do. Looks like curry tonight,' said Bea, processing a pack of chicken breasts, a bag of onions, some peppers and potatoes and a pot of very hot curry powder.

'Yeah. We're going to make it together, aren't we? My mum's teaching us both to cook.'

Bea looked with interest at Dean.

'It's true. It's a bit of laugh, actually.'

'I'm pretty good already,' said Tank, 'but Dean's . . .rubbish.'

'Thanks for that, mate,' said Dean. 'I can't be good at everything, can I?'

'I should learn to cook,' said Bea. 'I spend my life surrounded by food, and we're still eating crispy pancakes and oven chips.'

Tank got in a muddle with the cash, handing over way too much, but Bea dealt with it matter-of-factly and handed back the excess.

'He's doing well, isn't he?' said Dot after they'd left. 'Considering where he started.'

'Yeah, nice to see him out and about. And nice to see Dean helping him. Did you hear they're doing cooking together?'

'Yeah, I heard. Guilty conscience, I reckon.'

Bea could see Eileen, Dean's mum, who had moved to a closer aisle.

'Shh,' she said, and lowered her voice. 'That's a bit harsh, anyway, Dot. They're just mates. They were mates before his injury and they're still mates now.'

Dot grimaced. 'You're nicer than me, Bea. You've actually got a heart, where I've got a shrivelled old walnut.'

Bea snorted. 'Don't be daft.' She turned to her next customer with a smile. It wasn't just Tank's recovery that had cheered her up, but Dean's ongoing rehabilitation from sly, unsavoury little twat to somebody recognisably human. Not everything in the world was getting worse.

As she walked home, Bea rang Ant.

'Hiya, Bea. Been thinking about you today. You all right?'

'Yes and no. It's been a bit hideous. I'll tell you about it later. Tank was in, though. He said to say hi to you.'

'Ah, that's good. Sorry I missed him.'

'Had a nice day off?'

'Yeah, it was actually. Saggy's got a new toy, so we mucked about with that.'

'What sort of toy?' said Bea, then thought better of it. 'No, don't tell me. Listen, are you going to the library this evening?'

There was a pause. 'I dunno.'

'Go on, Ant, you said you'd give it a try. It's free and it would get you out of Saggy's place for a couple of hours.'

'Yeah, but—'

'Will you go if I come with you?'

'What are you going to do there?'

'Either help out or sit and read a book. I'll be there for moral support. If it's really awful, we'll go to the pub or something.'

'Yeah?'

'Yeah. Shall I come round to Saggy's?'

'No need to go out of your way. Let's meet by the clock.'

'Promise you'll be there?'

'I promise.'

She'd only just rung off when her phone buzzed again. Queenie was calling.

'Bea, where are you?'

'On my way home, Mum. I'm five minutes away. Why, what's wrong?'

'It's started, Bea. I've had people on the phone, asking questions, and a reporter knocked on my door just now. I told him to go away, but he's still there on the pavement outside. What should I do?' Bea could hear the note of panic in her voice.

'Don't worry, I'll sort this. I'm coming now.'

She put her phone back in her pocket, clutched her bag firmly to her side and started running. She was out of breath before she'd got halfway across the rec, but she kept going, fuelled by adrenalin and outrage. When she turned the corner into her road, she could see the reporter lurking outside her front gate. He had his back to her, but it was clearly the same young guy who had spoken to her at Costsave.

'Oi!' she shouted.

He turned around. Without really thinking, she clattered up to him and shoved him with both hands in the middle of his chest. He reeled away, arms flailing. The small garden wall caught the back of his knees and he folded over backwards and landed, bum first, in the flowerbed beyond.

'Oh my god!' said Bea. She clapped her hands to her mouth, delighted and horrified in equal measure at what she had done.

The reporter sat, blinking up at her in astonishment. Oh Jesus, thought Bea, I'm going to be up for assault. Then, he said, 'Fuck!' and started roaring with laughter.

'Are you all right?' said Bea.

He was almost weeping with laughter, unable to get up, feet resting on the wall.

'Oh God. Here—' Bea went through the gate and held her

hand out towards him. He wriggled sideways, got his feet away from the wall and grabbed her hand. She hauled him up to his feet, and he stood for a while, slapping his backside and legs, trying to get the soil off. 'I'm sorry. I'm so, so sorry.'

'It's okay,' he said, finally. 'No harm done. I was just winded. Jesus!' He started laughing again, and held out his hand. 'I'm Dan, by the way. Dan Knibbs.'

She took his hand and they shook briefly.

'Bea. Bea Jordan. But you already know that, don't you? You came into Costsave looking for me.'

'Yes, I did.' He had the grace to look rather shamefaced. 'I'm sorry. I shouldn't have sabotaged you at work.'

'No, you shouldn't. And you shouldn't harass my mum either.'

He held both hands up. 'No harassment, I assure you. I knocked at the door, and left when she asked me. I'm not a monster, Bea. I'm just doing my job.'

'Bit of a shitty job.'

'Aw, don't be like that.'

'Honestly, though. Do you really like doing this? Door-stepping people when they are distressed anyway?'

He shifted his feet a little, looking down at the ground. 'It's not the best part of the job, no.' Queenie was peering out of the front window. 'So, are you going to ask me in for a cup of tea?'

There was something so honest and open about Dan's face, that Bea almost said yes, but then she caught sight of Queenie's anguished expression.

'No, sorry. I can't. You won't get anything out of us, so you might as well leave.'

'Fair enough,' he said, 'but when you change your mind' – when, not if – 'these are my details. Give me a bell or text me.' He held out a business card. She looked at it in his hand. 'Please, take it. Just in case.'

She took the card. 'You'll leave us alone now?'

'Yes. I'm going. I'll see you around, Bea.'

She stayed in her front garden for a moment or two, watching as he got into his silver hatchback and drove away. Then she turned and walked into the house, where Queenie was waiting for her, dry-eyed, wrists scratched raw.

14

'Hello. You must be Ant. Come and sit down.'

Maureen was so welcoming and warm, Ant couldn't resist. He pulled out a chair at the nearby table and sat down. Bea stood next to him.

'Do you need any help?' she asked Maureen.

'Not at the moment, Bea. We've got more volunteers than clients.'

'Is it okay if I just stay and read?'

'Of course.'

Ant was looking deeply uncomfortable, as if he could bolt out of the door at any moment.

Bea flashed him an encouraging smile. 'I'll be over here,' she said.

She walked along the shelves, stopping now and again to inspect the spines and pull out a book. Fiction A-Z, Crime Fiction, Classics – a lot of the books were familiar to her. She'd been coming to the library since before she started school. Today, nothing took her fancy. Towards the back of the library there was a section she'd never visited before: Local History and Archive. She idly ran her eyes over the shelves and flicked through some of the books. Kingsleigh had a surprisingly rich history. There were studies detailing the Roman remains found in various locations and several accounts of the town during the first and second world wars. Then, she found a large rack of folders, labelled *Kingsleigh Bugle*, and dated by year. There were loads of them, stretching from last year back to 1985, when the paper was founded. Bea lifted the folder for 2005 out of the rack and put it down on the nearest table.

She opened the cover and started leafing through and was soon immersed in the reported life of her small town fourteen years ago. On the surface, it didn't seem much different from now. The lead story was often about parking charges and traffic. The *Bugle* normally steered clear of politics, but there had been a general election in May 2005, so there were photographs of all the candidates with a couple of paragraphs of biography below each one. Bea noted that Malcolm Sillitoe, now leader of the town council, was one of them. She shuddered to think of the heights his pomposity would have reached if he'd made it to Westminster. It was bad enough watching him lord it around Kingsleigh now. Most of the news concerned social or sporting events, many of them fundraising for charity. This was the lifeblood of the local paper. There were lots of photographs of people – Bea supposed that the editor liked to keep the headcount high, banking on anyone featured buying at least one copy.

Bea tiptoed to the end of the row of shelves and peeped at Ant. He was deep in conversation with Maureen, focused and calm. She smiled to herself and returned to her table, diving back into 2005. Towards the back of one edition (12th May 2005), there were a couple of photographs of another social gathering. The first one featured a large group of people, in two unruly rows, one standing in front of the other, and the second showed someone receiving a silver cup. The photographs were captioned with a full list of names of those pictured, and there was also a brief article under the heading 'Charity Skittles Night at the Factory Social Club'.

Bea looked at the group photograph more closely, and started to recognise some familiar faces. There was Bob, looking quite a lot slimmer, and Dot and a rather attractive man, who must be Darren. She felt an electric spark of excitement as she spotted a girl in the front row, smiling directly at the camera. It was Tina. This wasn't the stock photo that the media had been using, the one that had featured in the posters all those years ago. This was more candid. Her expression was more natural. She looked relaxed and happy. This was the Tina that Bea remembered. Someone had their hand on her shoulder. Bea looked at the people either side and behind her, and gasped. The hand belonged to the man standing slightly to the left in the back row. He was half-hidden by a tall woman next to Tina, but it was clearly Bea's dad.

She could see one side of his face. He wasn't looking at the camera. He was looking at Tina.

'Oh, Dad,' Bea said quietly to herself. 'What did you do?' She realised that her mouth was dry, but sharp tears were pricking her tear ducts. She was starting to think the unthinkable. There was some sort of connection between her dad and Tina. Did that mean – could it mean – that he was involved in her death?

She put her hand over the photo, palm down, obliterating the evidence and looked up at the wall facing her, the racks of old newspapers. She wondered if anyone else had dug up this article, in this sea of newsprint? She hoped not, and she wouldn't be showing it to Tom or anyone else official, but she did want a copy for herself. It felt important.

She took a couple of photos on her phone, then studied the names on the caption and read the article. The skittles evening had raised a hundred and thirty pounds for the club's adopted charity.

There was a noise, someone clearing their throat. She looked up and Ant was standing nearby.

'What are you looking at?' he said.

'Nothing,' Bea said, quickly closing the folder. 'You finished?' She put the folder back on the rack.

'Yeah.'

'Was it all right?'

'I'll tell you about it outside. Let's get out of here.'

They walked past Maureen. 'See you next week, Ant!' she called out.

'Yeah. Thank you,' Ant said, a touch sheepishly.

'So, tell me all about it,' said Bea when they were out in the precinct.

'You heading straight home? Or shall we get some chips?' The chip shop was only across the road and they could see that there wasn't a queue. 'Come on, Bea, I'm starving. Gotta feed my brain after all that.'

'Not sure chips are brain food.'

'No, but fish is. Gonna push the boat out and have me some cod with my chips today.'

He started jogging on the spot.

'What are you doing?'

'It's sitting still all that time, thinking. I've built up some energy, need to let off steam.'

He leapt onto one of the nearby benches and then stepped up onto the back of it and sprang off, landing unsteadily by Bea's feet.

'Okay, you wally, get over that road and get some chips before you break your neck doing something silly. Come on, tell me how you got on.' She linked her arm through his and they crossed the road and walked into the shop. They both ordered some food and mugs of tea and then sat down at one of the tables.

'It was all right, really,' said Ant. 'Maureen is really nice. God knows what she's doing with Neville. She's quite fun. Not stuck up at all.'

'So, you're definitely going back?'

'Yeah. She's given me some homework to do. Just some cards to look at and learn. I reckon I can do that.'

'I could help you, if you want me to.'

'It's a bit babyish.'

'Don't be daft. You can come round to mine after work, have some tea with Queenie and me.'

'Yeah? I'd like that. Can't hang around at Saggy's all the time. I've got to find somewhere else.'

'I wish I could help.'

'You do help, mate.'

'No, but with a room. Somewhere to stay.'

'That's okay,' said Ant. 'I'll find somewhere. Anyway, what were you looking at while I was making my brain hurt?'

'Oh, nothing really. Looking through old papers. Just confirmed how dull Kingsleigh usually is.'

'Old papers from 2005?'

She quickly met his eye and was surprised to find him looking at her intently.

'Yes,' she said.

He put down his little wooden chip fork.

'Bea,' he said, 'this is a big police investigation. You know you can't get involved, don't you?'

'I can if they're not doing it right, if everyone's already made up their mind about my dad. I can see it in people's faces when they look at me. People going quiet in the staff room when I walk in. I can't ignore it, Ant.'

'Bea, I don't think people are talking about it as much as you think they are. Anyway, sod them.'

'But it's the police as well, Ant. They want to interview Mum. They're coming tomorrow. It feels like they're just gathering evidence to pin on him.' She thought guiltily about the photo on her phone. That was evidence, wasn't it? 'I can't have it, Ant. I won't stand for it. If no one else is going to look for proof that he's innocent, then I am!'

She had raised her voice so much that the people at the next table *were* looking at her now. 'What?' she said, directly to them. They were a youngish couple with their two children. All four of them looked startled.

'Hey, buddy, cool down!' Ant turned to their neighbours. 'Sorry, guys, she's just had a bit of bad news.' He put his hand over Bea's. 'It's all right, okay? It's going to be all right.'

'It's not though, is it? Not unless I do something about it. He's not here to defend himself, so I'm going to have to do it for him.'

'Okay, okay. Eat your chips and let's get out of here, before you start a riot.'

Bea pushed the plastic tray away from her. 'I'm not hungry, Ant. You can have them if you want. I'm going to go home.' She got up, slung her bag over her shoulder and started walking towards the door.

'Wait! Bea, wait!'

Ant caught her up, carrying both trays of chips. 'You're not in this on your own, mate.' He held her chips out towards her.

'Feels like it.' Bea kept walking, almost barging the chips out of Ant's hand.

'Hey, this is me you're talking to! We've done two investigations already, you and me. If you're dead set on proving your dad innocent then you'd better count me in.'

Bea stopped walking. 'Really?'

'Yeah, course. Here,' he said, holding one tray towards her, 'eat your bloody chips before they're all cold and manky.'

They found a bench to sit on near the clock tower, and tucked in.

'If you're really going to help me, I'd better show you this,' Bea said, putting her chips down on the bench and getting out her phone. 'It's what I was looking at just now in the library.'

Keeping hold of his chips in one hand, Ant took Bea's phone in the other and squinted at the screen. 'What is it?'

'It's a picture from the paper, a week or so before Tina was murdered. There was a do at the club. It's a picture of some of the people there that night.'

'It's too small, Bea. I can't see a thing. Hang on, I'll zoom in.' He put the chips down, wiped his greasy fingers on his trousers and moved his fingers apart on the screen to enlarge the image. 'Wait, is that Tina?'

'Yes, and the bloke behind her, with his hand on her shoulder, that's my dad.'

'Yeah?' Ant held the screen closer to his face. 'I can only see half of him.'

'I know, but he's not looking at the camera. He's looking at her.' Bea let the significance sink in for a while. 'Ant,' she said, 'what if I've been wrong all along? What if my dad and Tina had a thing going on?' She went all hot as she said the words.

Ant's jaw fell open.

'I suppose, if we really are investigators,' he said slowly and carefully, checking her expression as he spoke, 'we should consider every possibility.'

'I know,' said Bea miserably. 'I've been so busy feeling outraged, I think I lost sight of that. I don't want it to be true, but what if it is?'

Ant gave her phone back.

'None of us are responsible for what our parents do or did. My dad's a burglar. It's what he does. But that doesn't mean I'm responsible for his crimes. If – and it's a big if – your dad was involved in some way, it doesn't reflect on you.'

'But it'll change everything. My whole childhood. My home. Everything. Nothing will ever be the same again.'

'That's true, and it would be awful. I'm not going to deny how bad it would be for you, and for Queenie. But whatever happens, Bea, think how much worse all this is for Tina's family.'

'Are you saying I'm being selfish? That I should shut up about it?'

'No, not at all. Just that there's always someone worse off. Maybe that doesn't help. I'm sorry. I'm not very good at this.'

Bea felt too churned up to give him the reassurance he was fishing for. They sat in silence for a while, picking at the chips that were rapidly cooling down. There was a group of teenagers nearby, skateboarding on the steps of the precinct. Bea recognised some of them as former friends of Ant's brother, Ken, who had moved to Cardiff with their mum and sisters.

'That's Ken's lot, isn't it?' she said, pleased to change the subject. 'Bet you miss him and your mum.'

'Yeah. It's weird. One minute I was part of a big, noisy, bonkers family, the next I'm on my own, kipping on friends' floors. I don't really know how it happened.'

'You could still move in with them, couldn't you? Go and join them in Cardiff?'

'I could do. I'd have to share a bedroom with Ken, though. Don't think either of us would want that. Anyway, I'll soon be reading and then I can really start sorting my life out.'

Bea doubted it was going to be that easy, but she didn't want to crush him. 'That's the spirit. How did your day off go?'

Ant crammed in the last of his chips and mopped up the last of his ketchup with his finger.

'Ha! It was a right laugh.'

'Oh?'

'Saggy's got a new toy, a drone. We took it out, filmed some stuff. It was pretty cool.'

'Bloody hell, I would have thought Saggy was one of the last people you'd want to have a drone. What were you filming?'

'We took it into the park and sent it up, filmed the beautiful sights of K-town.'

'Oh. Nice.'

Bea hadn't finished her meal, but she'd had enough. She looked around for a bin.

'They can go anywhere, you know, film anything. Turns out that topless sunbathing in your back garden is quite a thing in Kingsleigh.'

'You didn't! You pair of perverts.'

Ant grinned. 'Bloody did. That's not all. There was a couple, you know, at it on a sun lounger. Saggy said we should put it on YouTube, but I thought that might be a bit much. For a start, if they find out it's him, he could get a battering.'

'Someone should take that drone away from him. That's horrible, spying on people.'

Ant's grin became a leer. 'You got strong feelings about it, Bea? Like a bit of sunbathing, do you? Or a bit of extras in the fresh air?'

Bea tried to cuff the back of his head, but he ducked.

'No! Even if I wanted to, all the flats behind us can see into our garden.' Ant was still grinning. 'You can bloody well wipe whatever thought you're thinking out of your mucky mind, Ant.'

'Sorry, Bea. You can't blame a man for dreaming, though, can you?'

'Yes, you can. Especially if we're mates and it makes me really uncomfortable.'

'Oh.' The smile had gone now. 'Sorry. I don't want to make you feel weird. It's difficult, though, when one of your best mates is really fit. I can't help thinking sometimes . . .I mean, don't you ever think about me like that?'

Without thinking, Bea blurted out, 'No! We're friends.'

Ant's face fell. 'Yeah, okay. Message received.'

'Ant, I don't mean you're not fanciable, just not by me, 'cos we're mates.'

He shook his head. 'Keep digging, Bea, you're nearly down to Australia.'

'Give me your rubbish. There's a bin over there.' Bea took Ant's polystyrene tray and stomped over to the bin and back. 'Are you going back to Saggy's now?'

He thrust his hands into his pockets and kicked at a stray can. 'Yeah. S'pose.'

'You could come back to mine and go through what you did in class just now? Queenie would be interested.'

'Nah, it's all right. I'd better get back. I'll see you tomorrow, Bea.'

She watched him walk away down the High Street, hands still in pockets, shoulders slouched, and wondered if she'd really hurt his feelings. Their banter often had a slight edge of flirtation, but he didn't really fancy her, did he?

For a moment, she allowed herself to imagine kissing him. He'd taste of cigarettes and chips, which wasn't an altogether pleasant thought. She let the 'footage' play in her head but found it strangely unmoving. There was no frisson of excitement, not even the smallest butterfly in her stomach or anywhere lower. Ugh. She shook herself, like a dog shaking off water after a dip in the sea, and hurried home.

15

Bea spent the next day on edge. The police were coming to question Queenie. Bea had asked if she wanted her to be there, but Queenie had said no. 'No point you losing a day's wages.'

'I could take it as annual leave. I'm sure George would understand.'

'No, love. It's too short notice. I'll be all right.'

Bea couldn't help thinking that once again she was being shut out. Her mum didn't want her to hear whatever it was she was going to tell the cops.

She sat at her till and tried to act normally, to greet her customers with her usual smile, to remember to ask after her regulars' children or grandchildren. She was usually good at putting on an act in adverse circumstances, smiling through period pain, tiredness or a hangover. Today, however, it was almost more than she could bear. Life *wasn't* normal and she didn't want to pretend that it was.

At breaktime, the staff room was busy. Bea's antennae were working overtime, primed to detect slights, gossip or malice. It was a relief when Anna tapped her on the shoulder and beckoned her away from the others. 'Let's have a cup of tea in my office.'

Bea already had a cuppa, so she waited while Anna made

one and then followed her down the corridor. 'Shut the door, Bea,' Anna said.

'What is it?' said Bea.

'Officially, we're discussing staff rotas. I understand there was an issue with next week's shifts?' She looked at Bea meaningfully.

'Oh, yes, right. But really . . .'

'Really I wanted to tell you that my friend in the regional office ran a check on Julie's card. It hasn't been used for three weeks. No activity at all.'

'Anywhere in the region?'

'Anywhere in the country. The system covers the whole of the UK, Bea.'

Bea put her mug down on a coaster. 'That's not like her at all. She was in here most days.'

'But she's meant to be away though, isn't she?' said Anna.

'Yeah. Her husband said she was in Swanage. There's a Costsave there, isn't there?'

'Yes, but there is another supermarket in town, I checked, so this might not mean anything.'

'When's the last time her card was used?'

'The last time was right here, on the 16th May.'

'Oh, Anna, I've got a bad feeling about this. I think— God, I can't even say it. I think he's killed her. Killed all of them. Her and the kids.'

The temperature in the room seemed to drop.

'Seriously?' Anna put down her cup and sat back in her chair. 'That's a big thing to say, Bea. You'd better tell me why you think that.'

Bea took a long breath in and sighed it out. 'He used to beat her up. She'd come in wearing sunglasses on a cloudy day, with a black eye behind them. It's been going on for years. I tried to give her one of those domestic violence cards, you know, with the number to call, but she was too scared to take it. She said she'd remember the number instead. She said she'd call it.'

'Maybe she's done that then, Bea. Maybe she's at a refuge. Or she's gone to family. Has she got anyone?'

'I don't know. The thing is, why would her husband say she's on holiday, if she's left him?'

'Pride? Doesn't want to admit that she's dumped him. Maybe he's hoping she'll come back? Have you done anything about it? Reported it?'

'I talked to Tom, you know, the copper—'

'Oh, I know Tom. *Your* copper.' Anna arched her eyebrows.

'Not mine,' Bea said quickly. 'Anyway, I mentioned her name. Until it was identified, I thought that Tina's body might be her. When he said it wasn't her, we kind of left it. He's been so busy since then.'

'Maybe talk to him again, then. Nice excuse for a little get together. You like him, don't you?'

'No! Yes. Sort of. To be honest, I think I'm off men.'

'Don't blame you. Hard work, and then they let you down. Women aren't much better.'

Bea didn't know much about Anna's home life, except that she was fond of cats. 'Ha! Perhaps I should get a cat, or another dog. I miss Goldie.'

'Maybe a tame copper would be all right. At least talk to him about Julie. See what he says. It might put your mind at rest.'

'Yeah, I think I will. Thanks, Anna.'

She'd gathered up her cup and stood up when Anna said, 'Wait a minute, Bea. Are you . . .okay?'

'Yes, fine.'

'But really okay? You don't seem like yourself. You seem a bit down.'

Bea sank back into the chair, which creaked a bit on its castors. 'You know what people are saying about my dad?'

Anna was always refreshingly direct, and today was no exception. 'Yes.'

'It's not right, Anna. It can't be. I want to tell them all to shut up. I want to show them that they're wrong.'

'Of course you do. The police will sort this one out, though, won't they? And they should look into the Julie thing, too. Don't take it all on yourself, Bea. You did a bloody brilliant job finding the maggot who killed my Joan, but don't get tangled up in things you can't fix. I'm saying this for your sake, Bea. It's too much.'

As she was talking, Bea could feel waves of anger surging through her. She wasn't cross at Anna, who she knew was trying to be a good friend, she was furious at the rest of the world – the prejudice, the injustice, the indifference to truth, and the men who hurt and killed women and walked away.

'I can't just do nothing, Anna.'

'The thing to do is look after yourself, Bea. Look after you and your mum. The next few weeks aren't going to be easy. Pace yourself. Be gentle with yourself. Talk to Tom and then let him get on with it. And come to choir practice this evening. You are coming, aren't you?'

'Yes, I guess. I'm not really in the mood.'

'Give it a try.'

Anna's words – *Don't get tangled up in things you can't fix* – kept going round Bea's head as she dragged herself through the afternoon shift. Even one of her favourite customers, Charles, who owned Goldie, couldn't brighten her mood.

'Come and see Goldie soon,' he said. 'Take her out for a walk. She'd like that.'

'I will,' said Bea, absently. She'd spotted a bit of a spillage on her conveyor belt, so when Charles had gone, and with no other customers in the offing, she moved the belt round, then stood up and sprayed some cleaning fluid onto it and started wiping. Behind her, Dot's next customer was whistling quite loudly. Bea found herself listening, trying to identify the tune. She'd just realised it was Sinatra – 'I've Got You Under my Skin' – when he stopped whistling and started speaking. He had a deep, rather rich voice with a pronounced Bristol accent.

'Got the champagne, got the chocs, got the flowers, just need someone to give them to.'

Bea turned round. The man was quite tall, with dark, possibly dyed hair, slicked back over his head. He was wearing scuffed jeans and a leather jacket. The words 'ageing rocker' drifted into Bea's mind. His eyes, set in a decidedly rugged face, were dark brown and twinkly, but they weren't fixed on her. He was looking directly at Dot, who had been concentrating on taking the reams of receipt and vouchers from the till and handing them to her previous customer. Now she turned to the mystery whistler and gasped.

'Darren! What are you doing here?'

'Just breezing through, Dot. Couldn't pass K-town without calling in to see you, could I?'

Her hand went up to her hair, instinctively checking everything was as it should be.

'How did you know I was here?'

His smile twisted up a little further at one side. 'I asked around. You weren't difficult to find. So, are you going to accept these?' He tipped his head towards the flowers and chocolates.

'I don't know. What am I going to do with them? I'm at work, Darren, if you hadn't noticed.'

'Bung them through the till, and I'll keep them for later. What time do you get off today?'

'Five. But I'm staying on for something.'

'What? Overtime?'

'No, choir practice.'

Darren raised an eyebrow. 'You could skip that for once, couldn't you? We've got a lot of catching up to do.'

Dot seemed temporarily at a loss for words and Bea could have sworn she was blushing.

'I, um, I don't know, Darren. Actually, I do want to go to choir. I'll see you just after seven, in The Nag's Head. That'll be thirty-two pounds, sixty-five, please. How are you paying?'

Darren looked slightly taken aback, but he soon recovered himself. He paid for his shopping with cash, managing to hold onto Dot's fingers as he handed it over and quickly stooping down to brush his lips across the back of her hand.

'Go on with you,' said Dot. 'I'll see you later.'

She watched him walk away. Bea grabbed a laminated special offers price card and started fanning Dot, who swivelled round in her chair.

'What are you doing, you daft cow?' Dot said.

'It's suddenly got a bit hot in here. Thought I'd help cool you down.'

'Cheeky.'

'So that was your Darren, was it?'

'Yeah, that's him.'

'Good looking guy, Dot.'

Dot gave a pleased little smile, like Bea had paid *her* a compliment.

'When we were younger, he was smoking hot. He's still got it, hasn't he?'

'Yup.'

'He's bloody trouble, though, Bea. Always has been. I wonder why he's turned up now?'

Bea looked down the aisles towards the back of the shop. Bob was standing behind the meat counter. A customer was trying to get his attention, but he was staring, or rather glaring, at Dot. The customer rang the bell, right in front of his nose, and he went back to serving, but for the rest of the afternoon, whenever Bea looked up, chances were Bob was looking back in their direction.

At five o'clock Bea was ready to go home. Her shift had finished but now she faced the prospect of hanging around in the staff room with several others until choir started. Dot had rushed off to the locker room as soon as she'd logged off from her till. Bea followed her up there to get changed and pick up her bag. Dot was in front of the mirror with her makeup bag out, starting a full-on makeover session, layering foundation on top of what, to Bea, looked like already perfect skin. She almost offered to fetch Dot a trowel, but realised just in time how catty it would sound, and left her to it. It was nice, after all, to see her this excited.

'You look great, Dot,' said Bea. 'Making an effort?'

'Well, I like to look my best. Show him what he's been missing.' She dabbed some concealer underneath her eyes, then brushed some glossy powder onto her cheekbones.

'Do you think he's trying to get back together with you?'

'He's after something. I've got no illusions about him, Bea. He's always after something, but maybe I can have a bit of fun with him. Eyes wide open this time. Everything on my terms.'

Bea went downstairs and round to the side of the store, and rang home. 'Did the police interview you today?'

'Yes, it was fine,' said Queenie. 'It was just going over what I told them all those years ago. I've got nothing new to say.'

'Are you sure you're all right?'

'I'm fine, Bea.' Things were still a bit stiff between them. 'You staying on for your choir?'

'I'm meant to be, but I can come home if you need me.' She was half-hoping Queenie would say yes.

'No, we'll have dinner a bit late today, shall we? I'll get it ready for when you get in.'

'Okay.' She was about to ring off, but then she couldn't

resist sending some gossip her mum's way. 'Hey, guess what?'

'What?'

'Dot's Darren turned up. In the store!'

'No!' The awkwardness was gone in an instant. Bea could tell that, on the other end of the line, Queenie was agog.

'Waltzed up to her with champagne and roses!'

'Oh my word!' Queenie breathed. 'What did she do?'

'She agreed to meet him later.'

'Ooh. He's back! After all these years! You'll have to tell me everything later.'

'Will do. See you later, Mum.'

Ant was hovering nearby, waiting for her to finish. 'Was that Dot's ex in the shop earlier, then?' he said, apparently unashamed at listening to her call.

'Yes,' said Bea. 'Darren. They split up fourteen years ago, though. I don't think she's seen him since. Not recently, anyway.'

Ant pushed his lips forward, ruminating, and Bea suddenly remembered his brief fling with Dot, and wondered if he still harboured ambitions in her direction. 'She was gobsmacked to see him. Complete surprise.'

'A blast from the past,' said Ant. 'Interesting. That might explain why Bob's stomping about in the changing rooms. Thought he was going to rip the hand dryer off the wall!'

'Oh blimey. He's still sweet on her, isn't he?'

'Yeah.'

'Are you? Sweet on her?'

Ant gave a full-bodied laugh, and tipped his head up to the sky for a moment. 'Ha! No. She was a laugh, really good fun, but that's all over with. I think Bob's more her type. Or maybe this Darren fella.'

'She's trying to pretend she's cool about him, but she's in there now getting tarted up.'

'Maybe he's The One, then. First love and all that. Lucky

fella, if he is. Anyway, we'd better get inside. It's nearly time.'

Bea put her phone back in her bag and hoisted it onto her shoulder. 'I might just dip out, Ant. I'm not in the mood.' She took a few steps away from the store.

'No way, Jose, you made me go to reading class yesterday. You're coming to this.' Bea groaned. 'A deal's a deal, Bea. Come on!'

16

For a whole forty-five minutes, Bea forgot about her troubles and just sang. They started with a few vocal exercises and then Candy started teaching them 'Lean on Me', splitting them into two groups. At first Bea found it disconcerting to have two melodies running at the same time, but soon she managed to concentrate on her part and not worry about what the others were singing, and then she found the music was there, around her, and she was part of something rather magical.

She wasn't the only one to feel that way. At the end of the session she looked round the room and there were broad grins on everyone's faces, even Eileen, whose default expression was like a grumpy Persian cat on a bad day.

'Thank you, everyone! We'll be having our next session in a meeting room at the British Legion. As you know, this is a strictly no audition, open access choir, but if you would like to try out for a solo spot, then I'd like to hear you. I'll be there an hour before the main session, if you'd like to try.'

'Solo?' someone called out. 'Why do we need a soloist?'

'I wasn't going to tell you this until later, but –' she checked with George, standing next to her, who nodded, '– we're booked to perform on the community stage at the music festival in five weeks' time!' A ripple of discontent spread through the group, mutterings and grumblings. Candy held her hands up. 'I know, I know, it's a bit daunting, but I promise you we'll be ready to go public then.'

The groundswell of dissent grew. People were shaking their heads, pulling on jackets and gathering up bags, ready to leave. It felt like most of them wouldn't be coming back. George stepped in.

'Wait a minute. Before you go, I want to say something.' Everyone paused and looked towards the front again. 'It was my idea for us to take part in the festival. It's a way of giving something back to the town, showing everyone what Costsave is all about. I know it's a big ask, but I wouldn't ask you if I didn't think we could deliver. More than that, I'm confident that we'll do us, and we'll do Costsave, proud. Thank you, everyone! Have a good evening!'

'I didn't sign up for this,' said Bob, as he filed out of the room next to Bea. 'Singing in public. I don't think so.'

'Yeah, don't think anyone wants to.'

Bob sidled next to Dot at the top of the stairs. 'Like a lift home, Dot?' he said.

'No thanks, Bob,' she said, brightly. 'I'm sorted, thank you. I'm meeting someone.'

'Darren,' he said. 'I thought I saw him in the store earlier. Dot—'

'Don't, Bob,' she said. 'Don't get involved. He's back and he wants to talk, so that's what we're going to do.'

Bea followed them outside. They trailed round towards the side of the building. There was a figure waiting at the corner, with a large carrier bag from which the top of a bouquet of flowers was poking out.

'Dot!' said Darren, holding the bag out towards her.

'Thank you,' she said, taking the bag and inspecting the flowers, which were starting to droop a bit. Bob had come to stand next to her, instead of heading for his car.

'Darren.'

'Bob.'

There was an air of two gunslingers facing each other on a dusty street about them, thought Bea.

'You're back, then.'

'Looks like it.'

'Well . . .' Bob seemed to have run out of things to say, or unable to say the things he wanted to. 'Have a good evening.'

Darren simply nodded and offered an arm to Dot. She didn't take it, but started walking close to him. 'What are you doing here? I thought we agreed to meet in the pub.'

'Couldn't wait to see you.'

Bea looked at Bob, who was glowering as he watched them walk away.

'Is he bad news?' she said.

'Yes. He's bad news. I just don't want her to get hurt.'

This was a bit rich, considering that Bob had two-timed Dot only a few months ago, but Bea decided that discretion was called for. Unfortunately, she breathed in a small fly just at that moment, so she hiccupped a couple of times and then started a volley of coughing that resulted in the expulsion of the insect into her hand.

'You all right?' said Bob. 'Need me to slap you on the back?'

'No,' Bea gasped, trying to return her airways to normal. 'I'm okay. I'll see you tomorrow, Bob.'

Ant caught up with her as she crossed the car park. They both flinched a little as Bob drove past them with the engine revved far too high.

'He's in a stew, isn't he?' said Ant.

'Yeah. He's still got the hots for Dot all right. If he hadn't messed up earlier, I reckon they could be together now. It's his own fault.'

Ant grinned. 'Sly old dog.'

'It's not funny, Ant.'

'No.' He was having trouble wiping the smile off his face.

'Tell you what, though, he might not be the answer to Dot's prayers, but he could be the answer to yours. He's got at least one spare room.'

Ant raised his eyebrows. 'Bob!' He held his hands up in front of his face and crossed his two index fingers to ward off the name.

'Hear me out. He's got a decent sized house, his heart's in the right place, and you'll never go short of bacon.'

'He hates my guts, Bea. We've got history, remember?' Bob had been extremely jealous when Dot and Ant had had their brief dalliance. For a while there had been a great deal of seething amongst the sausages, and hard stares in the staff room.

'No, he doesn't. He's over all that. I reckon you two might get on all right sharing a house, actually.'

Ant still looked doubtful, then brightened. 'I could pick up some tips from him. He's a bit of a player, isn't he?' Bea batted his arm. 'Oi! Anyway, it's not a completely bad idea, I suppose. I can't stick it at Saggy's much longer. Reckon I'll ask him.'

They parted ways at the end of the High Street and as Bea set off across the rec, she texted Tom.

'Got time for a chat?'

He didn't reply immediately, but when she was nearly back, she heard the tone on her phone which signalled an incoming text. She stopped walking, fished it out of her bag and eagerly read the reply.

'Drink later? Pick you up at 9?'

She texted her acceptance and walked round the side of her house and in through the kitchen door, where Queenie was waiting for her.

'Tell me about Dot and Darren, then,' she said, before Bea had even put down her bag.

'Yeah, in a minute. I want to know about your interview with the cops. Was it Tom who came round?'

'No, it was a woman. Not the one who's been here before. Another one.'

'What did they ask?'

'Oh, just all the stuff they asked fourteen years ago, Bea. Honestly, I don't want to go over it all again. This morning was enough.'

'Have the press been round again?'

'No, thank goodness. I'm doing a shift at the launderette tomorrow, and I want to feel I can get out of the front door without being harassed.'

'You can't let this put you off, Mum.'

'I'm not going to. I spent too long shut away in this house after your dad died. There's no going back now.'

Queenie had suffered from anxiety and agoraphobia for close to six years, during which Bea became her carer and go-between. At the time Bea hadn't told many people about it, as she'd felt a weird sense of shame about how they were living, what they'd become. Things were much better now, though. Maybe she didn't tell her mum how much she admired her progress often enough.

'I'm so proud of you, Mum,' she said.

Queenie looked surprised. Little pink spots of pleasure appeared in the skin on her cheeks, and her eyes twinkled, perhaps a little moister than usual.

'Thanks, Bea. I'm proud of you, too. We're doing all right, aren't we?'

'We are, and we'll get through this current business. I know it wasn't Dad and soon everyone else will know too. When the truth comes out.'

'Yes,' said Queenie, but there was something hesitant about it, something about the way she looked away, that made the breath catch in Bea's throat.

17

'You look amazing.' Tom called at Bea's house at exactly nine o'clock, and his tired eyes lit up at the sight of Bea, which was a gratifying result for all the effort she had put in over the previous hour.

'Thanks,' she said. 'See you later, Mum!' She didn't need to have raised her voice, as Queenie had emerged from the lounge and was standing in the hall behind her.

'Bye, love. Have a good evening.'

'Right, where are we going?' Bea asked.

'I was thinking the Jubilee, unless you want to go somewhere quieter.'

In the past, Bea hadn't wanted to fuel the town's gossips by being seen with Tom, but she was past caring. 'Jubilee's fine.'

It was the nearest pub to Bea's house and it only took them a couple of minutes to get there. Walking side by side felt surprisingly good. Despite him being tall and athletic, they fell into step naturally and Bea noticed a little frisson – was this a taster of her future? Could she imagine spending the rest of her life walking next to this man? It wasn't an unpleasant thought and she let it stay in her mind, testing it out until Tom said, 'Penny for them.'

'Huh?'

'You're unusually quiet. What are you thinking?'

'Oh, nothing.' He was keen enough on her, she knew. No need to stoke the fire right now.

He bought the first round of drinks and they found a little corner to settle in. There was a moment of awkwardness as they looked at each other across the low wooden table. Bea sipped her spritzer and noticed the grey rings under Tom's eyes.

'You must be tired,' she said. 'Working flat out on this case.'

He rubbed his face, digging the heels of his hands into his eye sockets, as if he was trying to wipe away the fatigue.

'I'm knackered, Bea. It's great, though. This is exactly what I want to be doing. A case like this, it's so fascinating.'

'You know someone interviewed my mum today.'

'Yeah. Yeah, I do know. Look, Bea, I'm not gonna lie to you, this could all get really difficult. But I don't want it to come between us. Whatever happened in the past, whatever the outcome of this investigation, it's nothing to do with you and me, yeah?'

'You mean my dad, don't you? You mean, if it turns out he did it. Well, I can tell you now that he didn't.'

'Bea . . .' Tom reached forward and cupped his hand over the top of hers. 'You weren't there. You can't know what went on.'

She withdrew her hand. 'Neither were you!'

'I've been reading the case files, Bea.'

'What does that mean?'

'I've been going through all the interviews and witness statements of people who were there at the time. Including your dad.'

'And?'

He sighed, then bit the corner of his lip. 'I've got to be honest, it's not looking good, Bea.'

'My dad didn't do it, Tom. I know he didn't.'

'People were saying, still are, that your dad had a thing for Tina. Was maybe obsessed with her.'

'That's just gossip, Tom. You know what people are like.' She tried to mentally blot out the photo on her phone. She should show it to Tom, but there was no way she was going to.

'I'm sorry, Bea, but we've got to look at the evidence. When you eliminate all the other possibilities, what's left is the answer. He went AWOL that night. At least an hour and a half unaccounted for. He was interviewed three times, and he changed his story at least once.'

'He changed his story?'

'Look, I shouldn't discuss this with you. I'm sorry, Bea.'

'You've got to tell me now, Tom! You can't drop stuff like that into the conversation and then clam up!'

Tom glanced around the room, satisfying himself that no one was eavesdropping, then he shifted forward in his chair and leaned both elbows onto the table.

When he spoke, his voice was low and quiet. 'The first and second times he was asked about the time between leaving the club and arriving home he said that he was walking around the town. He realised he'd had too much to drink and was trying to sober up.'

'Okay, people do that, don't they?'

'Yes, but the third time he said he saw Tina with someone, a boy about her age, and then he went and sat in the park.'

'He saw someone with her? Did they find out who it was?'

Tom sighed. 'Chances are it wasn't anyone, Bea. He made it up, didn't he? To try and get the heat off himself. Otherwise why not tell us the first time? I'm sorry, Bea, he just cooked up a story.'

'You don't know that! Tom, this is my dad we're talking about. How would you feel if it was your dad?'

'Well, he's deputy chief constable, so I'd be pretty surprised.'

Bea stopped playing with her glass and looked at him sharply. 'Your dad's deputy chief constable?'

'Yeah.'

'No wonder you got your transfer to the CID,' she muttered.

Tom frowned and sat back from the table. 'Hey, I got that fair and square, Bea! It wasn't anything to do with him.'

'If you say so.'

'I think we'd better go. This wasn't a very good idea, was it?' Tom stood up, leaving his glass, still half full, on the table. Bea took a final swig of hers and stood up, too, but Tom was already walking away. She trotted across the room to catch up. He reached the door first, and very reluctantly held it open for her.

'Tom, I'm sorry,' she said when they were outside in the car park. 'I shouldn't have said that. This is a bloody nightmare for me. I feel like I'm losing my mind.'

He didn't say anything and she knew she'd really got to him.

'Tom, don't let my stupid big blabbermouth spoil things. I know you've got a job to do. I'm made up for you that you're in the CID now. I really am.'

His expression softened a little, but he still stayed silent.

'Look, I need to ask you something, not about Dad, something else. I could come down to the station, I guess, but I'd rather do it now.'

His interest was piqued now.

'Okay. Shall we start walking? I've left my car outside your place.'

'Sure. It's the woman I told you about, Julie. She still hasn't turned up. I got someone to check and she hasn't used her Costsave saver card for three weeks. I'm worried. I really am.'

'She's probably just lost the card. I do that all the time. It's not like a debit card or something, that you have to use, is it?'

'No, I don't think she has a debit card, though. I don't think her husband allowed it.'

Tom narrowed his eyes. 'Are you talking about coercive control?'

'Yeah, I guess. That and the rest. He beats her up.'

They were outside number twenty-three now.

'Everyone's super-busy on the factory case at the moment. If you want to make this official, you'll need to come into the station and report a missing person. Then, if we can get the resources, we'll ask around, have a word with the husband.'

'If it's formal, will he know it was me reporting it?'

'No. We can keep that confidential.'

'And you'll definitely follow it up?'

'At some point, but maybe not straight away. It's all down to resources. Bea, I'm not sure you've got any reason to worry.'

'I've got a hundred reasons to worry, about this and the other business.'

'Let us get on with the job, Bea. We'll get to the truth.'

'It's easy to go after someone who isn't around to defend themselves.'

Tom looked at her and it was clear he was running out of patience. 'And it's easy not to accept the obvious if you're too close to the case.'

The words hit home. Stung. Bea said, 'I'd better go in before I say something I regret.'

'Yeah,' said Tom. 'Goodnight, Bea.'

Not surprisingly, he didn't try to pinch a kiss, or cop a crafty feel, like he normally would. Bea was relieved and disappointed in equal measure. She hesitated at the top of the path and looked back. He'd already started his car and was drawing away. No sideways glance, no wave goodbye. Bea leaned against the pebble-dashed wall of the house.

She took out her phone and looked at the incriminating photo in her gallery. Tina smiled straight at the camera. She didn't look awkward or unhappy that her dad's hand was resting on her shoulder. She was comfortable with him. They were friends, right? Or maybe something more. No, she thought firmly, shutting the gallery down, putting the phone back in her pocket.

'I believe you, Dad,' she said, but as she walked towards the back door she thought perhaps she really meant 'I believe *in* you', and wondered if that was a different thing, and whether the blind faith of her childhood was really based on anything at all.

18

'Is that the Sea View Caravan Park?'

'Yes.'

There was a TV playing loudly in the background – *Homes under the Hammer*. Bea raised the volume of her voice.

'Have you got a Julie Ronson staying with you? I'm trying to get in touch with her, but I've lost her mobile number.'

Bea could hear someone on the telly saying, 'I've viewed a hundred properties and I haven't found the right one yet.'

'Who is this?'

'I'm just a friend of hers. I've got some news.'

Bono started singing, '...still haven't found what I'm looking for.' Bea wondered if it would be rude to ask the woman to turn the sound down.

'The park's really quiet at the moment. How long has your friend been here?'

'I'm not sure it's your park. It'd be three weeks. She's got two young kids with her.'

'No. We haven't had anyone like that here in the last three weeks.'

'Are there other—? Hello?'

But now there was only silence at the other end of the line. Bono and the woman at the caravan park had gone. The call had been cancelled. Bea turned to the next number and dialled, but after half an hour, she'd contacted all five holiday parks and camping sites on her list and nobody had seen Julie or were admitting to it. Bea stared blankly at the wall for a while, only brought out of her reverie by the sound of the doorbell, which reminded her that Ant was coming round for help with his reading homework. She got up off her bed, checked her reflection in the dressing table mirror, and went downstairs.

Ant and Bea sat either side of her kitchen table. It was just after eight and Bea had told Ant about the caravan sites while she stacked her and Queenie's dinner things in the dishwasher and made a cup of tea. Now she held up a card for Ant and asked him to read the word printed on the front. He looked and Bea could see him thinking, his lips forming the words, testing the sounds out silently before he said them out loud. She felt herself getting nervous for him, willing him to get it right.

'Bus?' he said, finally. Then, more firmly, 'Bus!'

'Yup,' said Bea. 'What happens if I do this?'

She covered the 'B' and he looked again. 'Us,' he said, grinning.

They worked their way through the pile of cards. He got a few wrong, or needed Bea's help, the first-time round, but then he asked Bea to go through them again and he got them all right.

'Fuckin' hell, Bea. I can do this!' he said, just as Queenie walked into the room. 'Sorry, Mrs Jordan. No offence.'

Queenie didn't bat an eyelid. 'None taken. I was listening to you in the other room. You're doing a great job. I'm proud of you, Ant.' She gave his shoulder a squeeze and bent down to plant a little peck on the top of his head. Bea cringed a bit, but Ant positively glowed, and Bea wondered how little warmth and approval he had in his life now that his mum and brother and sisters had moved away.

'I've got some biscuits somewhere,' Queenie said, rummaging in the cupboard. 'Here.' She handed a new packet of chocolate chip cookies to Ant.

'Don't open them for me,' he said.

'Don't be daft. Do you want a fresh cuppa to go with them?'

'Yes please, Mrs Jordan.' Ant tore the packet open and took a biscuit from the top.

'Don't let me stop you. Carry on with your reading.'

'We've done all my homework.'

'Do you want to watch some telly? *Gogglebox* is on later. We like that, don't we, Bea?'

'I don't want to get in the way. I should get back really.' He took another biscuit.

'You're not in the way, silly,' said Bea. 'Come on, let's sit in the lounge.'

Ant and Bea decamped to the other room where they sat at opposite ends of the sofa, with their legs curled up and their feet nearly meeting in the middle. Bea flicked through the channels.

'I was wondering if I should go down to the coast, ask around the holiday sites,' she said.

'They've told you she's not there, haven't they?' said Ant. He had the packet of biscuits balanced in his lap and was steadily working his way through it.

'Yeah. Well, four out of the five did. The other one wouldn't answer my questions.'

'So why would they answer face to face?'

Bea shrugged.

'I don't know. They'd see I was harmless. I could show them photos of Julie and the kids.'

'Have you got any photos?'

'No, I'd have to get some from somewhere. What do you think? Do you fancy a trip to the seaside?'

'Always, but I'd rather sit on a beach and eat ice cream than tour the caravan sites on a wild goose chase.'

His words hurt a little. 'I'll go on my own then,' said Bea.

'Hey, don't be like that.'

'You're like everyone else. You think I shouldn't do anything when I'm worried about things, that I shouldn't poke my nose in . . .'

'I'm not like everyone else. Here, have a biscuit. Peace offering.' He held the packet out towards her. There were only a few left.

'How many have you had?' she squealed. Ant's face coloured up.

'I'm s-sorry,' he stuttered, and leaned forward and put the packet on the coffee table, and with a horrible rush, Bea realised that he was actually hungry. Coming into the room with a tray and three mugs of tea, Queenie got there before her.

'Ant, dear, did you have dinner before you came here?'

'Um, no. Not tonight. But it's okay. I'm all right.'

Queenie and Bea exchanged worried glances. Queenie put down the tray, next to the biscuit packet on the coffee table.

'I've got some spuds in the cupboard. I'll bung one in the microwave for you, shall I? Do you like grated cheese?'

Ant shifted uncomfortably in his seat.

'No, honestly. Don't do that. I'm okay.'

'Do you like baked spuds?'

'Yes, but—'

Too late. Queenie was already heading for the kitchen and soon Bea could hear the sound of running water, as she scrubbed the potato and then the beep of the microwave as she programmed it and set it running.

Ant rubbed his hand over his head, trying to deal with his embarrassment.

'Just let her do it, Ant,' said Bea. 'She likes looking after people.'

He sent her a rueful smile. 'I've had a thought about the Julie thing. You're worried he's done away with her, aren't you? That's what's really bothering you.'

As he said it, Bea realised how real her fear was. 'Well, yes.'

'So, instead of going down to somewhere where she might or might not be, why don't we have a look closer to home?'

'But she's not there.'

'No, but if he has done something to her and those kids, he'll have had to get rid of the evidence, won't he? So why don't we do what the cops do and look for signs of recent digging.'

'Go round there when he's out?'

'Yeah, sort of. When's the next time we've got a day off together?'

'Dunno. Are you working tomorrow?'

'No, but he'll be around then. How about Monday?'

'Oh yeah. Monday's good.'

'I'll come round here. I'll let you know the time when I've organised it.'

'Organised what?'

'You'll see.'

A loud PING! from the kitchen announced that Ant's potato was ready. Shortly afterwards Queenie appeared with it sliced open and steaming on a plate. Butter glistened at the edges and there was a pile of cheese on top, starting to melt.

'Here you are, love. Dig in.'

'Thanks, Mrs Jordan.'

'You're welcome.'

Queenie settled into her armchair, but she didn't face the telly. She watched as Ant shovelled hot potato into his mouth, then sucked air in noisily to try and cool it. It was not, thought Bea, an edifying sight, but the expression on Queenie's face was soft and fond.

When Ant had polished off the lot, which didn't take long, she leapt up to take his plate.

'Cheers, Mrs Jordan. That was great.'

'You're welcome,' she said. 'I'm only sorry we haven't got room for you to sleep here, love.' She was about to go into the kitchen when she paused, 'Would it help if you came for your tea more often? Every day if you like.'

'Oh no, honestly, I'm all right. I'm normally okay. Saggy's mum's being great, but she's been out today.'

'Well, bear it in mind. You're always welcome.'

'Thanks. Can I wash my things up?'

'It'll all go in the dishwasher.'

'Okay. I'd better get off now. Thanks for dinner.'

When he'd gone, Bea made another cup of tea for them both. She and Queenie settled back into the lounge.

'I think we should keep asking him,' said Queenie. 'Did you see the way he demolished that spud? I don't think he's eating enough.'

'To be fair, he always eats like that,' said Bea. 'But you're right. I don't think he's very happy at Saggy's. I'm trying to get him to ask Bob if he could stay in his spare room.'

'Oh, that's a good idea. I'll put in a word, shall I? Maybe Ant'd do it if Bob actually asked him instead of the other way around. I want to talk to Bob anyway. I'll do it now.'

'Thanks, Mum.'

Instead of using the phone there and then, Queenie got up and took her mobile upstairs and into her bedroom. Hating herself for doing it, but not enough to actually stop, Bea turned the TV volume down and then crept upstairs, sitting about halfway up, trying to hear what her mum was saying.

'I know, Bob . . . I just can't . . . I can't do it . . . no, she doesn't know . . . do you think so? Yeah, maybe you're right.'

She doesn't know. Bea was pretty sure that she herself was *she*. What didn't she know? The conversation was moving on.

'. . . had young Anthony here. He was starving, poor lad,

hadn't had any tea. Could you take him in? Just for a week or two . . .you say that, but he's a good lad really. What do you think, Bob? Yeah . . .all right . . .see you soon. You too. Bye.'

Bea scuttled back downstairs and had just turned the telly back up when Queenie reappeared.

'Bea,' she said, standing in the doorway, 'I need to tell you something.'

Bea paused the TV. 'What is it?'

'Well, really, I need to show you something.' She was still standing there, looking like she wanted to run upstairs and hide. Bea kept quiet, waiting for whatever her mum had to say, but Queenie couldn't seem to find the words. The silence grew until it was unbearable.

'What is it, Mum? Are you ill? Is there something wrong with you?'

'No, darlin', it's not that.' Bea felt a wave of relief. She couldn't really imagine anything worse than her mum telling her she had a lump or an unexplained pain. But perhaps there was something worse, because Queenie was saying, 'It's about your dad.'

Bea's stomach tightened. 'Go on.'

Queenie was deathly pale now, scratching at her wrist compulsively. 'When he was ill, you know, when he knew he wasn't going to get better, he wrote some letters. One for you, one for me and one for the police.'

A tide of panic was rising inside Bea now, a sicky, fluttering, painful feeling.

'Letters? What's in them?'

'I don't know, Bea. I never had the nerve to open mine. I just hid them away, tried to forget about them. But I don't think I can pretend any longer. I think the time's come.'

19

'Pour us a drink, Bea, and I'll fetch the letters.'

Bea went into the kitchen and poured whisky into two tumblers. She added some cola to hers and left Queenie's neat. She heard a noise and turned around to see Queenie walking back into the room, holding three white envelopes. She laid them out on the table in a neat row. Bea could read the upside-down writing on each one – capital letters in her dad's unmistakeable sloping handwriting: 'MAGGIE', 'LITTLE BEA' and 'POLICE'.

Queenie sat down. Bea set their drinks down and sat opposite. She looked at the envelopes, then took a mouthful of whisky.

'What do you think's in them?' Bea said.

'I don't know.'

It was heading towards midsummer, but it suddenly felt cold in the kitchen.

'I'm going to have to say this,' said Bea, suddenly finding that her mouth had gone dry. She took a swig of drink. 'What if it's a confession? What will we do?'

Queenie looked up at her and it felt like they were facing each other over an abyss. They both knew that their lives could change forever in the next few minutes. Queenie reached out and took Bea's hands in hers.

'I would like to say we could burn them, but if that's what this is, you know we'll have to give them to the police, don't you?'

'Oh, Mum.'

'I know.'

Bea felt anxious tears pricking at the rims of her eyes. Queenie's face was puckered with pain. Without speaking, they stood up, moved to the side of the table and put their arms round each other. Bea let out a huge involuntary sob. Queenie rubbed her back.

'It'll be okay,' she said. 'It's been you and me for six years. It'll still be you and me, whatever's in those envelopes. We'll get through this.'

They stayed standing, hugging each other for a little while longer, then they broke away and sat down again. Bea wiped her eyes and blew her nose on a hanky.

'I'm scared,' she said.

'Me too,' said Queenie.

'We've got to do this, haven't we? Let's open our letters together.' Queenie nodded. 'Three, two, one . . .go.'

They both reached forward and picked up their envelopes. Bea turned hers over and put her index finger into the little gap at one corner. She exerted some pressure and it started to rip. She looked across the table. Her mum was doing the same. They reached into the envelopes and drew out the folded paper from inside. They looked at each other again, then both unfolded the paper and started to read.

For a moment, the words seemed to dance on the page in front of Bea. She was so panicked that her mind wouldn't settle down enough to read. Then a word came into focus. Her name. Her name written in her father's dear, familiar hand. She moved her eyes to the head of the paper and started to read.

My Dear Little Bea,

I'm writing this knowing that I will be gone by the time you read it. I wish with all my heart that I could be there to see you grow up, but it's not to be. Whenever you do read this, I know that you will be a fine person, because you have been the best daughter I could ever have wished for. You're clever, and brave, and you do your own thing, always have done. I'm so proud of you. You're going to have a brilliant life.

Bea let the tears trickle down her face. There was no point trying to stop them. There were more waiting to take the place of any she mopped up.

Bea, you may hear things about me when you are older and I want you to know—

Bea stopped reading. She wasn't sure she could bear it. She glanced across the table, where her mum was engrossed, her lips moving slightly as she read.

—that I have never physically hurt anyone in my life. I may have hurt your mum by being foolish once or twice, but I didn't mean to, and I think that she has forgiven me. She truly is a queen, Bea, as much as you are a princess. My Princess.

Look after each other. I love you so much.
Dad
Xxx

Bea read the whole thing again, then folded it up, slid it back in the envelope and put it on the table. She got out her hanky, wiped her eyes and gave her nose a good blow.

'You all right, love?' said Queenie. Her eyes were red-rimmed. A tear seeped out and she dashed it away with the back of her hand.

'Yeah. Think so. He told me he didn't do it. He never hurt anyone physically. You can read it if you like.'

'Maybe later.'

'He said nice things about you, too. What did yours say?' Bea could see that her mum's letter was longer than hers. Two full pages of his small script. 'Mum?'

Queenie was biting one side of her bottom lip.

'Mum? What did it say?'

'It's a sort of confession,' Queenie said, and Bea felt like her heart had missed a beat. 'Not the sort you're thinking of. And I kind of knew about it, but we never really discussed it, not properly. It's odd seeing it in black and white.'

Bea didn't want to ask, but she had to. 'What's he confessing to?'

'I'll read you a bit. Not the whole thing, that's personal. Let's see . . .' Queenie ran her index finger down the first page and stopped near the bottom. 'Yes. Here.' She cleared her throat, then took a quick sip of whisky. 'I want you to know the truth, even though it shows me up for what I am. Was. I think you know what a fool I was. I thought that I felt something – love – for Tina. I thought she felt something back. I was deluded, like I said, an old fool. She was just being pleasant, chatting, smiling. She did it with everyone. There was nothing there. Nothing at all between us.

'On the night she disappeared, I waited for her as the club was closing. I was going to say something to her, tell her how I felt. I saw her leave but there was someone else waiting, a bloke with his back to me. She kissed him, stood on tiptoes and kissed his cheek, but then it was odd. There were no raised voices, nothing like that, but there was something wrong. He was holding her arm too tight, hurting her. I started walking towards them. I shouted out, "Are you all right?" He didn't turn round, just shouted for me to mind my own effing business. I said I wanted to hear it from her. She looked at me, past his shoulder and said, "It's fine, Harry. Goodnight." And I walked away. I walked out of the factory grounds and then cut through to the park. I sat there, near the river, for ages, thinking how stupid I'd been. Feeling humiliated. I'm ashamed to say I thought about chucking myself into the water. I just felt so useless.

'Then I thought of you and little Bea.' Queenie's voice was catching now, but she carried on. 'My two shining stars, waiting for me at home. And I felt even more ashamed. I came home, and there you were. You pretended to be asleep so we wouldn't have a row and wake Bea. And in the morning, we just carried on being us, like normal.

'Us. You, me and little Bea – that's what's been most precious to me all these years. Our life together, just our normal everyday, wonderful life. I'm so sorry I ever thought I wanted something else, when what I had was everything. I'm so sorry I'm going to have to leave you two much sooner than I wanted to.

'I've written a letter to the police. I've told them it all before, but perhaps they will believe me this time.'

Queenie folded the letter up and looked at Bea. Tears were flooding down Bea's face. Snot was bubbling out of her nose. 'Come here, darling. It's all right.' Queenie came round to Bea's side of the table and put her arms round her, while she sobbed and shook. 'I know. I know. It's all right.'

They stayed like that until Bea's floods turned into sniffles. Seeing that her hanky was saturated, Queenie gave her a handful of tissues and made them both a mug of strong tea while she sorted herself out. She dolloped a spoonful of sugar into each mug.

'Reckon we need this more than the whisky,' she said, placing the mugs on the table and sitting down again. 'So that's that. I'd guessed he was, what's the word, infatuated with her, but I didn't know what to do. There's nothing you really can do when someone's eye goes wandering except carry on being yourself.'

'But he didn't actually cheat on you,' said Bea. She was feeling better for a good cry and the sweet tea was hitting the spot, too.

'No, he never. I don't know what he would have done if she'd been keen. Whether he'd have gone through with it or run a mile.'

'Doesn't matter now, does it? He didn't have an affair. He didn't hurt her. He's not the one who killed her and left her in the ground, all those years ago.'

Queenie cupped her hands round her mug and sipped at the hot liquid.

'No, but it doesn't stop people thinking he did.'

'Well, perhaps the letter to the police will help. You are going to give it to them, aren't you?'

'Yes, I will. But it feels like they made their mind up a long time ago.'

'What about the man Dad saw her with?'

'They all think he made that up to take the heat off himself.'

'But we know he didn't, and whoever it was is obviously the prime suspect. He didn't say much about him, did he?'

'No, and nobody else reported seeing her with anyone. That's why they all think it's made up.'

'I'm going to find out who it was, Mum. I'm going to do it.'

Queenie sighed.

'Oh, Bea. How can you? It was a long time ago. If the

police couldn't find who did it, then why on earth do you think you'd be able to? Besides, we're talking about a murderer. Don't go looking for trouble, darlin'. We've had enough drama round here recently. *We* know Dad was innocent. That's what matters. Let's just settle for that.'

'No, Mum. I can't bear other people thinking it was him. Where's the justice in that? We can't prove to everyone that Dad *didn't* do it, so we'll have to prove that someone else *did*.'

Queenie shook her head. She gathered up her own letter and the one for the police. 'I'm going to hand this in tomorrow, and then that's it. No more dwelling on it. No investigating,' she said, sending Bea a significant look. 'End of. Whatever anyone else thinks or does, it's over for us. It's over, Bea.'

20

Both Bea and Queenie slept in, then spent what was left of the morning cooking and eating a fry up and watching rubbish on TV. In the afternoon, they walked to the little police station, tucked away off the main road to Bristol, and handed in Harry's letter. They hadn't opened it.

The weather had started to behave itself, with blue skies, sunshine and fresh, clean air. If they hadn't both been preoccupied, they would have relished the chance to walk together, which would have seemed impossible less than a year before. The police station wasn't far from the town's cemetery, and Queenie suggested a diversion to visit Harry's grave.

As they entered through the cemetery gates, a bird flew up from the ground, squawking as it flew to the nearest tree. Bea saw a flash of turquoise on its wings, catching the light.

'There's a jay,' said Queenie, and Bea felt an instant pang at the word, couldn't help thinking about her Jay – well, not hers now – thousands of miles away.

She tried to push those thoughts away. 'I didn't know you knew about birds.'

'Only a bit. Did you see the blue on its wings? The body's a lovely soft pinky grey, too. They're cruel birds, though. Steal other birds' eggs and babies, if they get a chance.'

The bird hopped its way along a branch, stopping now

and again for an exploratory tap with its sharp beak. As she watched, the other Jay was in her mind. Stupid, faithless Jay, as cruel in his own way as this beautiful bird.

'Come on, let's go and see Dad.'

Harry's gravestone was modest – a plain rectangle, with his name and birth and death dates carved into it, and the words, 'Always in our Hearts.'

'We should have brought flowers,' said Bea.

'It doesn't matter,' said Queenie. 'He's got all this around him.' She crouched down and put one of her hands flat on the close-mown grass covering the grave, then closed her eyes. Bea left her to it and walked away to the nearest bench, which sat in pleasantly dappled shade under an apple tree.

Her phone rang in her pocket. She went to reject the call then saw it was Ant.

'Hiya,' she said. 'You all right?'

'Yeah, just checking you're still on for tomorrow morning. About ten o'clock?'

'Yes. That's fine.'

'Where are you? You sound weird.'

'I'm at the cemetery actually. Me and Mum are visiting Dad's grave. We've had a bit of an odd weekend to be honest. After you left the other night, she fetched out some letters that Dad wrote before he died. There was one for me.'

'Oh, mate. That's heavy shit.'

'Yeah. It's a nice letter really. He says lots of dad stuff, and also that he was innocent. He never hurt anyone. He wanted me to know that.'

Bea could hear Ant making a low whistling sound. 'That's cool. Does it really change anything?'

'Well, I can stop having doubts about him now. He wrote it when he knew he was dying. There's no way he'd lie to me in a letter like that.'

'Mm. Good on him. Have you shown your mate Tom?'

'No. There was a separate letter for the police. We dropped it round just now.'

'And you're all right?'

'Yeah.'

'I'll see you tomorrow then. Ten o'clock.'

'Okay. Bye.'

'Bye, Bea. Take care.'

Queenie was still crouched by the grave. The sun seemed to be growing in strength. The spots of light filtering through the leaves above her were dazzling. Bea closed her eyes and tried to think about her dad, the man she'd known, and the words he'd written to her, but, frustratingly, other thoughts intruded. She found herself remembering Tina and the evenings they spent together when she was her babysitter.

Tina had treated her like a little sister, chatting away quite normally, reading her stories, plaiting her hair and, yes, painting her nails. Bea had been slightly in awe of her. As an only child, she hadn't had either guidance or friction from an older brother or sister, and she lapped up the time they spent together.

Bea looked down at her hands. She had turquoise nail varnish on today, something a bit different, a bit more summery than her usual red. She spread her fingers out, remembering Tina holding her fingers loosely and gently brushing coral pink over her nails, one by one. Back then, Bea's hands were pudgy and she had dimples on the back of her hands at the base of each finger. To be honest, the dimples were still there, only not quite so noticeable.

'I like your earrings, Tina. They're really pretty.'

'Thanks, Bea. They were a present from my new boyfriend. Hold still. Don't wiggle your fingers.'

'Ooh, what's he called?'

'Oh, you wouldn't know him. He's new around here. He's really nice. There, we're nearly done.'

'You haven't got nail varnish on, Tina. Why aren't you wearing any?'

'My boyfriend doesn't like it.'

'But it's so pretty!'

'Well, he doesn't like me wearing too much makeup. Says it looks cheap.'

'I like makeup. I'm going to wear lots when I grow up.'

'I like it too, but he's got a point. Maybe I was trowelling it on a bit. You don't need any makeup, Bea. You're perfect just as you are.'

She booped the end of Bea's nose with her index finger. Bea wrinkled up her face, but she liked it really. She liked their girly chats.

'Bea? Are you ready to go?' Bea shivered. Queenie was standing in front of her, silhouetted against the sun, casting a shadow across the bench.

'Yes. I'm ready.'

21

True to her word not to be put off by the current upset, Queenie had gone to her shift at the launderette. Bea was enjoying having the house to herself when her mobile rang.

'We're round the front.' It was Ant.

'We? I'm not quite ready. Come round the back like normal.'

'It's okay. We'll wait out here. Come out the front door.'

Bea thought she could hear sniggering in the background. What the—? She put her keys and phone in her smallest cross-body bag, slipped her feet into some black sandals and headed for the front door. She checked her makeup in the hall mirror. She'd gone for a non-work, casual sort of look today. Brown mascara, neutral eyeshadow and a low-key pink lip. It all went nicely with her favourite grey asymmetric-hem T-shirt dress and leggings.

Not bad, she thought, as she opened the front door. There was something, a robot or something, like a giant bug, buzzing in her face. It was a foot from the tip of her nose, propellers whining. Bea yelped, jumped backwards and slammed the door shut, hearing raucous laughter above the noise of the bug. Her mobile rang again. She fetched it out of her bag.

'Bea! Bea, it's us! Me and Saggy – we've got his drone.'

'Well you can get the fucking thing out of my face. You're lucky I didn't swat it with my handbag.'

'Okay, okay. It's gone now. You can come out.'

Bea opened the door a fraction and squinted out. She could see Ant and his unsavoury friend, Saggy, standing the other side of the front wall now, grinning in her direction. Saggy was holding the drone. She opened the door fully and stepped out, closing it safely behind her and checking it was locked. She marched smartly down the front path.

'Is this your surprise?' she said. 'This drone thing?'

'Yes!' said Ant, eyes shining with excitement.

'What are we going to do with it? I've told you you're not allowed to use it to spy on sunbathing women.'

'It's not for that, Bea.' Saggy raised his eyebrows at Ant, but Ant continued. 'Not today, anyway. We're going to search Dodgy Dave's backyard.'

Bea's mouth formed a perfect 'O'.

'That, my friends, is a very good idea,' she said, nodding slowly. 'How far away can you be to control this thing?'

'Hundred metres or more. It's pretty good spec this one,' said Saggy, holding the drone in his arms a bit like a super-villain cradling a Persian cat. 'I've sussed out the location. We can send it up from the back of the garages round in Sutherland Avenue and fly it over that way. It sends pictures back to my phone – we'll guide it like that. No one will know it's us.'

'Blimey, I'm impressed.' Ant and Saggy both formed fists and touched knuckles. 'Okay, let's go.'

They trooped along the suburban streets, down alleyways, round the primary school perimeter and finally to the garages Saggy had identified. Saggy fiddled around with the drone itself and then handed it to Ant, while he checked the settings on his phone.

'Let's launch this baby,' he said.

Ant put the drone on the ground a few metres away from them, and he and Bea watched as it rose vertically for a few seconds and then started peeling away from them.

'Here, look,' said Ant. He held the phone so that they could all see the image the drone was sending back. It took Bea a little while to work out what she was seeing, but then the pattern of rooftops and gardens started to make sense.

'We're looking for the garden of number eighteen, aren't we?' said Saggy. 'That's the third block of houses up from the alleyway. 'That's the first one. Here's the second. Now, here we are. It's the garden further away. I'll drop it down a bit.'

Bea was fascinated to see the garden becoming bigger on the screen. Saggy moved the drone so that it scanned different parts of the plot, moving up and down to cover the whole thing. 'We can look at the footage back home on my laptop,' he said. 'We can zoom in, get a better idea. I can't see any obvious sign of digging. Oh shit!'

'What is it?'

'It's losing height. Hang on! No, it's not responding!'

The image on screen seemed to show the ground rushing closer.

Bea gasped.

'Bollocks! It's come down.'

The screen was blank now.

'It's stopped transmitting. I think that was a full-on crash. Shit!'

'I'm sorry, Saggy. What do we do now?'

'Get it back. See if it can be fixed.' He was already walking towards the exit from the garages. Ant and Bea ran after him.

'Get it back? What, go into the garden?' said Bea, horrified. 'We don't know if he's out.'

'That's my territory,' said Ant. 'I'll do it, Saggy. I'll go.'

'No, Ant!' said Bea. 'What if you get caught?'

'Nah, no danger of that. I'll be in and out before anyone

knows anything about it. You guys stay here. You'll just raise suspicion hanging about outside.'

Before anyone could argue, Ant had jogged out of the yard and was gone. Bea was left looking at Saggy. He wasn't an edifying sight.

'Sorry about your drone. Was it expensive?'

Saggy shrugged. 'I got it off a mate, who got it off a mate. Did a bit of trading.'

'Yeah?' Bea wasn't exactly sure what that meant.

'Swapped it for six dozen pairs of trainer socks.'

'Oh.'

'I'm in socks, you know. Or I was. Wasn't quite the money-spinner I thought it was going to be. I've still got ten boxes in my garage, if you want any. They're nice ones, white, top quality. I could do you a good deal.'

'Um, no thanks. Look, shall we at least walk to the end of his road? Keep an eye out for him?'

'Yeah. Can't do any harm, can it?'

They walked along the pavement, past one row of semi-detached houses and then turned right and right again to reach the end of Sutherland Avenue. There was a bus stop nearby, so they went under the shelter and perched on the angled plastic bench.

'How do you think he's getting on?' said Bea, realising as she said it what a pointless question it was.

Saggy didn't even bother to answer. They sat in awkward silence for a while until Saggy said, 'So why do you think this bloke's dodgy?'

'He's hit his wife loads of times, and now she just seems to have disappeared. It feels wrong, Saggy. I'm scared for her.'

'Fair enough. I'll have a good look at the footage when I get home.'

'Thanks. I appreciate it.'

'If he's done it, we'll get him, Bea. I've been hearing from

Ant about your investigations. Quite fancy myself as a vigilante.'

Bea looked at him again. He was wearing his usual uniform of T-shirt and jeans, with the waistband hanging perilously close to his genitals. There was a wide strip of underwear on display. Bea thanked her lucky stars that at least he was wearing pants.

'We're not vigilantes, Saggy. We do investigate things, but we don't take people on. Not on purpose anyway.'

Saggy held his weedy arms out, his hands palm upwards. 'Well, I'm available if you need a bit of extra muscle.'

'Thanks. I'll bear that in mind. Oh! Look! There he is!'

Bea stood up. Through the Perspex of the bus shelter she could see Ant strolling along the pavement towards them. She and Saggy emerged from the shelter, and they could see he was carrying the drone.

'Mission accomplished,' he said, when they met in the middle.

'Give it here,' said Saggy. Ant handed him the wreckage and Saggy stood, turning it over in his hands.

'Let's get out of here, though,' said Ant. 'Look at the drone properly at your house. This place is giving me the creeps.'

'What's wrong, Ant?' said Bea. 'What did you see?'

'I'll show you in a minute.'

He was glancing over his shoulder, obviously uneasy. Bea took the hint and started walking.

'Come on, Ant, what was it like in there?' she said, unable to wait any longer.

'It was pretty neat and tidy. A bit of grass, a kid's swing, a table and some chairs on a little patio thing outside the French windows at the back. No sign of anything being disturbed, but I didn't hang around, so it would be worth checking the drone film.'

'So why did it give you the creeps?'

He stopped walking. 'I found this,' he said, and put his hand into his pocket. Bea watched as he drew out a small pink plastic toy. She felt her stomach contract as she realised what it was. A little duck. The duck that Tiffany always clutched in her hand. That she was never seen without. 'It's the girl's, isn't it?'

'Yes,' she said. 'It's Tiffany's. Oh my god, Ant. What's happened to them?'

22

Bea hadn't seen Dot for a couple of days so she was very pleased to see her smiling face in the locker room before work on Tuesday morning. In fact, Dot wasn't just smiling, she was glowing.

'You look happy,' said Bea, as they stood side by side at the mirror, applying their lipstick.

'Do I?'

There was a definite twinkle in her eye.

'Yes. Had a nice weekend, did you? How's Darren?'

'He's great, actually,' said Dot, sending Bea a wink via the mirror. 'I'd forgotten how nice it was having him around.'

'He's staying with you?'

'Yeah. We went out for a drink after choir, and then one thing led to another, and . . .'

'. . .and he's moved in?'

'Sort of. Just for a little bit.'

Bea turned around and put her hands on her hips. 'Dot, you were all about taking things slowly and keeping him at arm's length when he turned up. What's happened?'

'He's a laugh, Bea. He knows me. We've got history. We've got a kid together.'

'And he gambled and got into debt and you kept falling out and—'

'So maybe he's changed. Everyone deserves a second chance, don't they?'

'Yes, but, I don't know, Dot. I don't want you getting hurt.'

Dot put her lipstick back in her bag, and the bag in her locker. 'Oh, Bea, you sound like my mum! You're twenty-one, aren't you? You should be having some fun yourself, not worrying about me!'

'Well, I was having fun with Jay, but that all went wrong. And Tom's not talking to me any longer.'

'Get yourself on one of those sites – you know, swiping left and right. There's plenty more fish in the sea, babe. Dangle your rod out there, see who you can catch.'

'Maybe.'

'Look, I know things have been tough recently, but maybe it's time to let it go.' Dot saw the warning look in Bea's eyes. 'No! Listen! You're gorgeous, Bea. You're bright and smart and young. But you take on other people's worries. You care about people, which is lovely, but I reckon it's time to start spreading your wings a bit. Think about yourself for once. Aim high.'

'And find someone on Tinder?'

'Not just that. But then again, why not?'

'I've got other things to do, Dot.'

'Like what?'

Bea sensed that now wasn't the time to tell Dot about her dad's letter, or her worries about Julie. Dot was on another planet today, or at least in happy orbit with Darren.

Halfway through the morning Bea looked up to see a group of three very pale teenagers in black T-shirts and ragged black skinny jeans, piling their shopping onto her conveyor belt; bottles of cider and fizzy water, family packs of crisps and a whole chicken from the hot rotisserie.

'Is this all together?' she asked them.

'Yeah.'

'Including the chicken?'

The lads all grinned. 'It's Tommo's thing.'

The shortest, bulkiest teen, at the back of the group – Tommo – held his hand up. 'Gotta fuel up,' he said. 'Long day ahead.'

'What are you guys doing?' said Bea, her curiosity peaked.

'Recording,' the lad at the front of the queue said, with more than a hint of pride in his voice. 'Putting down some tracks.'

'Oh, you're a band. That figures. Is there a studio in Kingsleigh now?'

'There's some equipment in the community centre. We've booked it for a day.' Bea checked her watch.

'Well, it's nearly eleven now. You'd better crack on.'

'Don't normally get up before two. Rock 'n' roll,' he said, while the others grinned and Bea wondered how their mums felt about them sleeping in until after lunch.

They shambled out and, as she watched them go, Bea tried to guess the sort of music they made. Something thrashy was her best bet. They were probably only a couple of years younger than her and yet they'd made her feel really old, as if she were from a different generation. They were kind of sweet in their intensity and seriousness, though.

There was no one waiting for her now. Bea tidied things up a bit, then watched the customers trawling round with their trolleys. A couple was approaching, their trolley half full, heading for her checkout. They both looked tired. The woman was leaning on the handle of the trolley and the man was trailing next to her. They were nearly at the end of her checkout when the man looked at Bea and she recognised him as Derrick Robbins, Tina's dad. He gently patted his wife's arm and Bea heard him say, 'Not this one. Let's go somewhere else.'

Nikki Robbins frowned. 'There's no one waiting here, love.' Then she, too, saw Bea. 'Oh.'

They started moving down the line. Bea stood up.

'Please,' she called out. 'Please come here. You're welcome.' She smiled encouragingly, even patted the conveyor belt.

Confronted directly like this, the Robbins were too polite to refuse. They checked with each other, then reluctantly pushed their trolley adjacent to Bea's checkout. Bea sat down and started processing the shopping as quickly and efficiently as she could, given that her hands were shaking. Derrick loaded the shopping on at one end and Nikki brought their shopping bags to the till end and started parcelling things up. Nobody made eye contact until Bea asked for payment.

'That'll be forty-seven pounds, fifty-three please. Do you have a Costsave saver card?'

'I've got a card somewhere.' Derrick fumbled in his wallet, but soon gave up. 'It doesn't matter. I'll just pay.'

Bea wanted to say something, anything, to make the situation easier, but the words wouldn't come. 'Do you need a receipt?'

'No. No, thanks. Come on, Nikki.'

He lifted the last of their shopping into the trolley and they set off without a backwards glance.

'You know who that was?' said Dot.

'Course I do,' said Bea. 'And they knew who I was, too. Bloody hell, Dot, that was awful.'

At the end of her shift, and before choir practice, Bea called in to see Anna in the office.

'Just need the loo. Can you hang on for a minute?'

Anna darted out and Bea walked over to the window and looked down on the earthworks that were now taking up most of the yard at the back of the store. There were workers in high-vis jackets dotted around the site, which consisted of a series of deep channels and heaps of soil and rubble. The workers were mostly wearing boiler suits, scruffy jeans and

T-shirts under their jackets, but Bea's eyes focused in on one man, picking his way across the site. He had a hard hat and jacket like the others, but he was wearing a suit and carrying a small clipboard with a sort of tablet attached.

As she was watching, he looked up, and their eyes met. He smiled and waved a hand. It was too late to pretend she hadn't seen him. Feeling exposed, caught out, Bea had no choice but to wave back. Dave carried on walking, looking pleased with himself. Bea wanted to turn away, but found herself thinking about the foundations at the factory and poor Tina's body lying there for all those years. If they hadn't been redeveloping now, she would never have been found.

At the far side of the site, men with diggers were filling in a trench with rubble and soil. Soon it would be concreted over. Sealed away.

Julie's there, Bea thought, with the cold dread of certainty. She's right there, and nobody else knows.

Dave had reached a cluster of men by an open trench quite near to the store. They stopped working as he approached and now stood, listening, as he talked to them, gesticulating with his arms to illustrate his point.

How do I prove it? What evidence do I need to get the police to stop the work and dig up the trenches already covered up?

'Bea? You all right?' Anna's voice brought her back into the room. 'We've got ten minutes. Shall we go down to the café and have a real cappuccino?'

'Um, yeah. That'd be nice.'

'You can tell me all about it then.'

'About what?'

'Whatever's making you frown like that.'

Bea wiggled her eyebrows to unlock her expression. 'I've just got an overactive imagination, Anna. That's my trouble.' She tried to laugh it off, but the feeling of certainty didn't leave her, neither while she and Anna were drinking their frothy coffee, nor as they walked over to the Legion hall where the choir was meeting.

'I've had a few brave souls try out as soloists, and thank you for that,' said Candy, holding her palms together almost in prayer and acknowledging several people around the room, 'but I'm not sure we've yet found that special someone.'

Ant leaned close to Bea's ear. 'She means they were all terrible. Do you know who tried?'

'Shh, Ant. Listen.'

'And so, I'm wondering if you would be open to something a little different. I've discussed this with George and she's happy. We want to open our doors to your friends and family. Do you know someone with a beautiful voice that needs to be heard?'

George, who had been standing as part of the choir, stepped forward and turned round to address them. 'We've always been a family at Costsave, and this is a chance to really involve our families at home with our family at work. There's no pressure and I know some of you like to keep your work life and home life separate and I absolutely respect that. But if you personally would like to extend an invitation to someone, then please do.'

Behind her, Bea could hear someone making little excited noises, a bit like a chicken about to hatch an egg.

'Yes!' said Candy, looking past Bea. 'Have you had an idea?'

Everyone turned towards Eileen, whose normally grim face was pink with excitement.

'My Dean's a wonderful singer. He's got the voice of an angel.'

Bea could see a magnificent range of expressions in the faces turned her way. Dean, who had worked in Costsave's stores, had been sacked the previous year for various misdemeanours, including supplying eggs to his mates for use in their Halloween mischief (or anti-social behaviour, depending on your point of view). He hadn't been a universally loved member of staff, and few people had mourned his dismissal. For her part, she and Dean had had a rocky relationship, but since their truce a few months earlier he had demonstrated a surprising level of empathy. Perhaps this was a way to bring him into the Costsave fold, maybe even back into employment. It would be better for everyone, and Kingsleigh generally, if he had a steady job.

'Great!' said Candy. 'Could you ask him to meet me before the next rehearsal? I'll have a listen.'

Eileen was positively glowing. There was a bit of low-grade muttering among the rest of the choir, but nobody actually spoke out against the idea.

'What are we going to sing at the festival?' someone called out.

'I'm glad you asked that. I've got some ideas and we'll start to learn one of them today, but, again, I'm happy to take suggestions. I'm looking for upbeat, cheerful songs. Songs that people will know and will sing along to.'

'If I might chip in here,' said George. 'I want us to sing something that says Costsave. That sums up what this place, this company, our colleagues and our customers mean to us.'

Bea could hear Ant sucking his breath in between his teeth, ready to call out his own suggestion. She put a hand on his arm. 'Don't, Ant,' she said.

He looked a bit surprised at her intervention but kept his counsel, while Candy announced that the first song they were going to learn was 'You've Got a Friend'.

There was a collective 'Ahh,' from the older ones.

'Ooh, James Taylor,' said Bob. 'Cracking song.'

'Carole King,' said Dot. 'Brilliant writer.'

'Okay, I've got some lyric sheets here. Hand them round please. Let's sing it all together and then we'll start breaking it into parts. Everybody ready? Now, take a few deep breaths together. That's it. Now, here's your note.'

After rehearsal Ant had said that he was heading Bea's way, so they walked together across the rec.

'What were you going to say?' asked Bea.

'I could only think of "Every Day I Love you Less and Less" on the spur of the moment.'

'Harsh.'

'I'll come up with something better if I have some time to think about it.'

'Try and think of something nice.'

'Yeah, right. Think we need something a bit more modern. That old stuff was a bit drippy, wasn't it?'

'I quite liked it.'

'Yeah, well, you're soft, you are. Are you going to ask your mum if she wants to join the choir?'

Bea was genuinely taken aback. 'Oh, I hadn't thought about it. Actually, she'd probably really like it. I will. You coming back for a bit of tea?'

'Nah, Saggy's mum is out again. Him and me are going out for a pie and a pint at the Jubilee. Then after that, I'm going to Bob's. I took my stuff over there yesterday. He pretty much begged me to stay in his spare room.'

'Yeah?'

'I wasn't going to ask, but it came from him. Think he wants the company. We spent last night having a beer and listening to a small part of his county and western music collection. Bloody awful, it was, but worth it for a room of my own.'

'That's better then. Did you get a good night's sleep?'

'Sort of. It was a bit odd being so comfy after Saggy's garden lounger. Funny what you get used to.'

'Is Saggy's drone fixable?'

'Yeah, he reckons. The footage didn't show anything, by the way. I don't think anyone's buried anything in Dave's garden recently.'

'That doesn't surprise me,' said Bea. 'I've had a thought about that. Dave's a surveyor, isn't he? So he's got access to all sorts of building sites. I reckon that's where he'd bury a body, or three of them. Could even be at Costsave.'

'Unless he didn't do anything.'

'Tiffany's toy, Ant.' It was still in the pocket of her black denim jacket. She brought it out now and held it in the palm of her hand. 'She literally never goes – went – anywhere without it. This is all the evidence I need.'

Ant snorted. 'Might not be enough to have him arrested.'

'What else can we do, though? Maybe we need to get inside the house, have a look round.'

'Breaking and entering?' He looked at her sharply. 'I don't do that anymore.'

'I don't necessarily mean that.'

'How else? Knock on his door and ask to have a look round? Get real, Bea.'

Ant peeled off to the pub. Bea put the toy duck back in her pocket, but she kept her fingers on it and as she walked round the shops to her street her worries about Julie wouldn't go away. If there wasn't evidence in the garden and she couldn't dig up all the building sites in Kingsleigh, perhaps she did need to get into Dave's house. It wouldn't be as easy as knocking on the door, but maybe there was another way.

23

Queenie was sitting in her usual armchair when Bea got home. The telly was on, but she wasn't watching it. She was busy with one of her word searches in a puzzle magazine.

'All right, mum?' said Bea, walking through the room on her way upstairs.

'Mm.' Queenie didn't even look up.

Bea halted behind her chair and peered over. Queenie wasn't training her brain at all, but she was studying something. Her magazine was on her lap, but she was holding her phone, on the screen of which was a photo of a man in his sixties. He had a bristly grey moustache and a warm smile. Bea watched as Queenie moved her index finger deliberately towards the screen and swiped right.

'Mum!'

Queenie jumped out of her skin. The phone flew out of her hand and landed on the carpet in front of her. She clutched at the top of her chest and twisted round in her chair.

'What are you doing, creeping up on me like that?'

'I wasn't creeping. You didn't hear me because you were busy ogling old men.'

'I wasn't ogling, and he's not that old.' Queenie turned around again and reached forward to pick up her phone.

'Lots of people do it. Jill at the launderette showed me. Then she signed me up.'

'Did she now? Do you ever do any service washes there, or are you both too busy swiping right and left?'

'Very funny.' She wiped the screen with the bottom of her cardigan. 'What are you so aeriated about? Everyone does it these days. I bet you have.'

'Maybe. Okay, yes,' said Bea, puffing out her cheeks, 'but I haven't looked for ages. Anyway, this isn't about me, it's about you.'

'And what's wrong with me doing it?'

Bea paused. What was wrong with it? Her dad had been gone for six years, and Queenie had nearly got back in the dating game with Bob a few months ago. It was actually a good idea, wasn't it? So why did she feel so put out?

'Nothing,' she said, aware she was sounding like a sullen teenager.

'Do you think I'm being disloyal to your dad?'

'Of course not. It's just . . .I don't know . . .an odd time to be doing it.'

'Maybe it's a good time. All this talk about what happened fourteen years ago, it's made me think how quickly time passes. I wasted six years sitting in this house, Bea, frightened of my own shadow. I don't want to waste any more time.'

'Fair enough,' said Bea, but a little part of her thought, yes, you are being disloyal. She started heading towards the stairs, when Queenie said, 'Anyway, I saved the local news for you.'

'Oh, that's all right, Mum. I'm not bothered.'

'There was a police statement about Tina.'

'Really? Is it on the planner?' Bea plonked herself down on the sofa and reached for the remote. She selected the news recording and fast-forwarded through to the item. The officer reading out the statement was the same one who had held the

140

original press conference with Tina's parents. This time he was standing outside the small police station in Kingsleigh.

'The murder of Tina Robbins has shaken this community to the core. We promised Derrick and Nikki Robbins that we would find out who killed Tina, and we are determined to do this. We can confirm that we have found traces of DNA which are being analysed at the moment, with the results expected soon. We would like to thank members of the public who have responded to our appeals for information. As a result of this we are following a number of lines of enquiry.

'Given the length of time that has passed, this may not result in a prosecution, but at the very least Derrick and Nikki will have the answers that they need. We are appealing again for anyone with information about the night of 25th of June 2005, to come forward. You can ring our hotline or email Avon and Somerset Police. You can do this anonymously if you need to, and all information will be treated in the strictest confidence. Thank you.'

Queenie looked at Bea. 'What do you reckon to that?'

'Well, the DNA thing is good, isn't it?'

'Is it?'

'Yeah, because that's hard, physical evidence. The sort of evidence you can't argue with. If they get a match with someone on their database, that's it. Case closed.'

'Will Harry be on their database?'

Bea sighed. 'I don't know. You'd know better than me if they took a sample. Did they?'

Queenie shrugged. 'I don't know, love.'

'But it's that other bit I don't like.'

'What other bit?'

'"This may not result in a prosecution." They're pointing the finger at Dad there.'

'Are they?'

'Yes, Mum. Read between the lines – they're saying they

might be able to identify the culprit, but not be able to charge him because he's dead. They've done everything except name him. Bloody hell!'

'I think you're being a bit oversensitive. I'm not sure other people will understand that's what they mean. I didn't pick up on it.'

Bea stood up. 'Yeah, but were you actually watching and listening, or were you busy swiping left and right?'

She just caught the hurt expression on her mum's face as she swept out of the room and upstairs. She knew she was being unreasonable, cruel even, but it did look like Queenie was really over Harry, and it felt like Bea was the only one still thinking the best of him. Still loyal to the best dad in the world.

She got out her phone and checked all the normal sites and apps. Then, almost as if it had a mind of its own, her thumb hovered over the Tinder icon. Dot thought she should go on it. Queenie was doing it. Yet, Bea didn't open the app. Instead she googled Julie Ronson, then searched on Facebook and Instagram. There was nothing. No record of her, or the kids. As far as the internet went, she didn't exist. Who doesn't leave any sort of digital trace behind? she thought. Someone who didn't have an online presence before they disappeared. You might expect it with an older person, who grew up before social media became a thing, but it was bizarre for someone in their thirties. This was a woman who was isolated, cut off. Controlled.

Bea was still at a loss as to what to do next. She got out her notebook and opened it at the back, so that these notes wouldn't get muddled with her records about the Tina Robbins case. Then she wrote down everything she knew about Julie's disappearance. It wasn't much. She tried to imagine what information could possibly give a clue to her whereabouts. Bank records? But she'd always used cash in

Costsave and Bea suspected she didn't have a bank account. Mobile phone records? Bea had certainly seen her with a mobile. How on earth could she access those records, though?

She sighed and set the notebook down on the bed beside her. This really needed to be a police investigation. Before they parted on bad terms, Tom had asked her to go to the police station and report Julie missing. She felt a pang of guilt that she hadn't already done so. Perhaps if she wrote her 'evidence' up, thin as it was, they would take her more seriously anyway.

She opened her laptop and did her best to write a professional-looking report. She spent an hour or so cutting and pasting and trying different formats. In the end, she settled on something simple and straightforward, with bullet points listing the facts as she saw them. She glossed over the drone incident, merely stating that Tiffany's toy had been found 'close to' Dave's house.

Satisfied with her work, Bea printed off a copy and sent it to herself in an email, as backup. She put the paper version in an envelope. She'd hand it in tomorrow. At least, she could tell herself that she was doing *something*.

She hoped that this would make it easier to sleep, but, alas, it didn't. Worries about Julie swirled around her head, somehow mixed up with the gossip and rumour surrounding her dad and Tina's death. Bea tossed and turned, trying to empty her mind, but it was no good. Just after two in the morning, she sat up and put the light on. She was pleased with her decision to report Julie as missing, but what could she positively do about her dad, presumed guilty by everyone including the police? She picked up the notebook that had fallen down one side of her bed, and went through the front pages. Then she turned to a fresh page and made some headings: Timeline. Suspects. What Do We Know? What Don't We Know?

She had a feeling that something significant had happened today. It wasn't seeing Dave on the building site, and it wasn't the police report, it was something else, something to do with her dad. She tried replaying the day in her head, but nothing stood out. She'd put her notebook down and turned out the light again when it came to her – the three lads in the band, with their crisps and cooked chicken. She'd never checked out the band that played in the social club the night Tina disappeared. Too tired to turn the light back on and write it down, she trusted that she'd remember to ask her mum about them in the morning.

24

The next day, however, that thought had gone, washed away by four hours' fitful rest. Bea felt like she was sleepwalking through breakfast and Queenie wasn't much better. Bea supposed she was still nursing the hurt and resentment from last night's spat, but she didn't have the energy to make up with her. They ate their cereal in silence and Bea took her mug of tea upstairs to drink while she was fixing her face.

They only managed cursory grunts as she left the house from the kitchen door. Walking round the side Bea stopped for a moment and leaned against the pebble-dashed wall. She hated having bad feeling between them. She took a couple of breaths of fresh morning air and went back.

She opened the door and popped her head through the gap. Queenie, still sitting at the kitchen table, looked up warily. 'Mum,' said Bea, 'I'm sorry. Sorry for everything.'

The muscles in Queenie's face relaxed. 'I'm sorry too, baby girl. Everything's just . . .it's all a bit . . .'

'I know. Let's forget about it. Friends again?'

Queenie smiled. 'Friends.' Then she flapped both hands at Bea, shooing her away. 'Off you go now. You'll be late.'

Bea closed the door behind her and went round to the front of the house. Her heart was a little lighter now, there was more of a spring in her step, which lasted for a few seconds before she spotted someone waiting for her on the pavement by her front gate. He was sideways on to her and was hunched over, checking his phone, but there was no mistaking the floppy hair and preppy clothes.

'Oh no,' breathed Bea. She picked up the pace, opening the gate and moving smartly past Dan, quickly looking left and right before walking across the road and heading for the rec.

'Hey! Hey, good morning!' She could hear Dan's footsteps as he jogged to catch up with her. 'Morning, Bea,' he said, as he drew level.

'Hi,' she said, keeping it brief.

'I wanted a friendly word. Do you have a minute to talk?'

'No, I don't want to be late. Some of us have got proper jobs.'

'Ow, stinger!' said Dan, with a grin, and Bea found herself grudgingly warming to him again. His good humour was infectious. If he went on the X Factor, he'd undoubtedly be told he had 'likeability'.

'Can we walk and talk?' she said.

'Sure.'

'So?'

'So I wanted to let you know that my editor wants to rehash some old stories about your dad. To be honest, we're struggling for angles on this case already. If we're going to do that, then I'd like to be fair to you, give you a chance to put your side of things, explain what all this is like for you.'

'I told you, we – Mum and me – don't want to talk to the press.'

'Yeah, I get that, but you do care about what people are saying about your dad, don't you?'

They were halfway across the rec. Bea stopped walking. She remembered the awkwardness with Tina's parents the day before.

'Yeah. I do.'

'And I don't know about you, but I thought the police statement yesterday was a bit of a dig at him.'

'Oh my god, so did I,' said Bea. 'Mum wasn't sure, but it totally was, wasn't it?'

Dan nodded. 'Yup. So why don't we write something that will make people change their minds? Or at least keep their minds open? Have you got anything, Bea? Anything that would help us.'

Bea noticed that he was using 'us' and 'we'. In someone else it might have sounded an awkward note, smelled of manipulation, but somehow, coming from Dan it sucked her in. Maybe they were on the same side. The side of truth and fairness.

'Actually,' she said, 'there is something. Could you use this?'

She fished in her handbag and drew out the envelope containing a copy of her dad's letter. She handed it over to Dan, who carefully unfolded the paper and read it.

'Whoa, powerful stuff,' he said when he'd reached the end. There was a note of disappointment in his voice, though.

'Sorry it's not a confession, if that's what you wanted,' said Bea.

'Hey, no need to be like that. A confession would be a brilliant scoop, but I'm glad it's not, for your sake. Like I said, maybe we can make people change their minds. Is this the original?'

'No, that's at home. Do you need it?'

'Probably not. I'll have to ask my editor.'

'You can keep this copy.'

'Great. Your dad, he died a few years ago, didn't he? So when did this letter come to light?' Bea told him an edited version of events. 'Your mum and you, you've been through the mill, haven't you? Would you do a little interview, the two

147

of you, to go with this letter? We could make a really nice article out of it.'

'I'll have to ask her, but maybe.'

'A little bird told me you're trying to investigate this, alongside the police. We could do something with that – "One woman's fight to clear her father's name."'

He was getting the bit between his teeth now and it was starting to make Bea feel uncomfortable.

'I don't know, Dan,' she said. 'I don't want any of this to be about me. I just want people to know that Dad didn't do it. That's why I showed you the letter.'

'Okay, but an interview, or even a quote or two, would really help. Just you, if you like, or you and your mum.'

'I'm not sure. When do you need to know by?'

'This afternoon? Print deadline's nine this evening. I'll need some time to write things up.'

'Okay, I'll ring Mum and get back to you.'

'Great.'

Bea checked her watch. 'Oh God, I am going to be late!'

'Sorry. Well, sorry not sorry. I'm glad we talked, Bea.'

'Yeah, me too. Gotta run, though, Dan. I'll ring you later.'

She set off jogging along the path. She didn't have time to ring Queenie before work – she only just made it to George's huddle by the skin of her teeth. When she rang during her first break, standing outside by the trolley park, Queenie was horrified.

'There's no way I'm talking to any of them,' she squealed. 'Vultures!'

'Okay, okay. Do you mind if I do, though? And show them my letter?'

Queenie sniffed loudly at the other end of the line. 'It's your letter, Bea. Yours to do with what you wish.'

It wasn't quite the endorsement Bea was looking for, but neither was it an outright objection. They said goodbye and she cancelled the call, then looked up Dan's number from the business card he'd handed her and dialled. It only took a few minutes' conversation, this time all on the record. Before Bea knew it, Dan was saying, 'That's great. I've got several good quotes there.'

'Are you sure that's all you need?'

'Yeah, it's all there. I'd better get on with it. Thanks, Bea.'

He'd rung off before she remembered to ask if she'd see the article before it went to print. What was that called? Copy approval? She was going to ring him back when she heard a tapping sound. She looked round and saw Neville standing on the other side of the plate glass window, rapping his finger against the glass like an over-excited woodpecker. When he saw her looking, he then moved his tapping finger to his watch. Breaktime was clearly over. Bea gave him the thumbs up and headed to the staff door to put her phone back in her locker.

25

'Aye-aye,' said Dot. 'Something's going on.'

There had been a flurry of customers after lunch but now there was a lull. Bea swivelled round to see what Dot was talking about. Eileen and Neville were both looking at the screen at the customer service desk. Eileen was pointing something out. Neville nodded and picked up the phone, then Eileen walked quickly towards the part of the store where the chiller cabinets held all the meat. She stopped when she came up to Ant, who was leaning on his mop on the corner of aisle four – Chicken, Pork and Lamb – and appeared to have an urgent word with him. He looked startled, then he shambled off to aisle two with his cleaning trolley while she lurked where he'd been standing. She trotted down aisle four and then crept along the end of the aisles, peering along each one in turn.

When Eileen was almost level with Bea's checkout, Bea could see Ant at the other end of aisle two – 'Crisps and Snacks' – sauntering slowly towards her. There was only one other person in the aisle, a woman in her thirties or forties, pushing one of the shallow trolleys with just a few items in it. When she stopped to examine a packet of crispbreads, Ant stopped too. He was shadowing her. Neville was obviously following the scene on the CCTV cameras. He was looking at the screen and then over towards Eileen. The woman got nearer to Eileen, who pretended to be arranging stock on the end-of-aisle display. The woman had a shopping bag dangling on the back of her trolley. She approached Bea's checkout.

Bea smiled at her as she loaded the shopping onto her conveyor belt. 'Good afternoon. Do you want any help packing?'

'No, I'm fine,' the woman said.

'Do you need any bags?'

'No, I've got these, love. Thanks.' She'd finished loading up now and pushed her trolley through to the packing area. She unhooked her shopping bags from the back and put them in the main body of her trolley, placing the goods that Bea had already beeped straight into them there.

Bea felt the eyes of the world on her as she finished processing the shopping and asked the woman to pay, but as she glanced up, it was only Eileen and Ant watching in a rather obvious way from the end of aisle four.

The woman paid in cash and Bea gave her the change. She noticed that Neville had left his desk and was standing near the exit, pretending to examine the buckets of cut flowers. As the woman trundled her trolley towards him, Eileen and Ant followed.

Bea grabbed Ant as he passed through her checkout, leaving his cleaning kit behind.

'Oi, what's going on?'

'Shoplifter,' he whispered. 'Gotta go, I'm the backup.'

The woman was level with Neville now. As she left the shop, Neville pounced, Ant and Eileen positioning themselves on the other side of her and in front of her trolley, blocking her in. Bea could see Neville talking to her and pointing at one of her bags.

Someone nearby cleared their throat. Bea looked round to

find a man waiting for her. He'd filled the belt with every single special offer that Costsave was featuring that week. Now he moved to the packing area and started pulling plastic bags out of other bags in readiness. Bea sighed inwardly. She wouldn't get to watch the show after all. She caught a glimpse of how things were unfolding when Neville, Ant and Eileen marched past her till with the woman sandwiched between them.

A little while later, Shaz, the community copper who used to partner Tom, appeared with her new workmate, a very young-looking lad with bulging eyes and a prominent Adam's apple. They reported to the customer service desk, which was being temporarily staffed by Kirsty, and she sent them to the staff door at the back of the shop floor. After a few minutes, they reappeared, escorting the woman out of the store, with Neville walking several paces behind.

As they passed checkout number six, Bea half-rose from her seat and called out, 'Shaz! Shaz, can you wait a minute?'

'Not really, Bea. I've got to get back to the station to fill out the fifty-seven varieties of form to deal with our friend here.'

'Just one minute?'

'Okay. I'll wait by the car.'

Neville's mouth gaped like a hyperventilating catfish as Bea logged out of her till. She heard him spluttering, 'Excuse me, Beatrice,' but ignored him and ran up to the locker room, where she retrieved her report about Julie. She overtook Ant on the stairs as she scampered back again.

'Hey, Bea, what's the rush?'

'Tell you later!'

She could see that Neville was still hovering near her till, so she went along the far end of the aisles until she was clear of him, then cut through the fresh fruit and veg display to reach the front door. Shaz was standing by the police car which was parked in the 'Keep Clear' area outside the entrance. Bea handed her the envelope.

'It's a missing person report. I've done everything I can to trace her but I've come up with nothing. She's disappeared with her two children.'

Shaz took the envelope and tucked it into the inside pocket of her uniform jacket. 'I'll read it, Bea, but you know sometimes people have reasons for disappearing.'

'Yes, I do know. And believe me, she's got good reason. But I want to know that she's alive and well and safe somewhere. I told Tom about it, but he's too busy on the Tina Robbins case.'

'Understandable. He's playing with the big boys now.' There was an unmistakeable note of rancour in her voice.

'It's a good move for him. It's a big case, but I think this could be just as serious, though, Shaz.' She noted Shaz's look of interest. 'There could be a lot of kudos for the person who finds out what's happened to her.'

Shaz gave a little smile and patted the front of her jacket. 'Noted,' she said. She opened the passenger door and got in. Bea didn't stay to watch them go but turned to run back to her till, instead cannoning into Neville, who let out an 'Oof!' as Bea's elbow caught him in the kidneys.

'Sorry Neville, but why were you standing so close?' said Bea.

Neville rubbed the area just under his ribs, grimacing. 'I was standing there to stop you running off through the car park.'

She turned on her smarmiest smile, and picked an imaginary piece of cotton from Neville's jacket. 'I was never going to do that, Neville. I just had—' she leaned closer to him and lowered her voice '—urgent police business to attend to, if you know what I mean.' She tapped the side of her nose with her index finger.

Neville backed away a little and swallowed nervously. 'No,' he said, 'I don't think I do know what you mean. Was it to do with that shoplifter?'

'No,' said Bea, then quickly, 'yes! Yes, I'd seen her before, acting suspiciously. I just wanted Shaz, PC Sanders, to know. So she had a full picture.'

Neville narrowed his eyes. 'Bea, you know that if you have suspicions about any customer, then they should be reported through the usual channels.' Bea knew by 'the usual channels' he meant himself.

'Yes, I know. I'm sorry. I never actually saw her take anything before, but there was something about her. I should have said. Sorry, Neville. Shall I get back to my till now?'

'Yes,' he said. 'Yes, you should.' He stood aside and Bea hurried past before he could quiz her any further.

Ant was lurking around her till, ostensibly fetching his cleaning trolley. 'Do you wanna know what she was nicking?' he said as Bea got settled back in.

'Go on, then.'

'Gammon. A big joint of gammon, stuffed into her tote bag. She was pleading with Neville not to report her. Kept saying she and her kids were hungry. It was a bit sad, really.'

'The thing is, though,' Dot chipped in, 'half these people are living in better houses than us, driving flashy cars.'

'Steady on, Dot,' said Bea. 'Have you been reading the *Daily Fail* again?'

'It's true, Bea! This is a way of life for some people. It's their actual job.'

Bea flashed a glance at Ant, whose father's 'actual job' was burglar and who was currently serving a hefty sentence in Bexton prison, as Dot well knew. He was already turning away, starting to trundle his trolley back to the storage area.

'Dot, shut up.'

'What?'

Bea closed her eyes and shook her head at Dot's lack of sensitivity. 'How are you and Darren getting on?' she said, to change the subject.

Dot took the bait. 'Still good,' she said, sending Bea a cheerful wink. 'He's a bit of a reformed character. Washes the dishes, puts the washing in the drier. He never used to do that stuff when we were together before.'

'Oh, nice.'

'Said he'd put a casserole in the oven for after choir practice tonight. We're going to have a quick drink afterwards, then go home and, you know, Netflix and chill.'

'Blimey, Dot. It's all getting very cosy. Is he back for good?'

'I don't know, love. It wasn't just his lack of domesticity that broke us up before. There were other issues, but he does seem to have calmed down. I like this Darren. I like him a lot.'

26

There were definitely more people at the next choir rehearsal. Bea ate a bag of crisps while she watched them file into the meeting room at the social club. Bob was on one side of her, and it felt as if he was standing under a big, black cloud.

'Wanna crisp?' said Bea, shaking the packet in his direction.

'No, ta. Oh, look who's crawled out of the woodwork now.'

He was talking about Dean, who was slouching into the room next to Eileen. She was looking as pleased as punch, her arm threaded through his, her chest puffed out a little, like a broiler chicken. Bob reached his hand absentmindedly into Bea's crisp packet and drew out a fistful of salt and vinegar Squares. He shoved them into his mouth, leaving Bea peering sadly at a little heap of crumbs left at the bottom of the packet.

'Oh great, now *he's* here.' Bob had caught sight of Darren coming into the hall, hand in hand with Dot. She looked immaculate. Her skin was glowing, her hair was just right, there was a definite spring in her step.

Everyone assembled into rows facing the front of the room. Candy breezed in on the stroke of six o'clock, made her way through the crowd and then turned to face them. She scanned the people in front of her and gave a quick thumbs up to someone on the left-hand side of the room.

'Great to see so many people here today, especially the friends and family who have joined us. You will be pleased to hear that my search for a soloist has been successful. Ladies and gentlemen, please give a warm welcome to Dean McKay!'

There was a smattering of applause as Dean stepped forward, a nervous smile twitching on and off, giving a workout to the unfortunate smear of a moustache on his top lip. He held one hand up.

'Hello, everybody. It's good to be back,' he said.

'Bloody hell,' said Bob in a whisper that everyone near him could hear, 'he thinks he's in Las Vegas. If he's got a good voice, I'll eat my ten-gallon hat.'

Eileen wheeled around and fixed Bob with a pugnacious glare.

'Now,' said Candy, ignoring the ripple of disturbance, 'some warm ups and then we'll start where we left off last time.'

Dean stepped back into line and the rehearsal got under way. Later, Candy asked them to move into four self-selecting groups – soprano, alto, tenor and base – and started teaching them harmonising parts.

'I'll never get the hang of this,' said Dot to Bea, but in fact, by the end of the session there were moments when the four sections gelled, and the sound was really quite pleasing.

Candy was announcing the date of the next rehearsal when someone called out, 'What about Dean? We haven't heard him yet!' There were murmurs of agreement. People were definitely curious to find out if his performance lived up to the hype.

'Come on, Deano!'

Everyone's focus was on Dean now. They were starting

to chant his name. He looked towards Candy, who held her hands up to quieten the throng.

'I'm going to be giving him a bit of extra coaching, so maybe we should leave this until next time,' she said. There were some moans and groans in response. And then a voice cut through them, a clear, pure voice singing the first line of 'Human'. It was a bit quiet to start with, and everyone hushed so that they could listen. People were looking at each other wide-eyed. The voice grew in power as it reached the chorus. Dean sang the second verse and just before he launched into the chorus, he shouted, 'Come on, everyone!' and people started joining in and the room swelled with joyful noise. Somehow, without being told, they stopped before the last line, and let Dean finish. 'Don't put the blame on me.' There was silence for a second or two and then the whole place erupted with applause and whoops and whistles.

'How are you going to tackle that hat, Bob?' said Ant. 'Need a fair bit of ketchup to help that bugger down.'

Bob smiled lopsidedly. 'Fair play to the lad. That was brilliant!'

'I told you!' squawked Eileen to anyone within range. 'I told you all my Dean had the voice of an angel.' She flung her arms round him and gave him such an almighty squeeze Bea could swear his eyes bulged a little.

'Oi, stop it, Mum!' Dean wormed his way out of her vice-like grip, looking pleased, nonetheless.

People started making their way out of the hall, some heading for the bar in the neighbouring room. Ant tipped his head at Bea, his way of asking if she fancied a drink there too. She smiled. 'Why not?' Then she noticed Bob hanging back a little from the rest. He was staring forlornly towards the door, where Dot and Darren were just leaving, still hand in hand.

'I'll join you in a minute, Ant,' she said, and walked back to join Bob.

'You all right, Bob?'

'What?' He looked confused for a moment. 'Oh. Yes.'

'You seem a bit upset. Do you want to talk about it?'

'No, it's okay.' Then, he looked at her, and Bea seemed to see a world of pain in his eyes. 'Actually, I would.'

'Shall we go in the bar here? Have a coffee? Or a drink drink?'

'I could murder a pint.'

The bar was filling up. Dot and Darren had found a sofa in one corner and looked very much like they didn't want to be disturbed. On the other side of the room, Bea spotted the unlikely pairing of Ant and Dean at a table, with plenty of spare chairs. Bob bought the drinks and carried them and a couple of bags of pork scratchings over to Bea. As he approached, Ant and Dean sprang up.

'Nothing I said was it, boys?' said Bob.

'Our turn on the pool table,' said Ant.

Bob sat down and sipped at the layer of foam on top of his beer, then took a long drink, sinking a good third of the pint.

'Ah,' he said, 'I needed that.' He licked the foam off his top lip. 'Do you know what, Bea? You're the first person to ask me if I'm okay for, well, I don't know how long. I don't know what it is. Because I'm a bloke. Or because I'm 'good old Bob' who's always all right. I've just started to notice it recently. No one actually cares whether I'm all right or not.'

'Maybe it's because you're busy caring for other people. You still do odd jobs for your neighbours and customers, don't you?' Bob nodded. 'And you've taken Ant in.'

'It's funny you should mention that. I did offer to take him in and he spent two nights at mine, but yesterday evening we had a couple of beers and at the end of the evening he said that he was sorted for digs. A mate's house, or something.'

'Oh? That's good. Still, you did offer, which was very kind. I guess people put other people into boxes. Caring and cared for. Okay and needy. We forget about the overlap, don't we?'

'True that. Very true,' said Bob, nodding sagely. 'All those years you looked after your mum. Who was looking after you?'

'Well, we managed.'

'Yeah, but I should have done more. I should have been a better friend.'

'We kind of tried to hide it. You didn't know how bad she was. Nobody did.'

'You're a little star, you are, Bea.' He held his glass towards her and she met it with hers, then took a swig of her white wine spritzer. 'None of this current bother can be easy for you.'

'No. It really isn't. I can't stand the thought that everyone thinks Dad did it. You don't think that, do you?'

'No, Bea, I don't. I never did, and your mum rang me up yesterday and told me what was in the letters. It rings true to me. I know he came back late that night, because Maggie rang us up near midnight asking if we'd pop round and babysit. She was worried something had happened to him and wanted to go out looking.'

'Did you do it? Babysit me?'

'We couldn't help, love, because Babs wasn't feeling well. That was why we left the club early.'

'But Dad came home anyway soon afterwards.'

'Yeah. He might have gone AWOL for an hour or two, but I'm sure he didn't do anything.' Bob was nearly at the bottom of his pint. He tipped his head back and drained the last dregs. 'There were other people out and about that night that could've, though . . .'

She leaned a bit closer.

'Who are you thinking of?'

Bob wiped his mouth with the back of his hand.

'Eileen's Alf for one. He was always a bit shifty. And then there was Darren.'

'Really?'

'He and Dot had a big row, I mean a big one, at the club that evening and he stormed out. He was raging, really wound up. That's the night he and Dot split up. Dot was in a hell of a state. Actually, your mum rang her, too, late that night, asking if she'd babysit, but she was too upset. And Darren just disappeared. The police found him a few days later in a B&B in Reading or somewhere.'

'So you think he might have run into Tina when he was angry?' Bea's mind was racing ten to the dozen.

'Who knows? He's a wrong 'un, Bea, I know that much.'

'I know you're not happy he's back.'

'No, I'm not. Look at the smug bastard now.' Bob glowered towards the sofa across the room, where Darren was whispering something into Dot's ear, making her blush and fan herself with her hand. 'If I hadn't messed things up at the beginning of the year, he wouldn't have got a look in. I'm a bloody idiot, I am.'

'Don't beat yourself up, Bob. Everyone makes mistakes.'

'But look what it's cost me. I like your mum, Bea, but I shouldn't have strung her along. Dot is the only woman who I can see a future with. Or *could*. Until he turned up again.'

Bea couldn't think of much to say to console him. The best she could manage was, 'Another pint?'

'Go on, then, but I'll get them. Same again?'

Bea looked round the club while Bob went to the bar. Ant and Dean's game of pool was getting very animated. Dot and Darren were so engrossed in each other that Bea suspected they would skip the casserole when they got home and go straight to afters. Her gaze travelled to a nearby noticeboard. There were posters for exercise classes and a board games club. There was also a 'Coming Events' section, which featured an A3 poster for a band: 'The Pindrop Twins – Kingsleigh's favourite acoustic duo. 7.30pm, Friday 20th June, in the Social Club bar.'

She noted it down in the diary on her phone. The new club was comfortable, and the drinks were cheaper than pub prices. Might be a nice evening out. Perhaps she could persuade Queenie to join her. Then she remembered that she'd never asked Queenie who the band was that played a gig in the old club the night Tina died.

Bob was heading back with their drinks.

'Cheers, Bob,' she said. 'Hey, do you remember the name of the band that was playing here the night Tina, you know . . .'

Bob slurped at the foam on his beer again, then sat back. 'Yeah, they were called the Peardrops. They were local lads, starting to make a name for themselves. They played nice indie sort of stuff.'

'Never heard of them. Are they still gigging?'

'Nah, they split up a year or so after the Tina thing. One of them died, I think, in a car crash. Sad.'

'Can you remember who was in it? Any names?'

Across the room, Dot and Darren were getting to their feet. Bob stared at them as they left.

'Bob. Bob!'

He came to. 'Sorry, love, was miles away.'

'Do you remember the names of the guys in the band?'

'No, no I don't, although I think a couple of them are still gigging locally. Pete Banner would know. He's been managing the club, more or less, for twenty years. Do you want me to ask him?'

'Yeah, if you don't mind.'

Bob looked round the room. A tall man with a bald dome was picking his way through the tables, picking up empty glasses expertly, carrying three or four with each hand.

'Hey, Pete!' Bob called out. The man looked up and started walking over.

'Yes, mate,' he said.

'Do you remember that band, the Peardrops, used to play at the old club?'

'Yeah, course.'

'Are a couple of them still going?'

Pete rested the empty glasses on the table. 'Yeah, they're going to be playing here in a few days, as a matter of fact. That's them, the Pindrop Twins,' he said, nodding towards the poster that Bea had just noticed. 'They're nice lads. You coming to it?'

'Yeah, maybe,' said Bob. 'What do you reckon, Bea?'

Bea smiled. 'Definitely. I'll be there.'

27

The next day, she met up with Ant at the opposite end of the High Street to Costsave. As she turned the corner from the path by the old people's bungalows, she spotted him coming out of the leisure centre on the other side of the road. He waved when he saw her and crossed over.

'All right, Ant?' she said. 'What were you doing in there?'

'Swim before work,' he said, casually, like it was something he did every day.

'What? Really?'

'Yeah. Why not? Set myself up for the day. Ten lengths. Might try for fifteen tomorrow.'

'Bloody hell, mate. I didn't even know you could swim.'

'Just goes to show, you don't know everything.'

'No, but I'm impressed.'

'You could join me, if you like, if you can swim.'

'I got my twenty-five metres certificate at school, but that was probably the last time I went.'

'It was nice, actually. There's a few show-offs ploughing up and down the fast lane with their Speedos and their nose clips, but apart from that, it's not too busy.'

'Mm, think I'd rather have the extra half an hour in bed. Let's see how long this health kick lasts.'

Ant grinned. They'd just left the High Street and were on

the path that cut through to the Costsave car park when Bea spotted a figure lurking by the wall; short, slightly hunched, wearing his brown, stained raincoat, even though it was a beautiful morning. Reg scuttled out to meet them, his familiar twang diluted in the open air to almost acceptable levels.

'Morning, Reg,' Bea said, disconcerted at this uncharacteristic behaviour.

'I need a word.' His gaze shifted from Bea to Ant and back again. 'With you.'

'Oh, right. What about?' Bea could only imagine there was some problem with Costsave, but she couldn't think what it would be.

Reg looked at Ant again and then said to Bea, 'It's private.'

Ant raised his eyebrows and pressed his tongue against the inside of his cheek so it bulged out. 'Don't mind me,' he said. 'I need an early morning fag, anyway. I'll be over by the trolleys.' He sauntered away, but stayed where Bea could still see him. Reg was still uneasy, tight-lipped.

'Over here,' he said.

He started scuttling towards a nearby bus shelter, which, as a commuter bus had just left it, was empty. Bea cringed inwardly at the thought of being in a confined space with him, but her curiosity was well and truly piqued now. She joined him inside.

'Sit down,' he said, parking himself on the sloping plastic bench seat and patting the area next to him. Bea perched a decent distance away from him. He slid along so that they were closer.

'What is it, Reg? What've you got to tell me?'

'It's your mum,' he said. If Bea had tried to predict topics that Reg might raise with her, Queenie was not one of them.

'My mum? What are you talking about?'

'I was there that night.'

'What night?' Bea said, even though she was certain she knew what he was referring to, and now she felt a growing sense of anxiety, like a gnarly, clawed hand scratching her from the inside.

'The night that girl, Tina, disappeared.'

'You were there?'

Close to, the evidence of Reg's lifestyle was all too clear – the yellow nicotine stains on his fingers, the trace of last night's booze on his breath.

'I was the nightwatchman. Worked there for eight years. Saw everything.'

'What did you see, Reg?'

'I saw people walking home from the club. And I saw your mum walking in. Just before midnight.'

'My mum? No, you've got it wrong. She was at home, Reg. She left early and came home to me.'

'And must have gone out again. She walked down to the club. Disappeared for a while. Well, it was all dark round there. Then came back again.'

Bea's mind was racing ten to the dozen. This couldn't possibly be true, could it?

'Are you sure it was her?'

Reg looked at her steadily. Bea could see a network of inflamed blood vessels in the whites of his eyes. She looked away, down to his grubby fingers which were resting on her arm now.

'I'm sure. She's a good person, your mum. That's why I never told the police. Never told anyone until now. It was her business what she was doing there. Your dad was a good person, too. He always said hello or goodbye to me as he walked past my hut. A lot of the others ignored me, like I was beneath them. Invisible. Not your dad. He was a gentleman.'

'He was Reg. I'm glad you think so too.' She'd always treated Reg's visits to her checkout as a sort of joke, always breathed a sigh of relief when he'd gone. She felt slightly ashamed now. 'Reg, why are you telling me this?'

'I heard you been asking around. Trying to find out what happened. I thought you should know. Up to you what you do with it now.' His fingers pressed into her arm a little more and Bea resisted the urge to squirm away. 'You're a good person, too, Bea. You'd better go to work now. Don't want to be late, do you? I'll be in in a minute.' He let go of her arm.

'For your *Racing Post*.'

He smiled. 'That's right,' he said. 'There's a good meeting at Kempton this afternoon. Might make a few quid.'

He stayed where he was as Bea got to her feet. Through the Perspex of the shelter she could see a tall man with a bald head coming out of the newsagents opposite. She recognised him as Pete Banner from the social club and remembered that the next choir rehearsal was going to be in one of his meeting rooms. She walked round to the car park. Ant was hovering at the entrance by the path.

'You all right?' he said. 'Wondered if you needed rescuing. It's nearly time for the huddle.'

'Thanks, Ant. I'm fine. He's a dark horse, our Reg.'

'Yeah? What did he want?'

Eileen and Kirsty walked briskly past them as they were talking. Eileen gave Bea a filthy look.

'Got time for a chat, have you?'

Bea checked her phone and yelped. They were cutting it fine. They started walking rapidly across the car park. There were a few cars pulling in to wait for the opening of the store, and a couple of builders in their high-vis jackets walking round to the back yard.

'He said he saw my mum there, at the factory, the night Tina went missing. He was a nightwatchman.'

'What, after hours?'

'Yeah, just before midnight.'

Ant made a low whistling noise.

'He's not the only dark horse, then. You'll have to talk to Queenie about that.'

'I bloody will, Ant. I thought she'd told me everything, but obviously not.' They'd reached the staff door now. 'Ant, what if she had something to do with it. What if she—?'

Rather surprisingly, Ant put his finger up against her lips. She could smell the swimming pool chlorine still clinging to his skin. 'Shh, don't even say it. This is your mum we're talking about.'

He moved his finger away. 'But Ant—'

'Have a chat with her this evening. Tell her what you know.'

'Yeah, you're right.'

'Uh-oh,' said Ant, 'Loved-up couple alert!'

Dot was approaching, hand in hand with Darren. 'I'll see you later, darlin',' Darren said, drawing her in towards him and planting a kiss on her lips.

'All right, love. Have a good day.' Dot patted his bottom, then broke away from him and headed for the door. Ant and Bea let her go in first, then followed her up the stairs. Bea didn't really listen to George's briefing. There was something about the choir, and something else about sales targets, but her mind was elsewhere. She needed to talk to Queenie, was tempted to fake some sort of illness so she could go home there and then, but it would wait, wouldn't it? Whatever it was, she'd kept this secret for fourteen years. Another eight hours wouldn't hurt.

28

Reg didn't come in for his *Racing Post*, after all. The shop was busy right from the get-go and Bea had only just remembered she hadn't seen him when something landed with a thud on the end of her conveyor belt and she heard Eileen's dulcet tones saying, 'Do you think this'll make a difference?'

Bea was in the middle of processing a week's family shop for a rather tired-looking woman. She glanced up and saw Eileen lumbering away towards the newspaper and magazine aisle, pushing a trolley loaded with papers. Bea peered over the mountain of goods yet to be beeped through and saw a new edition of the *Bugle* lying at the other side of the 'Next Please!' divider. She picked up the pace as much as she could, watching the paper inch closer to her with every twitch of the conveyor belt. Finally, everything in the heap was bought and paid for. As her customer put her debit card away and rearranged the bags in her trolley in an effort to keep them from spilling out, Bea reached for the *Bugle*.

'Oh God,' she murmured. 'Front page.'

'My Dad is Innocent,' the banner headline read, and underneath, 'Kingsleigh woman defends suspect in Tina Robbins case – reporting by Dan Knibbs.'

'You all right, love?' said Dot.

'They've printed it, my dad's letter. I'll just have a quick look. Keep an eye out for Neville, will you?'

'On it.'

Bea skim-read the article and, to be fair, Dan had done a good job. The letter was reproduced in full, which made her cringe a little. It was such a personal thing to be made public and it was there in black and white now – her dad's deathbed declaration. She was sure, though, that she'd done the right thing.

'Incoming,' said Dot, and Bea quickly stuffed the newspaper onto the shelf beneath her till, but it was only Eileen coming back, pushing an empty trolley this time.

'Going to have egg on your face if the DNA comes back and says it's him,' she said with a nasty sneer.

'Leave it, Eileen,' said Dot.

'Why are you being like this anyway?' said Bea.

Eileen stopped the trolley and put her hands on her hips. 'You're quick enough to point the finger at me and mine, aren't you?'

'Eileen, I've *never* pointed the finger at you,' said Bea, standing up now and, indeed, wagging her index finger towards Eileen's face. 'I've had issues with Dean, but that's all sorted now.'

Eileen screwed up her face and turned down the corners of her mouth, 'I've had issues with Dean,' she mimicked. 'You're so hoity-toity, you and your mum. You think you're so much better than everyone else. Well, I've got news for you, you're not.'

'Don't bring my mum into this!' Bea left her station and stomped round the end of her packing area, heading for Eileen.

'Eileen! Bea! That's enough!' Dot was on her feet as well,

trying to intervene, but it was too late. Shoppers had stopped at the end of the aisles to watch them, and now Neville was heading towards them like a ship in full sail.

'Ladies!' he called out. 'Ladies, calm down!'

They both ignored him.

'You can take your trolley, Eileen, and shove it where the sun don't shine.' Bea pushed the end of the trolley sideways, trying to clear a path directly to Eileen.

Neville jumped in between them. 'That's enough! Stop it!' His clipboard clattered to the floor as he held his arms out at either side, like a policeman directing traffic in the middle of a junction. 'Stop!'

Bea and Eileen glared at each other along the length of Neville's arms, both breathing heavily. Neville, in the middle, looked rather surprised that his intervention had worked, at least temporarily. He blinked several times, pushed his glasses back up his nose and said, 'Right. Let's all calm down. Eileen, please take this trolley to the stores and report to my office.' He held his hand further up as Eileen started to protest. 'No, I don't want to hear it. I'll see you in my office. Bea, are you all right to continue?' Bea nodded. 'Very well. Report to me at the end of this morning's session.'

He ducked down and retrieved his clipboard, which these days acted as a holder for his Costsave tablet and stylus, from the floor.

'Oh no,' he said. 'The screen's cracked.'

He blinked more rapidly and Bea wondered if he was actually crying.

'I'm sorry, Neville,' she said.

He swallowed hard, said quietly, 'Get back to work,' and walked slowly towards the back of the shop floor, to all appearances a broken man.

'Oh Bea,' said Dot. 'What've you done?'

'I didn't mean to, and it wasn't just me. She started it.'

Dot rolled her eyes. 'I know Eileen's a cow, but listen to yourself, love, and now look at poor Neville.'

Bea could just see him disappearing down aisle three. 'Oh God, he's going to tell George now, isn't he?'

'Bound to.'

'What am I going to do?'

29

Eileen didn't reappear on the shop floor that morning, and when Bea logged off from her till and went upstairs, there was no sign of her there, either. 'Eileen's going to be working in the stores for the rest of the day,' whispered Anna, as Bea waited for Neville to appear in the office. 'What was it all about anyway?'

'She was just winding me up about my dad and my mum. She's evil.'

'Bit harsh, Bea. She's just Eileen. Better to laugh her off than rise to the bait.'

'Yeah, I know,' said Bea. 'She just got to me.'

'Here he is. Good luck.'

Neville spoke to Bea more in sorrow than anger, and somehow she found that worse. It would have been easier to take the force of a full-on bollocking, apologise and move on.

'I'm very disappointed in you, Beatrice. I feel like you've not only let Costsave down, you've let yourself down.'

'Yes, Neville. Sorry, Neville.'

She received an official warning but was allowed to return to her shift after lunch. 'It can't happen again, though, Beatrice.'

'No, Neville. It won't.'

She slunk into the staff room and found a corner to hide in, where she read the front page of the *Bugle* again. Given the morning's kerfuffle, she was no longer confident that the article was such a good idea. Anna and Dot came and joined her, eating their packed lunches in companionable silence.

Bea leafed through the rest of the paper.

'Anything good in there?' asked Dot.

Bea stopped on page five and read out the headline. 'Leave our Spuds Alone – veggie vigilantes on the lookout for allotment menace.'

'Ooh, that's a good K-town story. Go on, tell me more,' said Anna, digging about in her Tupperware box and spearing what looked like raw cattle food with her fork.

Bea read the article and summarised, 'The allotment holders are up in arms because someone broke into one of the sheds up there. Didn't take anything, but they're all super-sensitive at the moment because the flower and vegetable show is earlier than usual this year, middle of July. They're talking about organising teams to patrol the place at night. Make sure all their cauliflowers and giant marrows are safe.'

'Vegilantes?' said Anna.

Bea snorted. 'I see what you did there. You're wasted at Costsave. You should be writing these headlines.'

Anna smiled. 'They'll be pacing round the paling in their wellies and jackets with a hundred pockets, pitchforks at the ready.'

'What was that?' said Ant, coming in at the end of the conversation.

'Nothing much,' said Bea. 'Angry spud growers patrolling the allotments at night. Someone's been breaking in up there. Kids probably.'

'Oh. Right.'

'It'd make the front page of the *Bugle* in a normal week, but it's my turn. Do you want a look?' She held the paper out towards him, eager to see if he'd accept the challenge and try to read the article.

'Hmm.' He took the paper, but didn't try to read it, or even look at the pictures.

'You all right, Ant?'

'Yeah. I'm fine.' But he wasn't, thought Bea. He was deep in thought, miles away. He stayed like that, subdued, uncommunicative, until the end of their lunch break.

'What are you on this afternoon?' Bea asked him.

He groaned. 'I'm outside breaking up cardboard again. Don't know why it's always my bloody job.'

'I thought you didn't mind it.'

'Well, it's okay normally, but now the sun's out the digging at the back's kicking up dust like nobody's business. It comes across in great clouds when they're piling stuff into a trench.'

'Ask Neville if you can wear a mask,' said Anna. 'We've got some in the stores.'

'Oh, right,' said Ant, brightening. 'Thanks, Anna. Reckon I'll take my top off – get a bit of sunshine on these guns.' He held up one arm, flexed his muscles and squeezed his biceps with the other hand. 'Rock hard, ladies. Do you want a feel?'

'All right?' The summer weather seemed to be bringing out the worst in Saggy. Bea had watched him shamble up to her checkout. He was wearing a loose vest which didn't quite cover his nipples, and his knee-length shorts were hanging so low Bea was worried that they might give up at any moment and descend to his ankles.

'Hi Saggy,' she said, trying to keep her eyes on his face. 'What's up?'

'Have you seen Ant?'

'He's breaking up cardboard. It's round the side, 'cos the back's still being dug up, but it's fenced off. You won't be able to get in.'

'Oh, right. Can you give him this?' Saggy held out a brown envelope. 'It came to ours.'

'Sure.' Bea slipped the envelope into the pocket of her tabard. 'Can't you give it to him later, though?'

'Nah, I'm not seeing him this evening. Got a date.'

Bea tried not to let her amazement show at this unlikely turn of events.

'Oh nice,' she said, 'but I meant later when you're both home. He's back at yours, isn't he?'

Saggy shook his head. 'He moved out a few days ago. Said someone at work had offered him their spare room. Can't remember who. Rob or Bob or something?'

'Oh,' said Bea. 'Okay, I'll make sure he gets the letter then.'

'Cheers,' Saggy said and sloped away towards the front door. Bea winced as his shorts inched downwards, then breathed a sigh of relief as he clutched the waistband and yanked them up.

Bea remembered the letter when she was putting her tabard in her locker at the end of the day. She fished it out of the pocket and went to find Ant. Despite his shift having finished, he was still breaking up huge cardboard boxes.

'Ant!' she called. 'Time to go home!'

He stopped what he was doing and looked round. He was wearing a white, surgical-looking mask, and despite what he'd said earlier, he had his Costsave polo shirt on and there were big sweat stains under his arms and across his chest. He moved the mask off his face and perched it on top of his head. 'I might as well finish this,' he said. 'You go ahead. I'll see you tomorrow.'

She walked towards him.

'Saggy was in earlier. He gave me this for you.' She handed him the envelope.

'What is it?' said Ant, turning the envelope over in his hands. 'Looks official. Oh Jesus, what now?'

'Shall I have a look?'

'Yeah. Not quite up to reading government bullshit yet. You open it. Tell me what it says.'

Bea took it from him and slit the envelope open with her finger. Inside was a sort of proforma with a few details hand-written into gaps. The heading was 'HMP Bexton'.

'It's a visiting order, Ant. You've got permission to visit your dad in Bexton on Saturday at 2.15. Were you expecting that?'

Ant frowned.

'No. I haven't seen him for a while, though. He usually uses his visits to see Mum and the others.'

'Must be missing you.'

'Doubt it. I wonder what's up.'

'Only one way to find out. Ant, do you want to come for tea? Mum'd be pleased to see you.'

He folded the letter back up and put it in his trouser pocket.

'No, it's okay. I really do want to finish this. It's collection day tomorrow.'

He put the mask back over his face.

'You could come after,' said Bea. 'Or are you eating with . . . who is it you're staying with now?'

She couldn't hear his reply properly, just a muffled string of words that seemed to include the word 'mate'. He turned to pull out a particularly large box from the heap and pull it apart.

'See you tomorrow, Ant!' Bea shouted.

He gave her the thumbs up and carried on with his work. As she walked home, thoughts of Queenie pushed worries about Ant from her mind. She wasn't looking forward to confronting her about what Reg had said, but there was no getting round it. Her mum had lied to her, and now it was time to find out the truth.

30

'Do you think we should just stop all this?'

'Stop what?'

'The lying. The half-truths.'

'I'm sorry, love, I don't know what you're talking about.'

'Where were you the night Tina died?'

Queenie's brow furrowed, as her confusion registered.

'I told you, I went to the club with your dad, but came home early. Then I was here with you.'

'That's part of the truth, but not the whole truth, isn't it?'

'Bea, sit down, you're bothering me with your pacing. Come on, sit down.'

'No, Mum. It doesn't matter if I'm standing or sitting. This isn't about me. It's about you. You went out again that night, after you'd come home. You rang Bob asking if he'd babysit.'

'And he couldn't. His Babs was in a bad way.'

'So you rang Dot, too, but she was in a state 'cos Darren had gone off.'

'Yes, that's right.'

'So who babysat while you went out?'

'I didn't—'

'Mum, you were *seen*!' Bea practically screamed the last word. Queenie's face froze, as if she'd been physically slapped. They looked at each other, Bea letting the growing silence between them push her mother towards telling the truth, force her into honesty.

'Sit down, love,' Queenie said. Bea sat. Her heart was beating rapidly. Her palms were sweating. She tried to keep things under control, to keep quiet, to let her silence keep doing the work for her. Queenie was fiddling with the edge of one of the sofa cushions, picking away at a loose thread. Bea watched and waited, until her mum spoke again. 'I did go out,' she said. 'I went out to look for your dad. I was worried about him, about the mess he might be getting into.'

'With Tina?'

She nodded. 'I knew he liked her. I saw it that night, kept catching him looking at her. I asked him straight out and he denied it. Said there was nothing going on. He was never any good at lying.'

'But there wasn't anything going on, was there?'

'No, only in his head. Something he thought he wanted.'

'So you went back to the club?'

'I walked the route I thought he'd take to come home, hoping to meet him. I got all the way to the factory site, walked round the club. It was dark. Everyone had gone, including your dad.'

'You didn't see anyone there?'

'No. Thinking back, I guess it was all over for Tina by then. Whoever did it had already moved her, put her in that trench.'

'So you came home again?'

'Yes. I walked back the same way. Got home ten minutes or so before Harry. I couldn't talk to him then, didn't want a row. I tucked into bed and pretended to be asleep. If I'd known he knew, perhaps we could have talked, but we didn't. We just sort of ignored it and carried on.'

'But why the big secret? Why not tell me this from the start?'

Queenie couldn't meet her eye. She was picking at the cushion again, working away at the loose thread with her fingernail.

'I couldn't find a babysitter. You were seven, Bea. I left you alone.'

She kept her eyes down as the seam on the cushion started to unravel.

'I guess I was asleep. You weren't out for long, right?'

'Forty minutes. Maybe more. But it was wrong, Bea. It was unforgivable. You should never leave a kid that age on their own. And I've never done it before or since.'

'Nothing happened, though. I was all right.'

'But what if something had happened? If you'd had a nightmare and woken up to find an empty house? What if you'd been sick and there was no one to look after you?'

'But it didn't. I didn't and I wasn't.'

'Sometimes you do things as a parent, even though you know they're not right. And then you torture yourself afterwards.'

'Mum, you can stop torturing yourself about this. Everything was okay. You never did it again. It's all right.'

'But I'm like one of those mums who leave their kids and go off on holiday to Spain.'

'Hardly.'

'It's the same thing, Bea. I put my needs before yours.'

'Once in twenty-one years. For forty minutes. It's okay. Honestly.'

'You're very kind. Forgiving. Harry was right. You're clever and brave and you do your own thing. I'm very lucky to have you.'

'Why do you think I am all those things, though?' Queenie shook her head. 'Because you and Dad raised me. You made me who I am.'

'No, love. You did that all by yourself. I'm just lucky I got to see it.'

'Stop it. You'll set me off. But no more secrets, okay?'

'No more secrets. Let's have a cuppa.'

It was still light outside, so Bea took her mug of tea into the garden and sat on the wooden bench overlooking a rather neglected flower border. She put her mug down beside her and started googling on her phone for 'the Peardrops'. She kept drilling down and following threads until she had names for the four members of the band, along with a potted history of the group which, she found, was marked by tragedy. In 2006, two members of the band died; one, Simon, in a car crash and the other, Trey, by his own hand seven months later. The Peardrops as such ceased to exist, but later Liam and Justin started gigging as the Pindrop Twins and were still playing in and around Bristol.

She scrolled back through the sites to an account of Trey's death. He had been living at home in Kingsleigh's Orchard estate, not too far from her own house. His parents had become worried when he went out for a walk one day and didn't come back. His body was found by a dog walker in the local woods, only half a mile or so from their home. He'd hanged himself from a tree.

'Blimey,' said Bea to herself. 'Poor bloke.'

There had been an inquest which heard that he'd had a history of depression. Even so, as Bea read further, she couldn't help asking herself a question. Why? Why had he taken his own life less than a year after Tina disappeared? Could there possibly be a connection?

She searched for 'the Pindrop Twins' and found their website. It was fairly rudimentary but there were dates for their upcoming gigs, links to some of their music, some music files and a couple of videos on YouTube. Bea ran her eye down the list of gigs. Of course, they were playing the Factory Quarter Social Club in a couple of days' time. She'd forgotten. Bea started clicking on the videos, only giving them her attention for a few seconds before trying the next one. She stopped when she found one viewed much more than any of the others. It was obviously their 'hit' or the nearest they'd come to one, 'Last Seen Wearing'. She pressed play. The music was gentle and melodic. One of the guys played an introduction on an acoustic guitar and then the other started singing. He had a beautiful voice, almost folky. It wasn't the sort of style Bea usually liked, but as she listened to the lyrics the hairs on the back of her neck started standing up.

'Oh my god,' she murmured. 'Oh. My. God.'

She exited the site and rang Ant, but her call went straight to his voicemail.

'Ant,' she said, breathlessly, 'call me back. I've got something on the band. We've gotta go see them. They're playing the club on Saturday. Ant, one of their songs – it's about her. About Tina.'

31

The next morning there was a knock at the door before Bea had even had her Coco Pops. Queenie, filling the kettle at the sink, looked round, scared. 'Who's that at this time of day?'

'Only one way to find out.'

Bea wrapped her dressing gown more firmly round her middle and went to the front door. She opened it a fraction and peered out. She recognised Shaz, with another officer, the young guy with a prominent Adam's apple she'd seen at Costsave. Bea opened the door fully.

'What is it? What's happened?' she said.

They both looked at her steadily.

'Can we come in, Bea?' said Shaz.

'Yes, of course.' She showed them into the lounge where they sat down on the sofa.

Queenie came through from the kitchen. 'What is it?'

'I don't know, Mum. They're just going to say.' Bea looked at Shaz, who cleared her throat.

'We've had the results from the forensics lab. We've got a DNA profile.'

'Oh. Does that mean . . .what does it mean?'

'It means that we can start eliminating people from our inquiries. Obviously, in the case of your dad, Bea, we can't ask him for a DNA sample but we can take one from you, as his nearest relative. If you don't mind.'

'Of course I don't mind. What do I have to do?'

Shaz produced a small plastic bag from her pocket. 'It's just a mouth swab. I can do it now. Is that okay?'

Bea's mouth had suddenly gone dry. She moved her tongue along the front of her teeth. 'Yes.'

'Don't worry,' said Shaz. 'Just open wide.' She bent down close to Bea, took what looked to Bea like a cotton bud attached to the lid of a glass tube and energetically scrubbed Bea's gums. It was quick and clinical and somehow made Bea feel powerless. 'That should do it.' She inserted it into the tube and twisted the top shut. 'I'll get that off to the lab. It'll take a few days to get the results.'

'Then Dad will be in the clear?'

'If the DNA doesn't match, then yes.'

Bea refused to countenance the obvious corollary. As she showed the two officers out, she asked Shaz, 'Did you read my report about Julie?'

Shaz nodded. 'Yes. I've passed it on, Bea. It looks like there's enough there for us to investigate, but we're really stretched at the moment. Leave it with us, though.'

Bea closed the door then checked her watch and raced upstairs. 'I'm going to be late at this rate!'

'Are you having your Coco Pops, though?'

'Don't know. I'll get dressed, see if I've got time.'

In the end, she had to set off without eating anything, a crime against routine which left Queenie tutting audibly. 'Shall I bring you something in later, Bea?'

'Mum, I work in a food shop, with a café attached. I think I'll cope.'

Bea didn't quite jog to work, but she did do her best power walking. Again, she met up with Ant as he emerged from the leisure centre.

'Two days in a row? I'm impressed!'

Ant's eyes were a bit bloodshot from the water, but he was looking quite pleased with himself. 'Got myself in the zone now,' he said.

There was a queue of people at the bus stop where Bea had talked with Reg the day before – the bus to Bristol was obviously running late. Bea noted a smattering of litter on the grass verge behind it and some rags in the bottom of the hedge. The street cleaner in Kingsleigh was usually pretty on the ball, but Bea knew from the *Bugle* that his hours had been cut recently. This was the result, she thought.

There wasn't time to grab anything to eat before work. Bea could feel her stomach start to grumble halfway through George's morning huddle. It was against the rules to eat anything on the shop floor but she rummaged in the pockets of her tabard anyway as she walked down the stairs and along the aisles, in case she'd left a packet of mints or a stray toffee there. No luck.

'Have you got anything to eat on you?' she said to Dot as they settled into their adjacent tills.

'No, love. Sorry. There was half a packet of rich tea biscuits in the staff room by the kettle. You could grab one on a loo break, if you're desperate.'

'I might have to.'

They went through their morning rituals before start of play. As she was rubbing in her hand sanitiser, Bea watched George walk towards the front doors jangling her big bunch of keys.

'Morning, ladies!'

'Morning!'

Bea saw her checking her watch then unlocking the door and activating the automation. The doors slid sideways and Cost-save was open for business. A smattering of customers spilled through, each heading purposefully towards their goals. Early morning shoppers meant business, no messing about. Bea kept watching until the first tranche were all in. There were a few workmen, a sales rep or two and a harassed-looking mother with a crying toddler in a pushchair, but no Reg.

'Dot,' she said. 'Did you see Reg in here yesterday?'

Dot twiddled her chair round to face her. 'No, love. He wouldn't come to me anyway, would he? It's you he's got a soft spot for.'

'He didn't come in, and he's not here today either.'

'Perhaps he's having a lie in.'

'Hmm.'

The morning went quickly enough. Dot wasn't as bubbly as she had been. Perhaps the first flush of excitement over Darren's return was wearing off, thought Bea. During a lull, Bea told her about her morning visitors.

'That's good, isn't it?' said Dot. 'They'll be able to rule out your dad and find who did it. This'll all be cleared up soon.'

'If they can find a match. I was thinking, if it was someone already on their books, they wouldn't have bothered with me, would they? So anyone with a criminal record or who's been questioned or whatever is off the hook. That rules out quite a few K-town residents, doesn't it?'

'Ha! Yeah, including my Darren.' Bea raised her eyebrows, but Dot brushed her unspoken inquiry away. 'Never mind about him. He's a liar, always will be, but he's not a murderer.'

There was something about the rather bitter emphasis to the word 'liar' that made Bea think that Dot wasn't just talking about his past misdemeanours, but now wasn't the time to press her.

'Mind you, babe,' Dot continued, 'I'm not sure what the rules are with DNA. Don't they have to chuck samples away after so many years?'

'Don't know,' Bea admitted. 'That's the sort of thing I could ask Tom, if he was talking to me. Uh-oh.'

Neville, seeing them chatting, was stalking towards them.

'If you've got time to gossip, ladies, you've got time to smarten up these workstations. Bea, your baskets are all higgledy-piggledy. Dot, your conveyor belt looks like it's suffered a spillage.'

Frustratingly, Bea couldn't think of a smart but acceptable riposte, so she simply sighed, got up and walked round to sort out the stack of baskets. Her empty stomach was rumbling now. 'While I'm up, can I just nip to the ladies, please Neville?'

'Can you deal with this influx first, please, Bea?'

Bea looked up. Sure enough, there was a gaggle of customers approaching the checkouts, including a couple of her regulars; Norma, with her tartan shopping bag and Charles, carrying a large bag of dog food, no doubt destined for her favourite pooch, Goldie. In fact, there wasn't a chance to take a break before lunchtime. Ant was sauntering past her till as she logged off.

'Chips?' he said, hopefully, and Bea's mouth started salivating at the thought.

'Yes,' she said. 'Shall we nip to the Golden Fryer quickly?'

'Let's do it.'

'Dot, do you fancy some chips?'

'No, ta, love. Can't pig out now. Darren said he'd take me out for dinner.'

'Okay.' Bea started walking quickly towards the back of the store. 'I'll just fetch my bag, then there's something else I want to do on the way to the chippy.'

Bag under her arm, Costsave tabard safely in her locker, Bea met Ant again and they trotted across the car park. 'What is it? The thing you want to do?'

'I just want to look at something. It's been bothering me all morning. Here,' she said. They'd reached the path which joined the High Street and Bea walked up the road for a few metres to the bus stop. It was empty now, but the litter was still there. She stepped behind the shelter, studying the ground.

'What are you looking for?' said Ant. 'Did you drop something the other day? Bea? Bea, what are you doing?'

Bea was bending down by the laurel bushes that formed the hedge at the back of the verge. 'God, it smells rank,' she said. She moved some of the lower branches aside. 'Oh shit. Oh no.'

Ant crouched next to her.

'What is it?'

'I saw it this morning. I should have done something then.'

'What?'

Ant looked down. There was a rag, caught up in the base of the hedge. Thick brown cotton or twill, but as he looked closer he could see it wasn't a scrap, it was the corner of a garment, the hem of a coat, and as he crouched down he could see that there was something underneath it, further into the dark shadow of the hedge. A leg sticking out. An ankle. A foot, wearing an old lace up shoe.

'Fucking hell, Bea,' he breathed. 'It's Reg.'

32

Bea made way as Ant shuffled sideways and reached through the trunks of the bushes to find one of Reg's hands. 'He's stone cold. There's no pulse. Should we try and get him out of there?'

'I don't think so. Leave that to the experts. We should call 999,' said Bea.

'I'll do it.' Ant dialled the emergency number and Bea listened as he stumbled through the conversation. 'I don't know...ambulance...or police. Either. We've found a body, you see. Yeah. No. Just off Kingsleigh High Street, behind the bus shelter outside Costsave. Yeah, okay.' He killed the call. 'They're on their way. I suppose I should check that he is, you know...'

Bea became aware of some noise behind them. She turned her head and there were half a dozen people gathered, including a grey-haired woman with a small child in tow, watching. She stood up and faced them. 'There's someone there. He's—' Bea looked at the tot and then at the woman '—I've called an ambulance. Best to get that one away from here.' The woman looked startled. She put her arm protectively round the child's shoulders, then ushered her away. The others stayed put, some of them craning round Bea to get a better look.

'God, Ant, this is awful,' Bea said. 'What should we do?'

Ant stood up, too, and spread his arms out, 'There's nothing to see here, folks. The ambulance will be here soon.'

'Who is it?' a man called out. He'd already got his phone out and was taking snaps.

'Hey!' Ant shouted. 'Show some respect.'

'It's news, isn't it?'

'I don't care, stop taking pictures or I'll take your phone off you.'

'Who the hell are you?'

'I'm the bloke who's teaching you nicely how not to be a dick. This is another human being here.'

His words hit home. The man put his phone away, and moved a bit further down the pavement. Bea was relieved to hear sirens now, and in less than a minute a police car drew up, followed quickly by an ambulance.

A cordon was set up. Brief statements were taken. They told the police officer Reg's name, and that Bea had seen him there yesterday morning. Then Ant and Bea were told that they could go back to work for the time being at least. As they turned to go back to Costsave, Bea took a last look behind her. Another police car had arrived and a tent was being put up to shield the whole site from view. Reg's body was still mostly hidden at the bottom of the hedge. Up to now, adrenaline had kept her fairly calm. Now, though, she started to feel sick and shaky.

Ant put his arm round her shoulders. 'Come on, mate. Let's go and get a cup of tea.'

They walked away, only to find Dan Knibbs running towards them. 'Hey guys,' he said. 'What's going on?'

'Someone's died, on the High Street,' said Bea, a violent shiver running through her as she spoke. 'We found the body.'

'You found them?' Dan's eyes widened and he whipped

his notebook out of his pocket. 'Can I ask you some quick questions?'

Bea put her hand up. 'No, honestly. I don't want to talk about it. I don't want you to put my name.'

'Okay, understood.' His eyes narrowed. 'You know who it is, though, right?'

'Leave it, mate,' said Ant. 'We can't say anything until the police have done their thing.'

'Listen, this is totally off the record. I'm just looking for a heads up, so I can hit the ground running when the police make their statement. Guys?'

Bea just wanted him to leave them alone. She badly needed to sit down somewhere quiet. 'Off the record, it's one of my customers. He's called Reg Firmin.'

'And do you know anything about him?'

'He was ...' Bea felt tired now, so very tired. 'He was a good man.'

Dan pressed his lips together in sympathy. 'Thanks, Bea. You look done in. Cup of tea with two sugars, if I were you.' He left them to get as close as he could to the police tent.

'Do we have to go back to work?' said Bea.

'Reckon the staff room will be pretty quiet now. We won't get badgered by anyone up there. I'll just ring ahead.'

Ant rang the Costsave office and talked to Anna. When he cancelled the call, he nodded to Bea. 'Anna's going to square everything with George. Let's go.'

They crossed the car park and made their way round the side of the building and into the staff entrance. Bea wondered if she had the strength to manage the stairs. She dragged herself up them, tottered along the corridor and sank down into the nearest armchair in the staff room. Anna was already in there, brewing tea.

'Hiya Bea,' she said, putting two steaming mugs down on the coffee table in front of her and Ant. 'Drink that.'

Bea took a mug, but it was too hot and she put it down again. She stared into the middle distance. 'I only saw him yesterday. He stopped me on the way into work. What the hell? I mean, seriously, what the hell is going on?'

33

'It must have happened yesterday, just after we spoke.' Bea was thinking aloud, trying to make sense of things.

'Do you reckon?'

'The last thing he said to me was that he'd see me in a minute, when the store opened. He was looking forward to picking some winners in his *Racing Post*, but he didn't show up. He must have collapsed between me leaving him and opening time. That's only ten minutes, Ant. What do you think happened to him?'

'We don't know, do we, Bea? Let's face it, he was pretty old and he wasn't the healthiest bloke, was he? Probably just keeled over.'

'The thought of him lying there for twenty-four hours. It's horrific. Oh no, you don't think he lay there, alive, for hours, do you?'

'Honestly, Bea,' Ant put a hand on her wrist, and, instantly, she remembered Reg's hand on her arm, 'I don't know. Don't torture yourself.'

'If I'd known he wasn't well, I would've stayed with him.'

'You can't think about "if onlys", Bea,' said Anna, fetching the biscuit tin and offering Bea a rich tea. 'None of us know what's round the corner.'

Bea took a biscuit absentmindedly and dunked it into her

hot tea. When she put the soggy end in her mouth the rush of saliva and a sharp pain in her stomach reminded her that she hadn't eaten all day. Somehow it didn't seem to matter. The mouthful of biscuit sat heavily in her stomach and she put the rest of it down on the table.

'Have your drink, at least,' said Anna. Bea sipped at the tea. 'You said he stopped you on the way into work. What did he want?'

'He was telling me about the night Tina disappeared. He used to be the nightwatchman at the factory.'

'Did he? I never knew that. Well, obviously I hardly knew him at all, sitting up here in the office. You saw him every day, didn't you?'

'Yeah and I'd never even thought about what he did before he turned into an old bloke who liked a smoke and a bet on the horses. I guess I just wrote him off.'

'Don't beat yourself up about it. You're not a social worker.'

'I know, but I sort of am. I like – love – my customers and they like me. I'm starting to think, no, it's stupid.'

'What?' said Ant.

'I'm starting to think checkout six is cursed or maybe I am. Bad things keep happening to people who use my checkout. There was Charles and his heart attack earlier in the year, Julie disappearing and now Reg. Maybe if they'd all stayed away from me they'd be all right.'

Bea started to cry and Ant shuffled closer to her and put his arm round her. 'Bea, they all flock to you because you're the best one. They all love talking with you. You make their day. None of this is because of you. It's just . . .life.'

George came into the room. She crouched down next to Bea. 'Anna told me about what's happened. I think you should both have the day off. It's been a shock. We'll pay for a taxi home if you need one.'

Bea was still snivelling into her tissue. She dabbed her nose and tried to compose herself. 'That's very kind. I'm all right to walk, though, if you'll walk with me, Ant?'

'Of course,' Ant said. 'Let's finish this tea and get off. Thanks, George.'

'You're welcome,' George said, standing up. 'It sounds like you both dealt with this perfectly. Calling the emergency services, keeping people away. You're a credit to Costsave, both of you. I'll see you tomorrow.'

They would have had to go all round the houses to avoid the place where they had found Reg, so, being brave, they linked arms and walked steadily and purposefully along the path. Bea couldn't help looking at the tent, which was still there, together with a whole team of people, some in uniforms, others in crinkly white jumpsuits. Tom was talking with one of the police constables, but he broke away when he spotted Ant and Bea.

'Hi Bea. You okay? I heard that you were the ones who found him.'

'Yeah,' said Bea, still feeling a bit wobbly. 'Ant's taking me home. We've been given the day off.'

'Good idea. Take it steady.'

'Tom,' she said, 'do you know how he died?'

'Not yet, not for sure. He stank of booze, though. He'd bashed his head open, so I'm guessing he stumbled and fell and hit a stone or something on the ground.'

Bea frowned. 'He did smell of drink a little bit when I saw him, but he wasn't drunk.'

'Well, the post-mortem will give us all the answers. Sorry it was you that found him.'

Bea pulled a face. 'In a way, I'm glad it was me. At least I knew who he was.'

'Not a nice thing to deal with, though. Take it easy.'

195

Bea and Ant crossed the road and set off down the High Street. It was a beautiful day. The sky was blue. The air was warm but not sticky. Away from the tent and the cluster of onlookers, Kingsleigh was going about its business. Outside the pie shop, a couple of workmen in high-vis jackets and enormous muddy boots were getting stuck into some sausage rolls, folding down the outside of the paper bags and breathing in as they ate to cool the food down and hoover up as much flaky pastry as possible. Bea's queasiness was going now and she realised she was very, very hungry.

'Do you fancy a sausage roll?' she said to Ant.

'Always. Let me get us some. We could eat them in the park.'

'Yeah, I'd like that.'

She waited outside the shop, standing close enough to the workmen to benefit from the intoxicating wafts of meat and grease coming from their food.

'Shame about that old bloke they found,' one of them said, cramming the last of his pastry into his mouth and crumpling up the paper wrapper.

'Yeah, that could be you or me in forty years' time – drunk and dead under a hedge.' His friend had finished too now and lobbed the ball of paper towards the bin. It arced gracefully through the air and fell onto the pavement nearby.

'Ha! You maybe, mate. Not me. I'll be sunning myself on the Costa Blanca.'

He, too, aimed his rubbish at the bin and missed. They laughed and turned to walk back towards Costsave.

'Hey!' Bea shouted. 'Aren't you going to pick that up?' They both looked at her as if she had taken leave of her senses. 'That litter. It's not a very good example to set, is it, if blokes like you just chuck it on the ground.'

She wondered if she was about to learn some new Anglo-Saxon, but instead they both looked rather sheepish, and one of them walked back, picked up their rubbish and a couple of other bits lying nearby and put them all in the bin.

'Sorry,' he mumbled.

'And another thing,' Bea was on a roll now, 'I don't think it's very nice to joke about someone dying in the street. He wasn't just an "old bloke", he was a human being, and you should show some fucking respect!'

Shamefaced now, they both muttered, 'Sorry.'

Ant had emerged through the shop doorway, carrying a bulging paper bag and a couple of bottles of pop, and was watching open-mouthed. The men shambled away, and he stepped towards Bea.

'Bloody hell, Bea, what are you doing? I leave you for two minutes and you're bullying two blokes the size of small mountains!'

'They just...I just...I couldn't help myself.' Bea realised she was on the edge of tears again. 'Oh, let's go to the park, Ant.'

They crossed the road and walked down the alleyway between the Indian restaurant and the now empty bank. The park was fairly busy, with a good-natured mixture of elderly dog walkers and parents with pre-school children. The café was open, doing a brisk trade in coffee and sandwiches, but Ant and Bea headed away, walking further down the hill towards the river, where they found a bench in full sun.

'What did you get?' asked Bea.

'Four for two quid. Bargain. And a couple of drinks.'

He tore open the packet and they sat in companionable silence as they enjoyed the feast. The sun warmed their faces and made sparkles dance on the top of the water. Quite a large number of ducks gathered in front of them, drawn by the prospect of pastry crumbs. When Bea had finished, she got up and held the wrapper out over the water, upside down, shaking it to get rid of all the bits. There was a chorus of appreciative quacking. She sat down again.

'I hate that people think that Reg was just another old drunk, who didn't matter,' she said.

'I know, Bea.' Ant wiped the grease away from his mouth with the back of his hand. 'But not every battle is your battle. Sometimes you just have to let things go. He did stink of booze when we found him.'

'And other stuff.' Bea shuddered.

'Well, yes, but that was just normal for Reg.'

'No, it was worse than normal, Ant. Different.'

'How do you mean?'

'Well, he'd, you know, soiled himself, but that happens when people die, doesn't it?'

'Does it? Jeez.'

'Yeah, it's one of the things no one ever talks about. But, you're right, he reeked of booze, like really strongly. It was odd because he didn't when I was talking to him. Not much, anyway. I know he drank, but that wasn't his big thing. It was smoking with him. A packet of fags every day and his *Racing Post*, and he smelled of stale cigarettes.'

'Perhaps he had a bottle or some cans in his shopping bag. Had a drink while he was waiting for the shop to open.'

'I suppose so. I just think that it wasn't his style. Out of character.'

'What are you saying, Bea?'

'I don't even know, Ant.'

They swigged at their soft drinks and watched the ducks squabbling over the last few soggy crumbs. The sun was getting stronger now, and Bea could feel herself growing sleepy in its warmth. Her eyelids started to feel heavy. She yawned, loudly.

'Here, lean on me if you're tired,' said Ant, offering her a shoulder. Some of the ducks had clambered out onto the riverbank and were fussing around on the ground near their feet.

Bea shuffled closer to Ant and tipped her head until it was resting on him, but he was only skin and bones and too knobbly to make a good cushion. She wriggled about a bit, then Ant put his arm round her and she found the comfortable place where his shoulder met his neck.

'Mm, that's better,' she said. She felt the weight of his head as he rested it on hers, and they both closed their eyes, basking in the sun.

'I suppose,' said Bea, only half awake, 'that it was natural causes. Just one of those things.'

'Shh,' said Ant, and she felt herself falling, the sounds around her blurring as she gave herself up to sleep.

She was woken by the flapping of wings and raucous squawking close by. She opened her eyes and squinted into the sun, finding it difficult to remember where she was or what time of day it was. Slowly the world came into focus. The noise was caused by someone at the next bench feeding sandwich crusts to the ducks, sending them into a frenzy. Ah yes, Bea remembered now: it was lunchtime, and this morning they'd found Reg's body.

Ant's arm was heavy across her shoulders.

'Ant,' she said, trying and failing to slide out from under it. 'Ant, wake up.'

His eyelids flickered open and now he and Bea were very close indeed, looking into each other's eyes.

'Hey, you,' he said.

'Hey,' said Bea.

Before she knew what was happening, he tilted his face further towards hers and slowly kissed her, full on the mouth. Caught by surprise, Bea went along with it, then realised she was liking it. There was nothing pushy or aggressive going on. It was gentle and loving and heartfelt. She made a noise, a low appreciative sound.

Mistaking it for a protest, Ant pulled away quickly. 'Shit.

Sorry.' He removed his arm and sat bolt upright, then rubbed his hand over the top of his head. 'Jeez, I'm sorry.'

'Ant—'

'No, I'm sorry. I didn't mean to—'

'Ant—'

He stood up and started pacing around in little circles. 'No, no Bea. You don't need to say it. I was out of order. It was just, you know, being all sleepy and just...I'm sorry, okay? Please don't let this fuck things up between us. You're one of my best mates.'

Bea listened to his apologetic rambling. The more he talked, the more she began to think that he'd hated it. The way he'd sprung away from her suggested the opposite of attraction – like two north poles of a magnet repulsing each other.

So that was that. Her surprising feelings didn't matter, and now that he was so embarrassed, she should smooth things over as best she could, shouldn't she? For both their sakes?

'Ant, calm down,' she said. 'It was just a kiss. We're mates, right? Let's forget about it.'

His face brightened. 'Will you? Can you?'

'Yes, of course. It never happened, okay?' She stood up, too. 'Come on, will you walk home with me, have a cuppa with Queenie?'

They headed towards the main park gates and then out along the High Street and across the rec, walking side by side but keeping a good distance between them, an invisible exclusion zone. They talked a little from time to time, but mostly walked in silence. Before today it wouldn't have bothered Bea, but now each time their conversation lapsed she worried that Ant would be feeling awkward. He, in turn, kept shooting little sideways glances at her.

Things felt more normal at home. With Queenie there, they fell back into their usual roles. They all sat out in the garden, drinking tea and Diet Coke and eating Magnums from Queenie's freezer. It was only at the end of the afternoon, when Ant said that it was time to go to his class at the library, that things got weird again.

'Do you want me to come with you?' Bea asked.

'No, I'm all right. You stay here. I'll be fine now I know everyone, and what we're doing.'

Bea walked round the side of the house with him, anyway.

'I'm visiting my dad tomorrow,' he said, 'so I won't see you at work.'

'Okay, but you're still coming to the gig at the social club in the evening?'

'Yeah, if you want me to.'

'Course I do. It's not a date, Ant. It's an investigation.'

'Yeah. Cool. I know that. If my buses work out. I'll be there.'

'Great.'

'Okay.'

He was hovering on the path now, obviously wanting to get away, but not wanting to be rude.

'Bye, Ant. See you tomorrow.'

'Yeah. Bye.'

Bea watched him walk away. He didn't head off into the estate but skirted along the right-hand edge of the rec. She realised she still didn't know who he was staying with. She'd ask him tomorrow at the club. If he turned up.

34

The visiting room was bleak. Over the years, Ant had been in several such rooms. Some prisons made an effort to create environments where families could feel comfortable. This was not one of them. Ant scanned the stark row of tables and spotted his dad at the furthest one from the door. His dad saw him at the same time and waved. Ant felt a familiar rush of emotion – relief, panic, affection, all mixed up together. He'd felt the same thing with every visit all through his childhood. The anticipation of seeing his dad. The worry that something might go wrong. The anxiety about what state he'd be in, what the other prisoners might do or say, the stress his mum would go through organising their transport, going through the searches. This time, though, he was on his own. Just him and his dad, man to man, and there was a different sort of anxiety. What did his dad want to say to him that couldn't be said with the others there?

He walked to the end of the room, past pairs of visitors and visited, huddled over tables.

'Hey Dad.'

'Hullo, Son.'

They'd never been huggers. Colin didn't attempt to stand up, so Ant just pulled out the grey plastic chair on the near side of the table and sat down. For one awful moment, he worried that that was all they'd got to say to one another, but then Colin said, 'Thanks for coming, Ant. It's good to see you. I swear you've grown again. Like a bloody bean pole.'

'Shut up, Dad,' he said, but they both knew he didn't really mean it. 'So, how are you?'

His dad ran a hand over the top of his balding head.

'I'm okay. You know me. I'm always okay. This place doesn't bother me. I've been in worse. How are you getting on? Can't be easy with Mum, and the girls and Ken in Cardiff. You coping all right? Where are you living?'

'It's all good, Dad,' said Ant, deliberately keeping things light. 'I was sofa surfing for a while, you know, sleeping on people's couches and in their spare rooms. People were very kind. But I've got my own place now.'

'Yeah? Nice is it? Council place?'

'Something like that. Got my own front door anyway and somewhere to lay my head.'

'Oh good. Bit young to be on your own but sounds like you're managing okay.'

'Yeah. Just got to get on with it. Quite nice not having anyone telling you what to do.' He sent his dad a wry smile. 'I've got something to tell you as well.'

'Go on.'

'I'm going to classes at the library, literacy. I'm learning to read, Dad.'

Colin's eyes widened. 'Yeah? Good on you, Son. How's it going?'

'Great. I can actually do it. Well, at least I'm starting to. It's exciting really.'

'That's brilliant. I'm so proud of you, Son. I know you didn't really get on at school. Neither did I. I've never been one for books and that. But being able to read will really help you.'

'Thanks, Dad. I think it will. It'll help at work. There's all sorts of stuff I can't do at the moment.'

'You still at Costsave?'

'Yup. It's all right there. Bit of a laugh, actually. They've started a choir.'

'You're singing?'

'Yeah. Sort of.'

'You're making a real go of things, aren't you? That makes me feel really good.' He paused. 'I'm sorry I'm not out there giving you a hand, but sounds like you're better off without me. You're doing okay.'

'I'd never say it was better without you, Dad.' Ant wanted to tell him how it really was. How everything had fallen apart. How life as he'd always known it had just been wiped out. How lonely he'd been. But there was no point being angry or trying to make him feel bad. 'Can't wait for you to come back, although I suppose you'll go to Cardiff, will you?'

'I don't know, Son. It's all up in the air, isn't it? And it's a way off yet. Got to keep my head down, get through the next eighteen months. That's what I wanted to see you about. Getting by in here.'

'I don't understand.'

'I could do with some help. Your mum . . . well, your mum was sending me money but that's stopped. I guess things aren't easy for her. The thing is, now you've got a steady job, could you send me a tenner a week? Twenty, even? I hate to ask, Son.'

Ant didn't know what to think. He was embarrassed to be talking about money with his dad, but also pleased his dad would ask him for help. 'I'm only a trainee, Dad. Get less than minimum wage at the moment. Stevo's working—'

'Stevo's turned me down.'

'Oh. Well, he's trying to get his own place with Natalie. Look, Dad, I'll send what I can, okay?'

'You can do it online. I'll need to give you the reference number, so it'll reach me.'

'I haven't got – never mind, I'll sort it out. I'll sort it, Dad.'

'Thanks, Ant. I knew I could rely on you.'

'Is that why you asked me here?'

'No! I wanted to see you, hear how you're getting on. I miss you, Son. I miss all of you. Home and that. Been seeing Kingsleigh on the telly news, though. That poor girl that got murdered.'

'Mm, nasty. Everyone's talking about it. Everyone thinks my friend's dad did it.'

'Who's that? Your friend?'

'Bea. You met her a couple of times. She came to the house.'

His dad sat back in his chair. 'Big girl?' He gestured with his hands, carving an hourglass through the air. 'Nice looking? I remember.'

'Not "big" no, whatever that means. God, Dad. What's that got to do with anything anyway?'

His dad started grinning and Ant could feel himself colouring up. 'Ooh, bit touchy. Are you two—?'

'No! Shut up. I can have friends, can't I?'

'All right, all right. Her dad was Harry Jordan, wasn't he?'

'Yeah, that's it. Do you remember anything about the girl, Tina, going missing?' said Ant, relieved to move the conversation away from Bea.

'Yeah. I remember it really clearly. I was working that night, out and about. In fact, I took a wander down to the factory. I knew there'd been a do on at the social club, thought the takings might be a bit tasty.'

'You broke into the social club?'

'I was thinking about it but when I got there, there was a bloke in the car park, right next to the back entrance to the club. He was sort of hanging about, looked a bit shifty to me, so I just turned round and went on my way.'

'What did he look like?'

'It was quite dark, but he was young, clean-shaven. Smart-looking, really. The thing is, Ant, afterwards I kept thinking about him, seeing him, and I broke the code. Normally I would never grass to the filth, but this was a young girl, so I rang them up. Gave my name and everything. Told them about him, in case, you know, he was something to do with Tina disappearing. See, there was something on the ground next to him. I just thought it was a tarpaulin or some bags or something. Now I keep thinking it was her.'

'Bloody hell, Dad. Do you really think so?'

Colin was looking down at his hands. They were clasped together in front of him, clasped so tightly that the knuckles were white.

'Yeah. I do.'

'What did the cops do about it? Did they take a proper statement from you?'

'Nope. Never heard from them. I guess they thought I was an unreliable witness.'

'Or what you were saying didn't fit with their theory. They interviewed Bea's dad several times, and they've just interviewed her mum again.'

'That'll be right, Ant. Never let the facts get in the way of an easy collar. I used to see Harry Jordan round the town, and the guy I saw wasn't him. No way. I did actually tell the cops that.'

A bell rang and people started saying their goodbyes. Visiting time was up.

Colin looked at Ant. 'Thanks for coming. Good luck with everything, Son. Keep up the reading. You can do it. I know you can.'

Ant scraped back his chair and stood up, then quickly sat down again and leaned across the table.

'Dad, have you ever thought of doing it? Taking reading

classes in here – they do that sort of thing, don't they?'

Colin looked at him sharply. The skin on his cheeks started to mottle, and Ant wondered if he was going to give him a bollocking for speaking out of turn, but then he just frowned and said, 'Old dog, new tricks, Ant. Think it's too late for me.'

Ant reached across the table and put his hand lightly on his dad's arm. 'Don't be daft. Never too late, Dad. Just think, if you did it and I did it, then we could, you know . . .we could write to each other.'

His dad made a strangled sound in his throat and Ant was shocked to see tears gathering in his eyes. Then he blinked hard a couple of times and said, 'I'd like that, Ant. I'd like that very much. Don't think it's going to happen, though.'

Ant became aware of a prison officer standing right next to their table. 'Time's up,' he said.

'Yeah, right. Sorry.' He realised he was the last visitor left in the room. 'Gotta go, Dad.'

'All right, Son. See you soon, yeah? Tell your mum I love her.'

Ant walked out of the room and collected his coat and phone. Emerging into the world through the prison gates, he felt like he could breathe freely again. The bus stop was a quarter of a mile away, but he hardly noticed the walk. He was replaying the conversation with his dad. It had been even more intense than usual and there was plenty to think about, not least his revelation about the night Tina died. He hesitated before ringing Bea, cursing himself for yesterday's misadventure. He didn't totally regret it, though. He'd often wondered what it would feel like to kiss her, and the reality had been everything he'd thought about, and more. Bea was bloody brilliant in every way – beautiful, smart, funny – but then she'd made that noise and he'd realised he'd just embarrassed himself. Of course someone that beautiful, smart and funny would never fancy him. The important thing now was to keep her as a friend.

He dialled her number and told her what his dad had said.

'Bloody hell, Ant. That's corroborative evidence!' Even at the other end of a rather poor mobile connection, Ant was gratified to hear the glee in Bea's voice.

'That's what I thought. He's backing up what your dad said, isn't he?'

'Yes, and he's adding a bit more to what we knew. Young. Clean-shaven. Smart. That rules out a hell of a lot of blokes in K-town.'

'It was fourteen years ago, though, mate. That's only what they were like then. They might look completely different now, or be living somewhere else altogether.'

'Or they might be in a band. You reckon you're going to be back in time to come to the social club?'

'Yeah, should be. I'll come to yours on the way, shall I? I should be able to get there about half seven.'

'Okay, see you later.'

35

The club was quite quiet when they got there. There wasn't a queue at the bar and they had no trouble finding a table.

'Did we get the wrong night?' said Ant.

Bea looked around the room. 'No, over there. I reckon that's them.'

There were two guys perched on stools in the corner, chatting with each other. Bea recognised them from their website. Liam, his long hair in a ponytail, was sipping a pint. Justin, sporting designer stubble but with his hair shaved at the sides, was quietly tuning an acoustic guitar.

'Oh,' said Ant, obviously underwhelmed. He scanned the room, then he nudged Bea's elbow. 'Hey, isn't that Dave Ronson just coming in?'

'Where?' said Bea, twisting in her chair.

'Don't turn round!' hissed Ant. 'He'll see you looking!'

'Well how can I say if it's him or not if I'm not allowed to look?' But it was too late anyway. She spotted Dave at the same time as he spotted her. He was just inside the main doorway with his arm protectively round a woman in her late teens or early twenties who bore a startling resemblance to Julie. He winked as he caught Bea's eye. She just stared for a second or two then looked away.

'He's got a nerve, hasn't he?' she said. 'Where's he found her?'

'I 'spect they both swiped right,' said Ant.

'Yeah,' said Bea. 'It's one thing being on there and looking. It's another going out on dates, when your wife and kids are "on holiday".' She made quotation marks with her index fingers.

'Bea, I know he's a scumbag, but if he'd got anything to hide, he wouldn't be taking women on dates in pubs in K-town, would he? He'd be skulking about in Bristol or wherever.'

'Unless he's completely brazen.'

'What does that mean?'

'Shameless.'

'Oh. Right. Look, are we having some crisps or not?'

'All right. Salt and vinegar, please.'

As Ant went back to the bar, Bea pretended to look at her phone, while watching Dave out of the corner of her eye. The room was filling up now and the only table free was near the toilets. Dave and his date sat down, moving their chairs so that they were both facing the musicians, which unfortunately meant that Bea was in Dave's eyeline. She shuffled her chair round a bit and put her phone back in her pocket. As she did so, her fingers brushed against something hard, and her stomach gave a little flip as she remembered that she was still carrying Tiffany's pink plastic duck around with her.

Ant threw a couple of packets of crisps onto the table and plonked himself down. He was tearing them open and spreading them out to share when, without any preamble, the Pindrop Twins started to play. It was very gentle music, the men singing in harmony to the accompaniment of the guitar, and Bea found it mesmerising. They were so relaxed, so comfortable with each other.

'Bit boring, aren't they?' said Ant.

'Shh, I like them.'

There was a ripple of applause as each song finished and

after half a dozen or so, Liam said, 'Thank you very much. We're going to do another one of ours now. Some of you will know this song. Tonight, of course, we're playing it for a special girl. Rest in peace, Tina. This is "Last Seen Wearing".'

Bea clutched Ant's arm. 'This is it,' she said. 'The song. Just listen to the words.'

Justin started picking at the strings, sending rippling arpeggios into the room. Then Liam came in with a simple, haunting melody.

> *'She's a face in the crowd,*
> *The sun behind a cloud,*
> *When I see her, the world's okay.*
> *Light's the room with her smile,*
> *I'm in love with her style,*
> *When she's there it's gonna be a better day.*
> *But like the clothes she was last seen wearing,*
> *The clothes she was last seen wearing,*
> *Yes, the clothes she was last seen wearing,*
> *She's still gone.'*

There was silence when they finished. Then the applause started, swelled and faded.

'Thank you. We're going to take a quick break now. We'll be back in half an hour or so.'

Justin propped his guitar up against the wall and they both headed towards the bar.

'I'm going in,' said Bea, getting up. She picked her way through the tables, avoiding eye contact with Dave, who was also heading towards the bar, and timing her walk carefully so that she ended up getting to the bar at the same time as Liam.

'That was great. Really,' she said, squeezing in next to him.

'Cheers.'

'You been gigging for a long time?'

'Yeah. Since we were teenagers.'

The barman set two pints down in front of Liam, obviously pre-arranged perks of the job.

'Cheers, mate.' He picked them up and prepared to take them to Justin, who was standing a little away from the queue. Bea stepped sideways, making it harder for him to move.

'Were you . . .were you originally the Peardrops?' she said.

'Yeah, a long time ago,' he said, but his guard was up now.

'Listen, what's going on? You're not just here for the music, are you?'

'Well, I am, and I love it, but I'm also trying to find out about Tina.' She held her hands up. 'I'm not a cop or anything. I just want to see if I can help them.'

'Ahh, I know who you are,' he said, looking her up and down. 'You were in the *Bugle*.'

'Yeah, that's me. Everyone's been saying that my dad did it and he didn't, so I just want to find evidence to back that up. Listen, can I buy you both another drink? We could sit with my mate.'

Liam looked over towards Justin and tipped his head, indicating that he join them. 'We're fine with these, but we could talk. We've got—' he checked his phone '—twenty-five minutes.'

They both stood away from the bar as Bea ordered drinks for her and Ant.

As she turned to take the drinks back, she realised that Dave was standing close behind her. 'Small world, isn't it?' he said. 'Having a good evening?'

'Yes. They're great, aren't they?' Bea held the two glasses near her chest. Her bag was threatening to fall off her shoulder. He made a show of making way for her, but put a hand on her waist as she passed. It wasn't anything, really, but Bea had a strong urge to spin round and tip the drinks over his head. She suppressed it and led Liam and Justin to the table where Ant was waiting. She made the introductions and the guys pulled up another couple of chairs and sat down.

'So, that song was pretty amazing. Did you know Tina?' said Bea.

'Yeah, she was a fan. We didn't have many then. Well, a bit like now, really.' He grinned ruefully. 'In 2005, it was a handful of girls we knew from school who came to every gig.'

'And Tina was one of them?'

'Yeah. She was a lovely girl, kind of happy-go-lucky, at least she was most of the time.'

'Not all the time?'

'Just the last few weeks before she disappeared, she changed a bit. Didn't come to every gig. Was a bit more reserved.'

'Really? What was going on? Did you ask her?'

'She just said she was busy. She was seeing someone new.'

'Did you meet them?' Bea kept her voice casual, even though there were pinpricks of excitement inside her head. Liam looked at Justin, seeming to check with him.

'No,' he said. 'She came to gigs on her own or met up with mates from school.'

Bea tried to hide her disappointment. Surely, somebody must have seen Tina's new boyfriend?

'Do you remember that evening she disappeared?'

'Of course. We kept going over it. The police questioned us, like everybody else who was there that night, and we talked about it too, amongst ourselves.'

'I know you said she was seeing someone, but before that were any of you—' Bea paused, not sure how to phrase her next question, but Ant helpfully stepped in.

'—shagging her?' he said.

213

Liam and Justin exchanged a quick glance. 'What's this?' said Justin. 'Good cop, bad cop?'

Ant held his hands up, worried he'd caused offence.

'Nah, it's all right,' said Liam. 'Don't worry, we've been asked this before, too. The answer's no. She was a sweet kid, but we were kids too, pretty naive really. It's weird, because that summer seemed like it changed everything for us, too. A few months after she disappeared, we stopped doing the band.'

'What happened?'

'We couldn't carry on as the Peardrops, not after we lost Si and Trey.'

'How come?'

'Si was driving the old van we used for gigging. He was on his own. The van left the road. There wasn't anyone else involved and he hadn't been drinking or anything, just took it too fast, misjudged it, whatever. He came off and there was a tree waiting for him. Trey died seven months later. It was a hell of a year.'

'I'm so sorry.'

'That was it for the group for a while. We stopped gigging, stopped writing, just didn't have the heart for it. We even stopped hanging out with each other. We got grown up jobs, got on with our lives.'

'What do you do now?'

Liam smiled. 'I'm in IT and Justin's an accountant. Not very rock 'n' roll.'

'What got you back together?' said Bea.

'I kept thinking about Tina, that summer, that awful year. One evening I got out my guitar again and I wrote that song. Just straight out wrote it in a couple of hours. It was about Tina, but it was about Si and Trey too. I rang Justin and sang it down the phone. That was it. We decided to start up again, as a duo. We've been gigging on and off since then. Keeping it simple. Acoustic guitar, couple of mikes and an amp.' He paused. 'No need for a van.' He and Justin gently bumped fists, and then each took a swig of their beer.

'Can I ask you one more thing?' said Bea.

'Sure.'

'You can tell me to mind my own business if you like, but what happened to Trey? I read online that he killed himself.'

Liam put his glass down but kept tracing patterns in the condensation on the side, looking at that, not Bea. 'He'd struggled with depression for years, all the time we'd known him. I guess Si dying was the final straw.'

'The accident must have been tough for all of you.'

'Yeah, worse for him, though.' He paused. 'He'd had a thing for Si. They'd never got it together. Trey had a couple of other relationships, but nothing stuck. He hadn't told his parents he was gay. They were pretty . . .old-fashioned.'

'Wow. That's so sad.'

'Yeah. It's a sad old world sometimes. You wonder if you could have done something, said something to make a difference. It was a terrible waste.' Liam checked his phone again. 'Listen, we'd better go and do the rest of our set. Are you staying?'

'Of course. Thanks for talking to us.'

'No problem.'

Taking their unfinished pints with them, they made their way back to their stools. Bea glanced back towards Dave's table and winced inside as he clocked her looking and raised his glass towards her. She looked away again, flustered.

'So I guess we can strike them off the list,' said Ant.

'Maybe,' said Bea, taking a big slug of her spritzer. 'We've only got their word for all this, though, haven't we? I mean, I'm not sure I buy all this "we were just sweet, innocent teens" stuff.'

'Yeah, how old were they? Seventeen, eighteen, and in a

band? I bet they were shagging anything and everything that came their way. That's what they were in the bloody band for. Why would they lie, though?'

'To protect themselves, or their mates that aren't here anymore. I guess I can understand that. Of course, they might have been telling the truth. At least Trey is off the hook, if he was gay and nursing a crush on Simon.'

'If that bit was true.'

Bea put her hands in her hair. 'God, Ant, this is too difficult!'

The Pindrop Twins were in full song again. Ant and Bea stopped talking and watched. After a couple of minutes, Ant's eyes glazed over. He leaned towards Bea. 'This is so boring, mate. They're a bit drippy, aren't they? Can we go now?'

Bea sighed. 'It's lovely, Ant. Have you got no poetry in your soul?'

Ant pulled a face. 'Apparently not.'

'I'm going to stay to the end. You can go if you want to, get back to Saggy's or wherever it is you're staying.' Ant looked at her and looked away quickly. 'Where are you staying, Ant?'

Ant found something interesting to pick away at on the surface of the table.

'Ant?'

Another song ended and applause rippled round the room. Now Ant joined in enthusiastically, putting his fingers to his lips and whistling, which brought smiles and a thumbs up from Liam and Justin. They thanked everyone and launched into another song and Bea forgot about Ant's domestic arrangements as she listened, appreciating the tone of their voices and the closeness of their harmonies. When the set was finished, Ant and Bea gathered up their things. Bea looked up and saw Dave's date heading for the Ladies.

'I'm just nipping to the loo,' she said and jumped up. She threaded her way through the crowd, who were now surging to the bar again, managed to avoid catching Dave's eye, even though she had to pass close to his table. He was absorbed in checking his phone as she sidled past.

She pushed the swing door open and made her way into the Ladies. There was a bit of a queue and she found herself standing behind Dave's date. Her top was made of something silky and had a gaping cut-out design at the back, revealing a thin black bra. It was quite a squash in the room, and it was easy for Bea to accidentally on purpose nudge the woman in the back as she manoeuvred her position to allow the door to close.

'Oh, sorry,' she said.

The woman turned around, checked out Bea, then smiled. 'It's okay. There's always a bloody queue, isn't there?' She got a red lipstick out of her bag and started applying an extra layer. Then she paused the lipstick in mid-air and looked over her shoulder at Bea. 'Did I see you talking with Dave at the bar before? Do you know him?'

She didn't miss a trick, Bea noted approvingly. 'Not really. I've just seen him around. I work in Costsave. Everyone comes through there.'

'Ah, I just wondered if I'd got competition. He's all right, isn't he?'

Bea hesitated. She wanted so much to tell her the truth. It was her duty, wasn't it, one woman to another?

'I . . . like I said, I don't know him.' She paused again. 'I know his wife, though.'

A hush descended on the room, like a fire curtain dropping down at the theatre.

The woman's face froze. She turned properly now. 'You what?'

They were crammed together. There was a fierceness in the woman's eyes that could either be outrage at Dave's duplicity or anger at Bea's input.

'He's married with two kids,' said Bea. 'I've seen them together in the shop.'

Everyone else in the room was listening too, even though they were pretending they weren't.

'He said single on Tinder. The fucking snake.'

A murmur of agreement swept through the assembled women.

'I'm sorry,' said Bea. 'I just thought you should know.'

'Too right,' someone called out from a locked cubicle. 'Kick the bastard into touch!'

She was met with laughter and a smatter of applause. There was the sound of flushing and the cubicle door opened. The woman who emerged was well over seventy, immaculately dressed in a floaty dress, with beautifully cut hair and long dangly earrings.

'Don't waste any more time on the fucker,' she said, setting off more laughter and some catcalls. The atmosphere in the room now was approaching that of an evangelical prayer meeting.

Dave's date sighed. 'That's it then. Over before it began. Does anyone know if there's another way out of here?'

Everyone agreed that there wasn't. She'd have to walk past his table to reach the exit. However, the earring woman said, 'Leave it to me. I'll create a diversion. When you're ready.'

Everyone got back to the business in hand. Bea was agog. She waited for her turn in a cubicle and nipped in and out as quickly as she could. By the time she was drying her hands, the earring woman had gone and Dave's date was lingering by the door. There was a loud crash from the bar outside. 'That's me,' she said, opened the door and ventured out.

Bea flapped her hands in the air to dry them and followed her. People were clustered around the earring woman to one side of Dave's table. Dave was standing up. His chair was on its side next to him.

'I'm so sorry,' she was saying. 'I don't know how it happened. I feel a bit faint.'

Bea could see the spattering of dark liquid all down one side of Dave's shirt and a layer of broken glass on the floor next to him. He was brushing his shirt with his hands, while others helped the woman to a seat and called out for a dustpan and brush. Away from the fuss and chaos, his date slipped out of the door, held open for her by another of the women from the toilet.

Bea squeezed past the huddle and found Ant. 'It's all been going on out here,' he said, cheerfully. 'Our friend Dave somehow got half his own pint all over him.'

'Really?' said Bea. 'Couldn't have happened to a nicer bloke.'

36

'I need your lottery money.' Eileen was doing the rounds of the staff room with her usual grace and charm.

'A tenner, like normal?' said Dot.

'Yes, please.'

'Hang on, I've got one in my bag.'

Dot rummaged in her enormous patent leather-look handbag. She found her purse and opened it. Eileen held out her hand.

'Oh. That's odd.'

Dot rifled through the compartments. Bea could see various store cards and a credit card, but no notes. Dot's face became pink and warm. She looked up at Eileen.

'Sorry, Eileen. I thought I had thirty quid in there. I must have spent it. Can I give it to you tomorrow?'

Eileen rolled her eyes. 'Tomorrow's the last day, otherwise you're out of the syndicate. I can't be chasing people up all the time.'

'No, course not.'

Bea dipped into her own purse. 'Here's twenty. For me and Dot.'

'You don't need to,' Dot started, but Bea waved her objection away.

'Pay me back whenever.' Eileen had moved on to bother someone else. 'You don't need her on your back.'

Dot's face was still pink, and now her mouth was twitching and her eyes were red.

'Don't be silly, babe,' said Bea. 'I know you'd do the same for me.'

Dot nodded, got up quickly and headed for the locker room. Bea followed. When she caught up with her, Dot was leaning against a wall, head tipped up to the ceiling, blinking back tears. Bea put a hand gently on her arm.

'Dot, what is it?'

Dot looked at her and a tear trickled down her face and dripped off her cheek.

'I've been so stupid, Bea.'

'Are you in trouble? Money trouble?'

'No. Well, sort of. I *did* have thirty quid in my purse last night. My scumbag ex-husband's taken it.'

'Darren? Do you think so?'

'I know so. Leopards don't change their spots. He's had money from the house as well. I keep some emergency cash in a drawer. Half of it's gone.'

'Oh Dot, I'm so sorry. Don't be upset.'

'I'm not upset, babe, I'm furious.' She dived into one of the cubicles and fetched a ream of toilet paper. She wiped away her tears and, looking in the mirror, dabbed at some stray mascara that had ended up under her eyes. 'That's it. I want him out. Out of my house. Out of my life. I should never have taken him back in the first place. What was I thinking?'

It was a rhetorical question, and Bea wisely stayed silent while Dot continued to rage.

'I thought it was love that had brought him back. Turns out he'd been kicked out of his previous place. Lost his job. Needed somewhere to stay. It wasn't his fault, of course. It never is.'

'Oh, Dot.'

'I'm a mug, Bea. A proper mug. He was a waster fourteen years ago and he's still a waster now. Time to get rid.'

'Are you going to tell him today?'

'Yeah, he's meeting me from work when I finish. I'll tell him then. We can go home, he can pack his bags and find some other mug to sponge off.'

'Shall I make you a fresh cuppa? We've got time.'

Dot checked her watch. 'Yes. That'd be nice. Just give me a chance to simmer down. I'll join you in a couple of minutes.'

Bea walked back to the staff room, where Ant was sprawling on the sofa with his eyes closed.

'Budge up,' she said. 'You're taking up all the room.'

He opened his eyes and sat up a little, but still had the appearance of something semi-liquid which had spilled over the surface of the couch. Bea jabbed him with her elbow.

'You're all arms and legs. What's up with you anyway?'

He groaned. 'I'm on trolleys and it's sooooo boring.'

'Why not practise your reading now then? Get your brain working?'

'Read what?' he said.

'I dunno. Look at something on your phone. I bet there are apps for people like you.'

'Thick people?'

'Shut up. People who are learning. Or just try reading Twitter or something. Here, look at my phone while I make Dot a cup of tea. Do you want one?' She gave Ant her phone.

'Yes, please. Where is she?'

'She's in the bogs at the moment. She was a bit upset because Darren's been messing her around.'

'Really? Damn. Poor Dot. Don't tell Bob, though. He'll flatten him.'

'Mm, I think he really would. I might just whisper in his

ear. I reckon Darren deserves a bit of rough justice. Oh, shh, here she comes.'

Dot was walking back into the room, makeup perfect, hair in place and a defiant look on her face. She sat at the opposite end of the sofa and got out a magazine from her bag.

'I'm sorry about—' Ant started, but she held her hand up.

'I don't want to talk about it.'

'Fair enough.'

Ant started looking at Bea's phone as she made the teas. As she held a mug out towards him, he frowned and said, 'Can you put it on the table? I think I've got something here.'

Bea put down the mug, pleased that Ant had deciphered a tweet on his own. This was real progress, but it was more than that. 'Does this say what I think it says?' He handed her phone back and she quickly read the tweet.

'What do you think it says, Ant?' she said, faintly, shell-shocked at what she'd just read.

'I couldn't get all of it, but I think it says that Reg was murdered.'

'What?' said Dot, putting her magazine down.

'Yup. That's it. "Police launch second murder enquiry in Kingsleigh after pensioner Reg is found dead on street."' She clicked on the link and scanned the article. 'They're saying he was bashed on the head and alcohol was poured over him. Bloody hell, Ant. Who would do that? And why?'

37

The news about Reg rippled through the staff room.

'Another murder?'

'It's like Midsomer round here.'

'What's going on?'

'Poor old Reg.'

Bea kept thinking back to the last time she saw him and their conversation. She found it difficult to believe that only a few minutes after she left him someone had hit him and dragged him into the bushes. Perhaps she even saw the murderer.

'Ant,' she said, 'you were keeping watch while I talked to him, weren't you? Did you see anyone hanging around?'

Ant rubbed his hands up and down his jaw. 'I dunno, Bea. There were just the Costsave people walking into work, and the guys working round the back, walking in ones and twos. Nobody out of the ordinary.'

'Why do you think anyone would do it? Why kill Reg?'

'Beats me. He was just harmless, wasn't he?'

Bea had whipped her notebook out of her bag and started scribbling in it. 'It's weird, isn't it? I mean, to bash someone over the head in broad daylight like that, at a bus stop. There could have been witnesses along at any time. It feels to me like it was impulsive.'

'It was what now?'

'Spur of the moment stuff. Someone saw him and decided to take him out, there and then.'

'Like a random act of violence?'

Bea paused. 'Maybe. But that's more likely to happen at night, isn't it? When people have had a drink. This was just after eight in the morning. This is odd.'

There were similar conversations going on all round the room. Once again, death had crept close to Costsave, too close for comfort. There was an anxious edge to the whispering and gossip, which was only ended by George appearing in the doorway and clapping her hands.

'Excuse me, everyone. I know some of you will have heard the latest about our customer, Reg, who was found just outside the Costsave car park. Obviously, the police are dealing with the matter, so the best we can do is keep focused and carry on. And, if your shift started at two, you're a minute late already.' People started leaping to their feet. 'Bea and Anthony, can you stay behind, please?'

Dot gave Bea's arm a reassuring squeeze as she got up from the sofa. 'See you in a bit, doll.'

George walked over to Ant and Bea. 'The police are here. They want to interview you both, separately. I don't think it will take long. Ant, why don't you wait here while I take Bea through to the office?'

Tom and another officer were waiting in George's office. She ushered Bea inside, then closed the door, leaving them to it.

'Bea, I know you spoke with officers yesterday, but can you please take us through it again – when you last saw him and how you found him?'

For a hideous moment, Bea wondered if she might be a suspect. If she was, she couldn't really blame them. She was the last person to see Reg, after all. The thought brought a panicky feeling with it. She had butterflies in her stomach, her breathing sped up, and the words that would explain everything seemed to slip and slide in her brain just out of reach.

She tried to tell them about Reg waiting for her, about him wanting to sit out of the way and about her being worried when he didn't show up when the store opened ten minutes later, but it all came out in a garbled mess. She could hear how mixed up it all was but couldn't seem to get a hold of herself.

'Okay, okay,' said Tom. 'Take a few deep breaths. Do you want some water?'

Bea sipped at a glass of tepid tap water and tried to breathe.

'So, you think Reg was waiting for you that morning?'

'Yes.'

She took another sip.

'What did he want to talk about?'

'Do I have to tell you?'

'Yes. I'm afraid you do.'

Bea breathed in and out, trying to relax the muscles in her chest. 'He wanted to talk about the night Tina disappeared. He told me he was the nightwatchman at the factory and that he'd seen . . .he'd seen my mum going in and out of the factory site around midnight.'

'Your mum?' Tom rested his pen, and leaned forward on the desk.

'Yes. I spoke to her afterwards, and she confirmed it. She'd gone looking for Dad when he didn't come home. She'd never told anyone about it and she didn't know she'd been seen.'

'I see.' Tom looked down at his notes, then up at her again. 'Bea, how did you feel when he told you that?'

Bea started laughing, a scattergun of inappropriate sound that seemed to fill the room.

'What's this, Tom? Have you turned into a therapist?' Then she saw his expression and her laughter stopped. 'Oh, you think I was so shocked and angry that I hit him? Well, I was shocked, and I was angry at my mum for not telling me, but I never hurt Reg. He was actually really kind. He said nice things about my mum and dad, and about me. It felt like, I dunno, like we were almost friends or something. You believe me, don't you?'

Tom was sitting, poker-faced.

'Thank you, Bea. We might need to follow this up, but you can go back to work now. Do you mind sending Ant in, please?'

When her shift ended Bea went to the locker room to get changed. Dot was in there applying another layer of war paint.

'I'm going to do it, Bea. I'm going to tell him to pack his bags.'

She slicked on a layer of lip gloss and checked herself in the mirror again, pulling a series of fierce expressions.

'You can do this, Dot. Do you want me to hang around in case he turns nasty?'

'No, it's okay, babe. He knows what he's done. When I confront him, he'll just slink away like the rat he is.'

'If you're sure. Give me a ring later, yeah? I want to know that you're okay.'

'Will do. Thanks, Bea.' She gave Bea a quick hug and they left the locker room together. Ant was waiting for Bea outside. They all trooped down the stairs. Bob had got wind of Dot's drama and was hovering by the back door.

'All right, Dot?' he said, holding the door open for her.

'Thanks, Bob. Yes, fine.' She wasn't giving anything away.

'Will you be at choir practice this evening? It's a bit later today, isn't it?'

'I don't know, Bob. I've got something to do first. We'll see.'

She stepped outside, and Ant and Bea followed her. Darren was waiting at the corner of the building. His face brightened when he saw her and he walked towards her and met her halfway. He bent down to kiss her, and she turned her face away.

'We've got time for a drink before choir,' said Bea, taking hold of Ant's arm. 'Tea or something else to oil the tonsils?'

'Something else, I reckon,' said Ant.

'Bob, have a quick half with us, before choir?' Bea said. Bob was standing gawping at Dot and Darren. 'Bob?'

He came to and said, 'Yes, love. That'd be very nice.'

They overtook Dot and Darren and walked round the building and across the car park.

'Looks like trouble in paradise,' said Bob, looking back over his shoulder. 'Do you reckon she's going to give him the old heave-ho?'

'Not for me to say, Bob, but, yeah, he's on his way out,' said Bea.

Bob rubbed his hands together. 'Yesss! Shall we nip into the Pioneer? I'm buying.'

Now they were passing the spot where Reg had died. 'Tom was questioning me like he thought I did it,' said Bea. 'Bloody awful, it was.'

'That copper? He doesn't think that, Bea,' said Bob. 'They have to ask these questions.'

'He was grilling me, too,' said Ant, thrusting his hands into his pockets. 'Like we might have done it together. I reckon they're bloody desperate to solve at least one of these cases. They're starting to look like right noddies, aren't they?'

'Yeah, but it's not easy, is it? I mean, we haven't got anywhere, have we? Not really.'

'Have you two been digging around then?' said Bob. They'd

reached the pub, which was only on the corner, opposite St Swithun's, and he was holding the door open for them. 'I don't know what you're like. Kids today. When I was your age it was just girls and music and pubs.'

He bought a round of drinks and they sat in a corner.

'I've been thinking,' said Bea.

'Dangerous that,' said Bob. He was in an irritatingly ebullient mood.

'No, seriously, I've been thinking about Reg. I reckon somebody killed him on the spur of the moment. I don't believe it was an act of random violence. I think they did it because they saw him talking to me.' She let that sink in for a while before continuing. 'So it was someone who knew that Reg used to work at the factory, who was worried what he might have seen that night.'

'They waited a long time to bump him off, then,' said Ant.

'Yeah, but maybe the investigation is getting closer to them. Maybe they're scared. I'm bloody kicking myself for not asking him who else he saw that night. He, of all people, clocked the ins and outs there, didn't he?'

'Bea, the police must have interviewed him at the time,' said Bob. 'It must all be in their files somewhere.'

'Yes, but if I'd asked him, there might have been things he'd forgotten to tell them, or things, like seeing my mum, that he deliberately withheld.'

'No good fretting over "if onlys". It's not your job to sort all this out, Bea. I know why you want to, but it really isn't.'

'If you're right, though, there's another thing,' said Ant. 'If that was really the killer's motive, then that means you're at risk, too. If they killed him to shut him up, they might try the same thing with you.'

'Unless they know it's too late and I've already talked to the police.'

'How would they know that unless they worked at Costsave.

Oh.' The three of them looked at each other, digesting the importance of what he'd said. They well remembered the atmosphere in the staff room just before Christmas, when another killer was roaming the streets of Kingsleigh and all roads seemed to lead to Costsave. 'Bloody hell, Bea, this is murky stuff. I think Bob's right. It's time to stop digging.'

38

Choir practice was scrappy and unsatisfactory. The day's news had unsettled everyone. On top of that, the date of the Kingsleigh Music Festival was edging ever closer and nobody thought they'd be ready in time, including, seemingly, Candy.

'Listen, people,' she said at the end of the session. 'I know you're all nervous and I know I was hard on you tonight, but the only way we're going to do this is to put in the time to practise. Don't rely on the person next to you to carry the song for you. You need to own this. I can't do this for you. Learn your parts at home. Come to the next session ready to sing your hearts out.'

The air of defeat must have shown in their faces, because she suddenly clapped her hands.

'Come on now. Heads up. Shoulders back. You can do this. I'll arrange some extra sessions. George, is that okay?'

George nodded. 'Of course, and I'll look at informal ones in the staff room. Ten minutes every day until we know it back to front.'

Somebody groaned at the back of the room. 'Hey,' she barked, 'you don't have to do this. It's not compulsory. Anyone who doesn't want to be part of it is perfectly free to walk.' She looked pointedly at the door. Ant glanced at Bea and raised his eyebrows. They knew very well, like everyone else, that anyone who left now would be a social pariah at work. 'No?' said George. 'Good. Listen, I actually think this is going to be great, but Candy's right. Let's put the work in. Let's make it happen. See you all tomorrow.'

They started shambling out of the hall. Ant offered to walk Bea part of the way home.

'I'm going that way anyway.'

'Where *are* you staying, Ant?'

'I've got somewhere up near yours.'

'What? A council place? Why didn't you say?'

'Not a council place. Maureen at the library told me how to put my name down for a flat but the chances of getting one round here are approximately zero.'

'What then? Bed and breakfast?'

'Bed. No breakfast.'

He wouldn't meet her eye.

'Ant?'

He looked down at the ground, and scuffed at some stones with his shoe. Bea thought again about his new early morning swimming regime and the penny dropped with a loud clang. It wasn't so much about fitness, more about using the showers.

'Ant. Look at me. Where are you sleeping?'

He dragged his eyes up to meet hers. 'In a shed,' he said, so quietly she could only just hear him. 'Up at the allotments. I break into them, but I don't do any other damage. I don't take anything. I just sleep on whatever's there, some potato sacks or whatever else I can find. I go up there after dark and I'm gone before anyone gets there in the morning.'

'Oh, Ant.' Bea found her eyes pricking with tears. 'Why didn't you say? There are loads of people with spare rooms. What went wrong at Bob's?'

Ant's face was red now. 'Bob's great. It's just he was crowding me, trying to teach me about godawful country and

232

western music, and talking about Dot all the time. I couldn't hack it. And I didn't say anything because I didn't want this.' He gestured towards her face. 'I didn't want people's pity. People feeling sorry for me.' Bea dashed her own tears away with the back of her hand. 'I don't want to be a charity case. I just want a bit of peace and quiet and my own space.'

'I'd rather you slept on our sofa than in a shed. What about the allotment holders? Weren't they going to start patrols up there?'

He shrugged. 'They haven't done it yet. I keep an eye out for torches at night. If anyone comes up, I'll just scarper.'

Bea stood with her hands uselessly by her sides. 'Ant, what can I do?'

'Nothing, Bea. You're doing it anyway. Keep treating me like a human being. Like a normal mate.'

Fresh tears gathered in Bea's tear ducts. She took a deep breath in through her nose, trying to suppress them. 'But how are things going to get better?'

Ant flung his arms out. 'I dunno. I'll have to make them better. Once I can read, maybe I can get a better paid job, like in the stores or something. If I've got a bit more money, I could get a room somewhere, although my dad wants me to start sending him some.'

'Really?' said Bea.

'Leave it, Bea. It's all right. Something'll come up.'

'In the meantime, can you please swallow your pride and stay with Bob?'

'Not if he's going to get back with Dot, I can't. I couldn't stand listening to those two shagging in the room next door. Can't think of anything worse.'

'I wonder if she's actually dumped Darren?' said Bea, checking her phone. 'She didn't turn up to choir, did she? There's no message from her, though.'

'I think someone should've gone with them, if she really

was kicking him out. What if he refused to go or lost his temper?'

'Mm, I read in one of my magazines that that's the most dangerous time, when you tell someone it's over. Ask them to leave or say you're moving out.'

'She was pretty confident Darren wasn't like that, he wouldn't hurt her or nothing, but I was thinking, he *was* around when Reg got thumped. He walked Dot to work, didn't he? He'd have been walking out of the car park again around the time it happened.'

'Bloody hell, Ant. Do you really think it could have been him?'

'It *could* have, that's all I'm saying. I reckon I'll ring her in a minute, check she's all right.'

Bea agreed. Dot had seemed confident and she did know Darren inside and out, but people were unpredictable. She mulled over what she knew about Darren. He'd gone AWOL the night Tina was murdered, hadn't he? He'd turned up in Kingsleigh just after her body was found. Was he really here to make things up with Dot? Had he just run out of money and options? Or was he keeping an eye on the investigation?

Her mind wandered further to someone else who'd wanted to leave a relationship. To Julie. Still missing. Still apparently having disappeared off the face of the earth. Dave was someone who definitely wouldn't take that sort of news well. Is that when it happened? When he killed her?

She thought, too, about the woman in the club last night, making a swift exit and leaving Dave in the lurch. How many other women had Dave dated since Julie disappeared? How many more had he got in his sights? Whatever had happened to Julie, he was a danger to women. Something had to be done about it. She thought of the older woman with the dangly earrings. She'd been bloody brilliant. Perhaps it was time to take her cue from women like her and step up.

'Ant,' she said. 'You know that woman in the pub yesterday?'

'Yeah, the one who dropped Dave's own drink all over him?'

'No, the other one. Dave's date. The one who got away.'

'What about her?'

'She told me she met him on Tinder.'

'It's what everyone does now. Except me, of course. "Hey, wanna come back to my shed?"'

'So, what if I swiped right? With Dave? What if I went on a date with him? Tried to get him to talk, to open up.'

Ant stopped in his tracks. 'Have you completely lost your mind? We've all seen the bruises he gave his wife. We don't know what happened to her, or the kids. You should keep a million miles away from that psychopath, Bea, not date the bastard.'

'But if you came too. I mean, sat at the other side of the pub or wherever and kept an eye on things. Backup.'

'No, Bea. He's evil. Don't let him think you're interested in him. He's creepy enough at work, already. I've seen how he slimes up to your checkout and chats you up.' He put his hands on her shoulders. 'Promise me you won't go on a date with him. Bea, promise me.'

'Okay, okay. I promise.'

Ant let go of her shoulders. They were halfway across the rec now. 'Actually, things might be getting a bit hot at the allotments. Reckon I should leave it for a few nights till it's all calmed down up there.'

'So you'll ring Bob?'

'I've got a better idea.'

'Ant—?'

'Don't worry about me. This one's pretty sound. I'll be all right. I'll see you tomorrow, yeah?'

'Okay, you take care, though.'

They parted ways; Ant heading back towards the town centre and Bea covering the short distance across the rec and home. Before she got there, though, she'd taken out her phone and opened up Tinder. She may have promised Ant not to meet up with Dave, but promises didn't count if you crossed your fingers behind your back, did they?

39

'I knew you were keen,' said Dave, his eyes confidently holding Bea's. 'Knew it the first time we really spoke. Do you remember? When Costsave used to do date nights. There was a spark between us. Animal attraction.' Bea did remember and he was right. There had been a frisson between them. 'That was months ago, Bea. What kept you?'

It took all of Bea's self-control not to say, 'Your wife', tip her drink over him and leave.

'I knew you had . . .commitments,' she said carefully. 'I'm not the sort of girl who goes for married men, but they're gone now, aren't they, your commitments?'

'Yes,' he said, with a touch of bitterness in his voice. 'They've gone.'

'I know you said they were on holiday, but it's been a while, Dave.' She scanned his face, trying to read his expression, gauge her words.

He looked at her sharply, and she thought he was going to snap at her. She'd seen the results of his temper in Julie's bruises, but she was pretty sure he wouldn't lash out here. He kept that sort of thing behind closed doors. She reached across the table and gently touched his hand with the end of her sharp, glossy red nails. He looked down at their hands together on the table and then back up at her. Desire softened his features.

'What's happened? You can tell me,' she said.

'Do you really want to know?'

She dug her nail in a little more firmly, tracing a line along the length of his thumb, leaving a faint white mark which his pulsing blood removed as it flushed through his veins.

'I really do.'

He looked down again as he spoke.

'She's left me. Bitch walked out four weeks ago, taking the kids. I didn't want to tell anyone because, you know, wounded pride and all that, so I made up the story about the holiday.'

'Oh Dave, I'm so sorry. That's awful. Where have they gone?' She caressed his hand some more.

'I don't know. I haven't heard from her. She didn't leave a note or anything. Just packed up some things and went when I was out.'

He was so plausible. His words felt like they had the ring of truth about them. Bea felt her spirits lifting at the thought that Julie had really left and gone somewhere safe. Somewhere Dave didn't know about.

'Must have been a shock,' she said.

'Yeah. You could say that. Miss the kids like mad.'

'Of course. You're a good dad. I've seen you with the two of them in the shop.'

She'd seen him confiscate a toy from Mason, seen his barely controlled irritation at Tiffany whining in her trolley seat. He moved his hand now so that he could interlace his fingers with hers. Bea felt a wave of revulsion, but fought hard not to show it.

'Thanks, Bea. No idea when I'll see them again. What sort of monster uses their kids as a weapon like this?'

'Is that what she's doing?'

'Of course she is. I'm the injured party here, but I don't know where my kids are or when I'll see them again.'

If he was putting on an act, he was doing a good job, thought Bea. She was starting to believe him.

'Have you reported them missing? You've got rights as a dad, after all.'

'Rights? Hardly! I don't want the police involved anyway. She'll come back one day, I know she will, and then I'll deal with things my own way.'

His words chilled her to the bone. She wanted to take her hand away from his, leave as quickly as possible, go home and lock the door. Even if he hadn't killed Julie, if he was telling the truth, she didn't want to spend one minute with him, breathing the same air as him. It was time to call it quits. But he had hold of her hand quite tightly now, his tanned fingers linked with hers, holding on. He put his other hand on top. The weight of it was oppressive.

'But it does mean that I'm free right now, Bea. Free to do what I want, when I want, with who I want.'

He was staring into her eyes now. It was quite clear what he did want. She tried gently removing her hand. He held on.

'I'd better be getting back,' she said.

'You're kidding? It's still early.'

'Late enough for me. I've got work in the morning.'

'So have I,' he said. 'That needn't spoil our fun.'

'Really.' She pulled her hand away. 'I'm going to go now.'

'I'll give you a lift back.'

'No, it's okay. I'm happy to walk.' She wanted to get away and she didn't want him knowing where she lived, although he could easily look it up.

'Bea, I've got the car here.'

'It's not a bad evening and I like a bit of fresh air.'

They parted outside the pub door. Bea set off along the main road into town, all the time feeling his eyes boring into her back as she walked away. She tried to keep it casual, walk with confidence, fighting the urge to run. She wouldn't be able to run fast in these stupid shoes, anyway. Why on earth had she chosen these red stilettos? After a minute or so, her nerves were settling. The evening had given her a lot to think about and the walk would give her the chance to do so. A minute or two later, she heard a car approaching behind her. It drew level and the passenger window glided down. Dave was leaning over, looking out of the window, driving at the same time.

'Bea! Get in!'

'No, I'm fine, honestly.'

'Stop a minute, then.'

Reluctantly, she stopped walking and the car pulled in and parked. Dave opened the driver's door, stood up and addressed her over the top of the car. 'Look, I know what's going on here.'

'Do you?' She felt a spasm of anxiety in her stomach. Did he know about the drone? The report she gave to the police?

'You're scared.' She didn't say anything, tried not to react at all, even though her heart was racing now and her throat was dry. 'You're scared of the attraction between us. I get it. I feel it, too. Haven't felt like this since I first met...never mind. Listen, can I be honest with you?'

'Please.'

He glanced behind him. Another car was approaching. He was in a bit of a vulnerable spot, with the door open. 'Let's talk in the car.'

It seemed rude to say no. There was something vulnerable about him now, and so, against her better judgement, Bea got in, aware of her skirt riding up as she lowered herself into the passenger seat. She tugged at the hem, then wished she hadn't as the action clearly drew his attention there, but he didn't leer. He glanced down and then up at her face, sitting back in his chair.

'Bea, I'm not the guy you think I am.'

Her stomach lurched. Where was this going?

'You haven't seen me at my best. When I was with Julie, in the shop, well, we've not been happy for ages. She brings out the worst in me. Maybe we bring out the worst in each other. I was angry when she left, gutted too for the kids, but now I think it could be the best thing that ever happened to me. I can start again. Start again with someone good, cheerful, generous. Someone like you, Bea. I can finally be myself.'

He sounded sincere, but all Bea could think of now was getting out of the car again without pissing him off.

'It's too soon, though, isn't it?' she said. 'They haven't been gone long. You probably need to decompress for a bit, come to terms with it.'

'Like I said, it's been over for ages, except we were still living in the same house. I'm ready to move on.'

'Well, can you move me back home, please? I really do want to go home, but let's meet up again soon, yeah?'

He pressed his lips together and tilted his head to show it wasn't what he really wanted, but he was smiling too. 'Okay,' he said, starting the engine. 'Where are we going?'

'Poplar Street, on the Orchard estate, please.'

It would only take five minutes to drive through the town centre and out the other side to Bea's estate. Bea was still on edge, but she was pretty confident she'd got things on an even keel now. She'd be home soon.

40

Ant waited for a full ten minutes after the library had closed. It was cramped and uncomfortable in the ceiling space above the cubicles, but it was a genius hiding place. He moved the loose tile a fraction and listened. When he was sure the coast was clear, he put the tile aside, braced his elbows on the supporting ceiling struts and lowered his legs down, pointing his toes and feeling for the top of the cistern below. When he found solid porcelain he tested his weight gradually, then released his grip and clambered down onto the toilet lid and then the floor. He stopped and listened again, then crept out of the cubicle, past the sinks and into the library.

Being nearly midsummer, it wasn't dark yet, and the glass sides of the modern building – one of the jewels in the redevelopment of Kingsleigh town centre – left him exposed to discovery. Ideally, he would have slunk in here at the end of the evening, but he'd had to get in before closing time – he hadn't worked out a way of getting in once it was all locked up. However, he'd also spent a bit of time sussing out angles and blind spots and he reckoned that if he kept close to the floor, he could establish a sort of camp in the reference section, with cushions dragged from the children's corner. He spent a happy twenty minutes or so wriggling backwards and forwards, fetching cushions like a mother cat carrying kittens. He also brought back a handful of picture books from the book train, a series of open boxes on the floor, and set himself up in a sort of nest to see if he could read them. To his surprise and delight, he could. He would never have done this in the full light of public scrutiny but he became happily absorbed in working his way through, taking time on each page to enjoy both the words and the pictures. They were actually quite clever. The pictures pretty much told the story themselves and if he was getting stuck with a word, they helped him to work it out.

When he'd finished the last book in his pile, he checked his phone and was amazed to find that two hours had gone by. He got out the chicken and bacon sandwich he'd bought earlier for his tea, and cracked open his first can of cider. The cushions were surprisingly comfortable. He reckoned he was in for a good night's sleep. The only thing he'd have to be careful about was waking up and removing all traces of his occupation before the staff opened up in the morning. Thinking ahead, he put down his sandwich and set the alarm on his phone.

Sandwich eaten and the first can of cider drained, he wondered what to do next. It was getting slightly darker outside, but he didn't feel sleepy yet. He looked around him, and spotted the rows of folders holding the *Bugle* archive that Bea had mentioned. He slithered up the side of a stack and ran his finger along the row of files.

'Two thousand and five,' he said out loud, noticing how weird his voice sounded in this empty place. He pulled out the file, slunk back down to his nest and started leafing through. His success with the picture books had boosted his confidence, but now, faced with pages and pages of dense small print, his nerve failed him. The words seemed to dance in front of his eyes, mocking him and his new-found skills. He tried to focus, and picked a word at random to decode, but panic had set in and he couldn't work it out.

'Bollocks,' he said. He was going to put the file back when a series of pictures caught his eye. It was obviously a set of photographs taken at that year's music festival – images of bands, marquees, crowds. Ant studied them in turn, thinking that not much had changed over the past fourteen years. It was still a good day out, attended by young and old, families, groups of mates. There was something for everyone. He looked carefully at a crowd scene, half expecting to recognise his family, camped out on the grass with picnic chairs and blankets – it was something of a tradition. For some reason he felt a sense of urgency. It was really important to find the Thompsons all together one last time and he felt a sting of bitter disappointment when he couldn't. He took another look – surely they usually parked themselves near the community tent – and then he stopped.

'Holy shit,' he murmured. 'Holy fucking shit.'

He had recognised someone, but it wasn't his mum or dad, or Ken, Stevo, Britney or Dani. There was a couple on one side of the picture, almost falling out of the frame. They were holding hands. The girl had her back to the camera, but he was pretty sure it was Tina. The boy, or rather young man, was facing her. He was smart, neat and tidy, clean-shaven.

Ant rested the file on his lap, got out his phone and dialled Bea. The call connected, but went to answerphone after three rings. 'Bea, I need to talk to you urgently. Call me back!' He looked at the photo again then found Bea's home phone and tried that.

It rang for a while. 'Come on, come on,' he muttered to himself, then felt a surge of relief as someone picked up at the other end.

'Hello?' It was clearly Queenie's voice.

'Hi Mrs Jordan, it's Ant. Can I speak to Bea, please?'

'Hello Ant. She's out on a date this evening. Someone she met online.'

'Oh, right. Did she say a name or anything?'

'No. She said they were meeting in the Boatman, you know, down by the river. It was funny because she doesn't always tell me where she's going, but she made a point of it. That was a while ago, though. She's been out since just before eight.'

'Okay, tell her I called, please. I need to talk to her.'

'Will do. Bye, Ant.'

'Bye.'

He killed the call. The display on his phone said, '10:47'. He wondered if Bea was still at the pub, or whether they'd gone on somewhere else. Perhaps she'd got lucky. But who would she be out with? Then he remembered. *What if I swiped right? With Dave? What if I went on a date with him?*

'Oh no, Bea. No, no, no, no.'

Not thinking about his visibility now, he left the file on the floor and jumped up.

'I've gotta get out of here.'

41

'You thought I'd hurt them, didn't you? Julie and the kids?'

Bea was taken aback. She blinked rapidly and tried to keep her voice light and even.

'No, course not.'

Dave snorted. 'You're such a bad liar, Bea, but I kind of like you for that. Here, let me show you something.'

Without indicating, he took a sharp left into the next side road, making the car tyres squeal gently in protest.

'Wait! Where are we going?'

'I want to prove to you that I'm telling you the truth. That you can trust me.'

'You'll prove that if you take me home like I asked,' she said, firmly.

'Yes, and I'll do that after I've shown you this.' They were drawing up outside Dave's house. 'Just for a minute. Come on!'

He jumped out of the car and went around to open the passenger door. Bea hesitated, but was glad, after all, to get out of the car. She stood on the pavement and watched him walk up to the front door and unlock it.

'Come on, Bea. It won't take a minute,' he said.

She looked up and down the street. A young woman was pushing a child in a buggy along the opposite pavement. A middle-aged man was walking towards her with a chihuahua skipping along beside him. Everything seemed so normal, so unthreatening, and this was the chance she'd wanted, wasn't it, to see inside the house. Look for evidence. She followed Dave up the path and he ushered her inside the front door. There was a row of pegs in the hallway, with a mixture of big and little coats still hanging there, and underneath, on the carpet, was a sheet of newspaper and two pairs of tiny wellington boots.

'Come on, up here!' He squeezed past her and started bounding up the stairs, past a series of family photographs hanging on the walls.

'You're kidding. I'm not going upstairs.'

He stopped near the top and looked down at her. 'Not my room, the kids' rooms. I want to show you that their stuff's gone.'

Part of her was itching to look, but she didn't want to go anywhere upstairs with him.

'It's okay, Dave. I believe you, okay? I don't need to see.'

'Okay,' he said, starting to come back down the stairs, 'let's have a drink instead.'

'I'll take a rain check. I really want to get home.' She started moving back towards the front door. He didn't try to stop her. She put her hand up to the latch, glad that she was able to leave so easily.

'The thing is, Bea, I hate it here now. It's so empty without them.'

She stopped and looked back at him. He was standing at the bottom of the stairs. His hands were by his sides. His shoulders were rounded. He looked smaller somehow, defeated. He looked like a man at a loss.

Afterwards, she wondered why she hadn't remembered Julie's bruises, the guarded, wary look in Mason's eyes. She knew Dave could be brutal, but at that moment all she saw was a guy who'd been hurt by life, who needed someone to listen.

'Just one drink,' she heard herself saying.

A smile started playing at the corners of his mouth.

'Just one,' he said. 'Let's go into the lounge.'

42

Ant scouted round for windows to open, ways to escape, but the ground floor windows were solid and unyielding, designed to stay shut and let the building's fancy warm air heating system do its thing. He ran to the front doors, which were firmly locked. He looked wildly around for something to break the lock with. There wasn't anything – books and more books, computers, tables, chairs. He picked up a chair. It was a sturdy thing with a cushioned seat and metal legs. He held it as high as he could and threw his weight into smashing it against the door lock. The doors moved a bit on impact, but the lock and the glass remained intact, and now an alarm was wailing, rattling Ant's ears.

A man passing by on the other side of the door looked up and straight at Ant. Ant banged on the door and shouted, 'Help!' The man grinned, raised his phone and started videoing him.

'Fucksake!' Ant yelled. 'Get some help! I'm stuck in here!'

The guy gave him the thumbs up and started to fiddle with his phone, typing quickly and frowning with concentration.

'Stop fucking uploading it to the fucking internet and get some help!'

Another couple of people had joined the man outside. They were pointing and smiling, as if Ant was their own personal entertainer putting on a show. 'Jeez!' Ant got his own phone out and checked for messages from Bea. Nothing. Increasingly desperate, he picked up the chair again and, using it as a kind of sledgehammer, he started battering the door.

Adrenaline was giving him strength and stamina he didn't usually possess. At last something gave way. One of the doors moved a little. Ant heaved the chair at the lock one more time, then let it fall to the floor. He ran at the door and cannoned into it, shoulder first. He let out a squawk of pain as the door opened and he staggered out into the forecourt. The crowd which had gathered there parted as he reeled about, flailing his arms wildly.

'Thanks for bloody nothing, you bunch of muppets!' Ant yelled and started running through the precinct. The Boatman was on the stretch of river on the other side of the park. Ant raced down the steps and across the road towards the main gates to the park. It was dark in there, but he pressed on, taking a straight course. The ground was uneven and he couldn't see where he was putting his feet. When he went over on one ankle, the pain brought him up short. He stood for a moment, breathing hard.

'Bloody hell, what am I doing?'

The pub would be shut by now. He rang Bea's mobile again and hung up when it switched to answerphone. He wanted to ring Queenie again, but thought it would worry her too much. If Bea had got home, her mum would have passed his message on, after all, and she would have rung him.

'Think, Ant. Think!' He smacked his head hard with the flat of his hand.

He set off back the way he'd come, testing his weight on his ankle and then breaking into a tentative run. He jogged out of the park and up the steps to cut across the precinct. When he got near the top he saw a blue flashing light. He peered around the corner. A police car was parked near the entrance to the library. Shaz and her colleague were interviewing some of the 'muppets' who had gathered there. He considered telling them about his discovery but couldn't risk getting arrested for the damage to the library. Was it breaking and entering, if you broke *out* of a place?

Ant nipped quickly out of the cover of the building and scuttled along in the opposite direction, skirting around the back of the library and then away down the High Street. He ran through the streets and alleyways, and round the garages until he came to Sutherland Avenue. He could see lights on in number eighteen, but the curtains at the front were drawn.

He had no idea what he was going to say, but he needed to know that Bea was safe, so he went up to the front door and rang the bell. It opened a little. Dave peered out, then opened the door wider.

'Yes?' he said.

'Is Bea here?' Ant blurted out, realising he sounded like a boy calling round to ask if his friend could come out to play.

'Bea?' Dave looked genuinely puzzled.

'She works at Costsave. I do, too. She said she was going on a date with you this evening.'

'Oh, that Bea! No, it wasn't me she was seeing this evening. Sorry, mate.' He started to close the door. Behind him in the hallway Ant could see a woman's shoe lying on its own at the foot of the stairs, a peep-toed shiny red affair, with a stiletto heel. He hadn't seen it before, but it looked like the sort of thing Bea might wear. Acting on instinct, Ant put his hand out to stop the door closing and shouted, 'Bea? Bea! It's Ant! I need to talk to you!'

Dave reacted quickly. He shoved both hands into Ant's chest, pushing him out of the doorway. 'She's not here. Now fuck off or I'll call the police.'

The door slammed shut. Ant stood looking at it for a

moment or two, then retreated to the pavement. He rang Queenie again.

'Sorry to bother you. Is Bea home yet?'

'No. No, she isn't. Has something happened, Ant? Should I be worried?'

'No, everything's fine. Just tell her I rang, okay? Oh, Mrs Jordan,' he said, trying to keep his tone casual, 'what's she wearing this evening?'

'What's she wearing? A nice summer dress, I think. Red and white.'

'And red shoes?'

'Yes. Too high to walk in, silly girl. Why, Ant?'

'No reason. Just so I can spot her easily in the pub. Bye.' He rang off quickly, aware that his questions had been none too subtle and that he had probably catapulted Queenie into a frenzy of anxiety now.

'Shit, shit, shit,' Ant said to himself. He dialled '999' and waited. 'Police, please.'

He reported his suspicions, that a woman had been abducted and was being held at Sutherland Avenue. The operator at the end of the phone line kept quizzing him and her reactions grew more and more sceptical the longer their conversation went on.

'Are you going to send someone out?'

'I'll add it to the incident log.'

'What does that even mean? Oh, never mind.'

Ant rang off. He made another call, this time to Saggy.

'Mate, I haven't got time to explain but I need your help at Sutherland Avenue. Bring anyone else you can think. I need a fucking army.'

He walked a few paces along the pavement. Having done it once before, it was no big deal to vault over the fence and into the back garden. Unfortunately, this time he landed awkwardly on the already weakened ankle. It gave way and he ended up in a heap on the ground. All at once he was bathed in light. He'd triggered a security light, and there he was, centre stage, for anyone to see.

The French windows at the back of the house were uncurtained. Ant saw Dave come to the window and cup his hand over his forehead to see through the glass. He frowned, then flicked a catch at the side of the door, reached down to grab something leaning nearby and slid the door sideways.

Ant tried to get to his feet, managed to get halfway, then had to crouch down again. His ankle wouldn't hold his weight. Dave was in the garden now, advancing towards him across the patio.

'You again. I told you to fuck off.'

Ant looked up at him. He was silhouetted against the light from the French windows, and it was clear that he was carrying some sort of weapon, a poker or something. He held it with both hands, and as he got nearer, Ant could see it was a baseball bat.

'I think my friend's in there. I want you to leave her alone.'

'That's her decision, isn't it? Nothing to do with you.'

'So she is there. Bea? Bea!'

'Shut up, she can't hear you.'

'Why? What've you done to her?'

Ant was scuttling backwards on his hands and feet, trying to draw Dave away from the house. Dave took a swipe at him with the bat, missing his head by a few inches. Ant slithered faster. There was a little brick shed at the end of the garden. Maybe he could make it inside, or find something to fight back with in there.

Dave took aim again, this time raising the bat high in the air before bringing it down onto Ant's already injured ankle. Ant let out an agonised yelp. 'Stop it! You can't do that. You're a fucking maniac!'

'You're an intruder. I'm defending my property.'

Ant's shoulder found the cold hard wall of the shed. And now, of course, he was trapped. Nowhere else to go. He'd managed to pin himself in a corner. He watched as Dave swung the bat backwards. This was it. Nothing to lose now.

'Is this what you did to Julie?' he said.

Dave held the bat where it was.

'What?'

'Is this how you killed Julie? Did you hit her with something? What about the kids?'

'You're talking out of your backside. They left me. Bitch packed a case and went when I was at work.'

'What about Tina?'

Ant's heart was hammering away in his chest.

'I don't know what you're talking about.' Brave words, but there was a tell-tale edge of uncertainty there and now Ant knew his hunch was right.

'Yes, you do,' he said. 'You didn't move to K-town in 2006. You were here in 2005.'

'No. You're wrong. Do you think I don't know when I moved here?'

The angle of the bat was drooping as Dave hesitated and gravity pulled on the heavy wood.

'I've found a picture of you. Of you and her together.' Now Dave rested the end of the bat on the ground. He was listening. 'You were her secret boyfriend. You were the one who killed her and buried her in the factory groundworks.'

'Absolutely not. You're talking rubbish.'

Ant was listening hard to Dave's words, but also trying to hear the sound of help coming. Much as he disliked the cops, he'd give anything to hear a police siren right now, but there was only a faint murmur of traffic and a high-pitched whining noise which he couldn't identify. He'd just have to keep him talking.

'What did Tina do to deserve that, Dave? What could she possibly have done?'

'You don't know anything.'

'Did she dump you? Was that it? Did you lose your temper?'

The whining was becoming louder.

'She would never have dumped me. Never.'

'So it *was* you. You and her. If she didn't dump you, what was it?'

'She needed to be taught a lesson. She was flirting with other men, giving them looks. I just wanted her to stop it.'

'And you argued?'

'She tried telling me it wasn't flirting, but I saw it. Saw it with my own eyes. I didn't want to hear excuses. So I slapped her. And she started screaming, really loud. It was dark, but there were still people on site. I had to stop her. Stop the noise. I didn't mean to— What the hell is that?'

Dave looked up just as Saggy's drone appeared over the fence. 'What *is* that?' He took hold of his bat and swung it at the drone, which appeared to hop out of his way, hovering overhead.

With Dave distracted, Ant spotted a hosepipe, curled up on a bracket on the side of the shed. It was attached to a tap. It wasn't the rake or spade he'd been hoping for, but it was all he'd got. He dragged himself closer, reached up and turned the tap as far as it would go.

The drone was dipping up and down, teasing Dave, like a bull making passes at a matador. He took another swing and came within a gnat's whisker of hitting it. Ant pulled himself up on the hose's bracket and leaned on the shed wall. Then he grasped the nozzle of the hose and directed it towards Dave. The water didn't feed through for ages, but when it did it came out in a fierce concentrated jet and hit Dave in the back of the neck. He wheeled round and Ant angled the nozzle a little higher, aiming for his eyes. Dave put both hands up to his face, dropping the bat, and at the same time he heard a loud bang and the sound of wood splintering. A Doc Marten boot attached to a leg like a tree trunk appeared through the fence and was withdrawn again. It reappeared and the wood above the hole splintered and came away and the substantial figure of Tank stepped through the gap. Dean followed behind him, and Ant had the impression he was using him as a human shield.

'Hullo, Ant,' said Tank.

'All right, mate. Could you sit on this bloke, please? Don't hurt him, or not much anyway.' Ant pointed to Dave who was still cowering with his hands up to his face as a jet of water blasted him.

'Okay.'

Tank walked towards Dave. He grabbed him round the waist and bundled him to the ground. Ant directed the hose away from them, but kept the water running until he was sure that Tank had him under control. He was impressed to see he had him pinned on the ground with his hands behind his back. Dean stood a few feet away, out of harm's reach if any trouble started kicking off.

'Dean, can you turn this water off?' Ant handed him the end of the hose, and started running towards the house. By now Saggy had also entered the garden and was landing his drone on the grass.

'Well done, Sags,' called Ant. 'Can you call the police again? I tried earlier, but I don't think they took me seriously.'

'What's he done? Is it his wife and kiddies?'

'I'm not sure about them, but he killed Tina Robbins fourteen years ago.'

'Holy shit.'

'And I think he's hurt Bea. She's in there.' Ant had reached the French windows now. He took in the sitting room as he ran through it, but it was the shoe at the bottom of the stairs he was haunted by. She was in one of the bedrooms, he was sure. He raced up the stairs, three at a time.

'Bea! Bea, it's me!'

The first door he saw had a little ceramic name plate on it – 'Tiffany's Room'. The next one was bare, but when he pushed it open a robot-themed duvet cover on a small single bed told him this was Mason's. Still shouting her name, he pushed open the third door.

She was lying on top of the bed, fully clothed. The top light was on, and there was a camera and tripod set up near the bottom of the bed. Bea, however, was sound asleep. Asleep or . . .? Ant felt a stab of panic, then his first aid training kicked in. He checked that she was breathing and had a pulse. She was and she did, but she seemed to be completely out for the count. He called her name quite loudly and there was a little flicker of her eyelids.

'Bea! Wake up! It's time to wake up, Bea! Oh my god, please be all right. Please, please, Bea!'

Her eyelids fluttered open. She looked at him without seeming to recognise him. Her pupils were huge.

'Bea, it's me. Ant.'

She frowned and licked her lips, which were dry and crusty.

'Where am I?'

'You're at Dave's house. He brought you here. Did you have a lot to drink?'

She looked confused. 'Only had one and a bit drinks. I'm very tired, Ant.'

'I think you've been drugged, mate.'

'She all right?' Ant looked behind him. Saggy was in the doorway.

'I think she's drugged up. Can you ring for an ambulance? Are Tank and Dean all right with that tosser? We mustn't let him get away.'

'They've got it all under control. Dean wanted to give him a kicking, but Tank wouldn't let him.'

'Are the police coming?'

'Yeah, they said so.'

'Police?' said Bea, trying to sit up. 'What's happened?'

Ant stroked her forehead. 'It's all right, Bea. Don't worry about it now. I'll tell you everything later.' She stopped struggling and lay her head back down on the pillow, but her face was still etched with concern. 'Bea, it's all right. Honestly. I know who killed Tina and it wasn't your dad. Everything's going to be all right.'

43

The next day Bea set up camp on the sofa in a nest of pillows and duvets. Queenie gave her full charge of the remote control and kept up a steady stream of cups of tea, plates of toast and packets of biscuits. Towards the end of the morning, Tom came round, bearing a huge bunch of flowers and an equally enormous box of chocolates. Queenie showed him into the lounge and discreetly withdrew to the kitchen.

'Bea, I'm so glad you're okay. I should have listened to you. Shouldn't have dismissed your worries about Julie.' Tom was sitting opposite Bea in an armchair.

Bea sat up. 'Tom, is there any news? Did he kill her and the kids too?'

'No, turns out he was actually telling the truth about Julie. She did leave him. She and the little 'uns have been living in a refuge. She was so scared she didn't tell a soul, but when she saw he'd been arrested she sent a message through. I don't know if she'll have to testify against him. Hopefully we'll be able to spare her that, unless she wants to, of course.'

'She was very brave to leave.'

'Yes. I spoke to her on the phone this morning for a couple of minutes. She bundled a few things and some of the kids' clothes and toys into a case and left. At one point she thought Dave had come home from work, but it was just her taxi – it turned up early and gave her a fright. But she did it, Bea. She got out. She said to say thank you to you. She rang the number you gave her. That's how she found the refuge. Oh, Bea—'

Bea had started to cry. 'They're really okay?'

Tom came over to Bea, knelt on the floor and put his arms round her. 'Yes, they're really okay.'

He held her until she stopped crying, then gallantly gave her his hankie and returned to his armchair while she dabbed her eyes and blew her nose. Queenie popped her head round the door.

'You all right, Bea?'

'Yes. Just . . . you know . . .'

'I'll put the kettle on.' She disappeared again.

'Can you open those choccies, Tom?' said Bea, looking towards the coffee table. 'Box that big was made for sharing.'

Tom picked at the cellophane wrapping and, eventually, unpeeled it and opened the cardboard box. He handed it over to Bea, who took great delight in examining the rather superior contents and choosing the first one, before handing it back to him.

'Mm, these are lovely,' she said, through a mouthful of salted caramel truffle.

'Only the best for you, Bea,' he said, letting his fingers hover over various chocolates before choosing a bobbly log-shaped one. 'I was going to come and see you anyway today. We got your DNA results through yesterday. I was going to tell you that your dad was in the clear.'

'I *did* say, didn't I?'

'I know, love, but we had to prove it. The DNA certainly eliminated people, like your dad, but we didn't have Dave on our database. It needed something like Ant finding that photo, or you doing your thing, to make the breakthrough. Got to say I'd rather your thing wasn't quite so risky, though.

What were you thinking?' He clutched at his forehead in exasperation.

Bea sighed and took another chocolate. 'I had no idea he was anything to do with Tina. I was just hoping to get some information on Julie. It was Ant that made the connection.'

'Yeah, bit of a surprise that. He's always struck me as a picnic short of a sandwich.'

'Ant? No, he's sharp as a pin. Well, sometimes. Is he going to be in trouble over the library thing?'

'Not sure yet. Partly depends whether the council want to press charges. With any luck, they'll show a bit of heart.'

'Is there any chance that Dave will get off?'

'No. I'm a hundred per cent sure we'll get a DNA match for him. He confessed about Tina to Ant, too, of course, and it looks like there's some blood on his work clothes that will link him to Reg. He was starting to get really rattled by then. When he saw you talking to him, I reckon he just panicked.'

'So it was my fault?'

'No, course not. None of this is your fault. It was an evil man trying to cover up what he'd done. We can charge him for what he did to you, too. If he's got a shred of decency, he'll plead guilty to everything but scum like him rarely do.'

'But one way or another he'll be locked up for life?'

'Yes, Bea. I can't see how he wouldn't be.'

Bea sank back into the sofa, suddenly feeling like all the stuffing had been knocked out of her. Tom got up again and tucked the duvet round her legs and balanced the box of chocolates on her covers, so she didn't have to reach over for it.

'I'll get off now, Bea. I can see you're tired. I expect it'll take a day or two to properly get over the drugs he gave you. I've been thinking, though, you've got a good instinct for investigating, even if you sometimes go about it the wrong way. Have you thought of joining up?'

'Joining the police? Honestly, no I haven't.'

'Perhaps you should. You'd look great in uniform. Anyway, think about it. In the meantime, it's time we got back on track.' It was an announcement, rather than an invitation, and it threatened to take the edge off Bea's enjoyment of the cappuccino mousse enrobed in white chocolate that she'd just popped into her mouth. 'I'm sorry we fell out over your dad. But that's over now. And I reckon we should go out on a proper date.'

Bea tuned out his voice and let the mousse dissolve on her tongue, enjoying the accent of bitterness mingling with the melted sweet white chocolate.

'Mm . . .' she said.

'Is that "mm, yes" or "mm, I'm thinking about it"?'

She came to and found him perched on the far arm of the sofa, looking anxiously at her with puppy dog eyes. She felt curiously unmoved. Perhaps Dave had cured her of falling for seemingly vulnerable men.

'It was "mm, I think the coffee ones are my favourite",' she said, aware how callous it would sound.

'Oh.' He sat back in his chair. 'Did you even hear what I said?'

'I heard. It's just, I dunno, Tom. It's all stop-start with us, isn't it? It's never quite right. Perhaps we should just be friends.'

'Friends is good, Bea,' he said. 'More than friends would be brilliant. I can wait, though.'

He stood up and selected a dark orange disc. Bea watched as he started moving the chocolate towards his mouth, then swooped down and popped it into Bea's, kissing her on the top of her head as he did so. She was too startled to resist. He straightened up again, grinned, said, 'See you later, Bea,' and walked into the kitchen.

That was a bit extra, thought Bea, as she heard the kitchen door close. Queenie came into the room.

'He's in a good mood,' she said. 'He just gave me a bit of a squeeze on the way out. What have you done to him? Are you two an item?'

Bea swallowed the chocolate down and said, 'No. That was just Tom being Tom.'

'Oh,' said Queenie, who was now inspecting the selection box. 'What are they all? I haven't got the right glasses with me.'

'I'm not going to read the whole lot out for you. It'll have to be lucky dip,' said Bea.

Rather unnecessarily, her mum closed her eyes, waved her hand dramatically in circles in the air and then plunged her fingers into the box. She put a chocolate in her mouth and then opened her eyes wide, like a startled owl. 'Ugh! Marzipan! Pass me that tissue to spit into.'

They shared a tin of tomato soup for lunch and then Bea slept for most of the afternoon. Dot popped round just before five. Seeing how tired Bea was, she didn't stay long but she did report that Darren had left Kingsleigh.

'I told him I knew about him taking my money. Didn't try to bluster his way out of it or anything, just packed his bags and went. His parting words? "Well, it was good to catch up." Catch up? Like I was someone he used to know down the pub or went to school with.' Dot had shaken her head. 'Anyway, he's gone. I don't know where and I don't care. I've warned our Sal he's on the road, though, in case he pitches up at hers.'

Soon after Dot had gone, Bea's phone rang. She was pleased to hear Ant's voice, but alarmed at his apparent distress.

'Bea, you've got to help me. Can I come round to yours?'

'Um, yes. Of course. What's up?'

'It's Neville. He's bad enough at work, but at home he's fucking hilarious. It's killing me not to laugh. I might actually burst a blood vessel.'

After breaking out of the library, Ant's homelessness was common knowledge. Neville and Maureen had insisted on Ant coming home with them, and Ant had been powerless to refuse.

'What's he doing?' said Bea, selecting another chocolate from the box Tom had left.

'Well today, for instance, he'd called us into the dining room for lunch and then he actually asked me if I'd washed my hands, like I'm one of his kids. I just lied and said yes, of course, and then we sat down and he said, out of the blue, "Will you say grace, Anthony?"'

'Ha!'

'I had no idea people lived like this.'

'They mean well.'

'Yeah, I know, but now he's announced that tonight, like every Saturday, it's board games night. I can't do it, Bea. I just can't sit there and rattle a dice in a pot, taking turns nicely with little Heather and James, and not cheat or swear or drink or smoke. It'll kill me, Bea. I might actually die.'

Bea laughed. 'Come round here, then. I think one of those *Mission Impossible* films is on. Shall we watch that and have a bag of chips?'

'Oh, sweet. I'll pick some up on the way round, shall I?'

Later that evening, after Ant had reluctantly left to walk back to Neville's, Bea and Queenie were both snoozing gently as the ten o'clock news played in the background when Bea's mobile rang. Bea jerked awake and looked around.

'Oh, my phone's ringing. Nobody rings.'

'Better answer it, love,' said Queenie, rubbing her eyes with the side of her index finger.

Bea fumbled down between the cushions and retrieved the phone. She looked at the screen. 'It's Jay.' Her thumb hovered over the 'reject' button, then curiosity got the better of her and she stood up unsteadily and took her phone into the garden.

'Hey Bea, how are you?'

'I'm okay.'

'So what's been happening in Kingsleigh?'

'Nothing much,' said Bea, too tired to go to the bother of explaining exactly what had been going on. 'The weather's turned at last. We've got a new range of choc ices in at Cost-save. They're doing a bomb.'

'Ha! Nothing changes. Good old K-town. The weather's pretty good here too. That's what I was ringing about.'

'You were ringing to talk about the weather?' She rolled her eyes and then stayed looking at the sky. It was actually a beautiful night – a little residual warmth in the air and above her a deep blue blanket, studded with stars.

'No. Listen, Bea, I was ringing to say that I miss you. I made a silly mistake. Come on, Bea, hop on a plane, come out to Thailand and let's pick up where we left off.'

All it would take was a quick search on the internet, a loan applied for, a phone message left on Anna's answer machine in the Costsave office, and she could be there. Instead of leaning against a pebble-dashed wall in Kingsleigh she could be lying on a beach with Jay, looking up at these same stars to a soundtrack of waves washing onto the sand.

But this time it was easy to say no. 'I'm sorry, Jay, I've got a gig to perform.'

'A gig? You in a band now? Hey, tell me all about it.'

'Something like that. I'll tell you when you get back.'

44

Bea went back to work after a couple of days. Bob gave her a lift in and insisted on dropping her right next to the staff door before he went and parked the car. Eileen, arriving on foot at the same time, held the door open for her.

'Good to see you, Bea,' she said, gruffly, and Bea found herself strangely moved.

'Thanks, Eileen,' she said. 'Good to be back.'

People were gathering for the morning huddle in the staff room. A little murmur rippled through them when they spotted Bea. She made a beeline for Ant who was lurking near one of the sofas.

'Sit here,' he said, brushing some crumbs off one of the sofa cushions.

'I don't want any fuss,' said Bea.

Thankfully, she was below George's sightline, hidden by people standing in front of her, so there was no official mention. Instead, there was another pep talk about choir practice and a five-minute run through of one of their songs, as well as the usual notices, sales updates and targets. As the throng dispersed, George spotted her and came over.

'Welcome back, Bea,' she said, extending her hand, inviting Bea to shake it. A bit nonplussed, she did, and again she felt the stirring of emotion.

'Better get to my checkout,' she muttered, and scuttled out of the room and down the stairs to the shop floor. She settled into her seat at checkout number six, and she and Dot went through their morning routines.

'Ready, love?' said Dot.

'Yup,' said Bea, but as George unlocked the front door, she felt an achy sort of pang in her stomach, and then, as the first customers came through and Reg wasn't amongst them, a lump pressing at the back of her throat.

Dot glanced at her. 'No Reg,' she said, seeming to read Bea's mind. 'Takes a bit of getting used to.'

'Mm,' said Bea, unable to say any more. Dot passed her a surreptitious extra strong mint and they both put on their Costsave smiles to greet their first customers.

Just before lunchtime, Dot swivelled her chair round and gave Bea a nudge. 'Look who!' she said. Bea looked up and saw Julie pushing a trolley in through the front door, with Tiffany in the little seat, and Mason walking alongside. Julie spotted them and waved. When she'd trawled up and down the aisles, she headed for Bea's checkout.

Strictly against regulations, Bea got out of her seat, went around the end of the packing area and gave Julie a hug.

'I'm so pleased to see you.'

'You, too, Bea. The police told me what happened to you. I'm so glad you're okay.'

They stood looking at each other, lost for words.

'We should have a coffee sometime,' said Bea. 'Talk it all over.'

'Yes. I'd like that. I'm buying, though.'

'Don't be silly.'

'No, Bea. Seriously. I need to find a way to say thank you. I'd never have got out if you hadn't given me that number. I honestly think you saved my life.'

Bea could feel tears welling up. She bit the inside of her

mouth to try to stop them, made her way back to her seat and started processing Julie's shopping.

'Are you back at home now?' she said.

'Yeah, for the time being. I don't know if we'll stay there. Lots of ...you know ...memories, but it is the kids' home. We'll see. Let's have that coffee soon.'

'Yes, let's.'

Dave's arrest and the role Ant and the others played in rescuing Bea was front page news in that week's *Bugle*, of course. Bea couldn't help smiling when she saw the main picture, which took up the whole of the top half of the page. Under the heading, 'Local Heroes' was a photograph of Tank, Dean, Saggy and Ant posing awkwardly outside Dave's house.

'Don't reckon much to this new boy band, do you?' said Queenie as she picked up the paper from the coffee table.

'Ha! They're a rum looking lot, aren't they? The new cast of *Avengers Assemble*!' Queenie snorted her approval. 'They really are heroes, though. All of them.'

'Yes, they are. They all did their bit but especially Ant. He should get some sort of medal.' They both fell quiet, thinking about what might have been. It was too awful to contemplate, but it was difficult not to. Queenie looked back at the photo. 'Look at them, though. They remind me of those bags of misshapes they used to sell in the factory shop.'

'Harsh, Mum, harsh,' said Bea, giggling. 'They were great, those bags, weren't they?'

'Mm, funny lumps of chocolate and bundles of choccy bars without their wrappers on. Probably not allowed to sell them like that now.' She seemed to be lost in thought for a while. 'Some things were good in the good old days.'

'And some things weren't.'

'It's worth remembering the good times, though.'

'Yes,' said Bea. 'We can remember Dad properly now, can't

we? Without those memories being tainted by the gossip. Feels like we've got him back.'

'Mm,' said Queenie, 'he's ours again. The rest of the world can bog off and leave us in peace.'

'I hated people thinking badly of him, Mum. I don't even mind knowing that he wasn't perfect. He was my dad, and the best dad anyone could have.'

'He was.'

Tom's box of chocolates hadn't lasted more than about twenty-four hours, but Bea had had all sorts of gifts and flowers from well-wishers. They were halfway through a large box of Maltesers chocolates, which Dot had brought round.

Now Bea took a handful of Maltesers and worked her way through them as Queenie flicked through the channels on the telly, trying to find something good.

'One thing, though,' said Bea. 'Why did you forgive him so quickly?'

'Real answer?' Queenie looked at Bea, who nodded.

'Yeah, I can take it.'

'Well, I loved him, of course. Although love waxes and wanes a bit like the moon. It's not constant, Bea, not with anyone. But the important thing was that he made me laugh. Every day we were together. Well, not every day, but nearly. If you can have a laugh with someone, share a sense of humour, it'll take you through a whole lifetime together.'

'I hope I find someone like that one day.'

'You will. Maybe I will again. Who knows?'

45

'It's all right to have nerves, but you've got to control them. Channel them into your performance.'

It was five minutes until the Costsave choir was due on stage. There was quite a crowd in the community tent. The Dorothy Dempsey Dance School had just performed, and what seemed like a hundred small girls and boys, apparently dressed as flowers of the field, were filing out of the tent flap that acted as a stage door to be met with hugs from their proud parents.

Bea was regretting having the bag of sugary doughnuts half an hour before, as they were now threatening to reappear. She didn't feel as bad as Dean looked, though. He was as white as a sheet. Candy moved through the crowd and spoke quietly with him, then she turned and said, 'Come on, everyone, let's join hands. We're all in this together. Long breath in. Hold it. Long breath out.' They all did as instructed. Candy had that sort of aura, Bea thought, that they would have all followed her into the river at the bottom of the park if she'd told them to. 'And one more time. Remember, when we get in there, we'll take our time, get settled and I'll give Dean the starting note. Let's do this, people!'

The performance went in a blur. All Bea could remember afterwards was Dean's voice ringing out, clear, assured and really rather beautiful, and then a swell of noise around her. To start with she just saw a sea of faces, but as her nerves calmed, she saw Julie with Tiffany on her lap and Mason jigging around next to her. They were beside Keisha and Kayleigh, in a big group of parents and kids. Queenie had nabbed an empty fold-up garden chair. She was towards the back of the tent near to Tom who was leaning on a pole, chatting with Shaz and her new partner who were in uniform and on duty.

The first two songs – 'Lean on Me' and 'You've Got a Friend' – had people singing along, but when they got to 'Can't Stop the Feeling', everyone was up on their feet and having a good old dance. At one point, Candy, who was standing in front of the choir, conducting, turned round and pretended to conduct the audience. When the song finished, the whole place erupted.

The Costsave choir filed out into the sunshine. People were tottering around, high-fiving each other. George found Candy and hugged her, then appealed for some quiet.

'Everyone! You were brilliant! Dean! What a voice! We need to thank Candy. Thank you. Thank you for everything you've done for us. Come on, everyone, three cheers! Hip, hip—'

Two little girls ran up to George and clung onto her legs.

'Mummy, you were great!' George beamed at them and lifted the smaller one up and balanced her on her hip, while a woman came up next to them and put her arm round George's shoulder, smiling proudly.

'Everyone, this is Charlie, my wife, and these are Ella and Claire.'

'Do you think we should give three cheers for George?' Bea muttered to Ant.

'Nah. Too sucky,' said Ant, but someone else obviously

disagreed, and another round of hip-hip-hooraying got underway. When that had died down, they all heard Eileen piping up.

'Three cheers for my Dean. What did I tell you? Voice of a bloody angel! Hip, hip—'

By now the cheers were rather ragged. 'Jesus,' said Ant. 'Time to hit the cider tent. You coming?' But Queenie was threading through the crowd in their direction.

'You were marvellous!' she said 'All of you! Quite brilliant!' She gave both Bea and Ant a squeeze.

'Thanks, Mrs Jordan. Thirsty work, though, all that singing. Time for a drink,' said Ant. 'Anyone else want one?'

'Yeah, go on, then,' said Bea. 'Mum, are you coming?'

'I'm going to nab a deckchair down by the bandstand,' said Queenie. 'It's the brass band in ten minutes.'

'I'll see you down there in a bit then. Shall I fetch you something?'

'Do I look like the sort of person who comes to the music festival to sit on the grass and get trollied?'

Bea burst out laughing. 'I don't know, Mum, but I reckon I am.'

'Just a half for me, then. I'll see you in a minute.'

'I quite fancy an ice cream,' said Dot, fanning herself with the festival programme.

Bob swooped in. 'Madam,' he said, offering Dot his arm, 'would you allow me to buy you one?'

'A ninety-nine, with a Flake in it?'

'You can have as many Flakes as you like.'

Dot took his arm and they started strolling towards the ice cream van. Ant and Bea headed for the cider tent. On their way in they met Dan Knibbs coming out.

'You working today?' said Bea.

Dan grinned. 'Yes and no,' he said. 'I've already written my piece on the festival, so I'm free to enjoy the rest of it.'

'How can you have written it? It's only just got going?'

'I just take the press release and change the tense – "The brass band performed, the crowd enjoyed the sunshine" – all that sort of thing. Let's face it, these things are the same every year. Nothing really happens at them. I'm going to find me some really thrashy music now. The metal tent's got some great bands on. See you later, yeah?'

Ant and Bea queued up at the bar.

'Not sure about the metal tent,' said Bea. 'I was going to check out the acoustic tent in a bit. The Pindrop Twins are playing. Feels kind of appropriate to go and listen to them. What?'

Ant was rolling his eyes. 'You're on your own there, mate,' he said. 'I can't sit through another hour of their dirgy nonsense. I'd rather gnaw my own leg off and escape.'

'Really?'

'Really. Saggy's terrible dogs make better noises than them, out of both ends.'

Bea started giggling. 'Harsh,' she said. 'Our choir thing was good though, wasn't it?'

'Yeah,' said Ant. 'I thought the idea was a bit lame to start with, but I reckon we smashed it.'

'Yeah, we smashed it all right! Pretty good feeling.'

'Shall we have one pint here and then get another to take with us?'

'I was only joking about getting trollied, Ant.'

'Come on, Bea. It's the one day of the year you can get really rat-arsed in the park without getting arrested. I'll look after you, and you'll look after me, won't you?'

'True.'

'You're twenty-one. It's summertime. We've caught a murderer and saved your dad's reputation. That's worth a celebration, isn't it?'

'When you put it like that, yes, Ant, it is.' They ordered

four pints and raised the first two plastic glasses, which disappointingly made no noise at all as they knocked them together.

'Cheers, Ant.'

'Down the hatch.'

At the end of the evening, Ant and Bea lay flat on their backs on the hillside which sloped down to the river. The remains of their pints were resting unsteadily in dips in the grass next to them. For a long time they didn't speak, both listening to the sound of the final band on the main stage drifting across the park, the whoops and cheers from the crowd, the shouts and squeals of revellers straggling out of the park or seeking its darker corners.

The sky was clear and Bea watched the stars getting brighter every minute, almost as if someone was turning up a dimmer switch. She was pleasantly pissed, drunk enough to feel mellow and happy and blurry at the edges, but not yet at the point where the world was spinning.

In the distant tent, the music blasted to a series of false climaxes and then, with a final elongated chord and a crashing of drums, it was over. The audience roared their approval and gradually the noise died down as the crowd started to disperse.

'I love you, Bea,' Ant said, out of the blue.

Caught by surprise, Bea started laughing, her back and legs shaking against the ground beneath her. 'No more cider for you. You've had enough.'

'No such thing as enough cider. Hang on, I've got a bit left.'

Out of the corner of her eye, Bea saw him prop himself up on one elbow and drain the rest of his pint. Then he lifted his arm and threw the plastic cup as far as he could.

'Oi! Litterbug! Go and pick that up!'

'You can't make me.'

'I bloody can.'

Bea propped herself up with the thought of tickling him, but then she looked at the grass below them, which was studded with a sea of discarded cups.

'Have a job finding it in that lot, mind,' she said, and started to giggle. Ant joined in this time, and they both fell back onto the ground, laughing themselves silly until Bea had to curl up and squeeze her legs together to stop herself peeing there and then.

'Stop, stop, I can't cope!' she wheezed.

They lapsed into silence again, and somehow Ant's hand found hers. His fingers curled around hers, and although she kept looking at the sky and the stars, all her other senses were concentrated on the places where their skin touched. In that moment, their fingertips and palms and wrists were at the centre of the universe.

'I know I'm pissed,' Ant said, 'but I mean it. I bloody love you.'

Bea thought about faithless Jay, on a beach somewhere under the same sky, about Tom and his car and his prospects and his baby boy – even about Dan Knibbs, last seen topless and glistening with sweat in what passed for a mosh pit in the heavy metal tent. And she thought about what Queenie had said. *He made me laugh. That's why I stayed with him. He made me laugh every day.*

She turned her head and found that Ant had flipped onto his side and was looking at her.

'You daft bugger,' she said, reaching her free hand out and touching the side of his face.

Acknowledgements

As ever, I'd like to thank the whole team at Sandstone Press, especially Kay, my brilliant editor, and Ceris, who has worked tirelessly on this series. I'm so proud to work with this small but mighty publisher. Thanks also to my agent, Kirsty McLachlan at David Godwin Associates, who has such faith in Ant and Bea (and me).

The writing community is a kind, supportive one and I'm very lucky to have writer friends who cheer and support me along the way. On Facebook, Twitter or in real life, this is much appreciated. I'd also like to thank the lovely readers, librarians and booksellers who have taken And and Bea to their hearts.

Last, but not least, my little family, Ozzy, Ali and Pete, continue to be my biggest supporters. I hope that I support them back, and that we help each other to pursue our dreams.

www.sandstonepress.com

f facebook.com/SandstonePress/

𝕏 @SandstonePress